Forty Years
and
Forty Fathoms

by

Cass Howell

International Standard Book Number 13: 978-1-60452-106-1
International Standard Book Number 10: 1-60452-106-6
Library of Congress Control Number: 2016931054

BluewaterPress LLC
52 Tuscan Way Ste 202-309
Saint Augustine FL 32092
http://bluewaterpress.com

This book may be purchased online at -

http://www.bluewaterpress.com/forty

To Summera, for her keen insight and advice.

Chapter 1

Honolulu, 1980

He shoves the door open with just enough authority to let it know who's boss. The whupita, whupita, whupita of a passing Huey helicopter pushes past, announcing his entrance. The bar is in twilight, no windows and few lights, a welcome contrast to the harsh tropical sun and heat outside. A glance around makes it clear this isn't a tourist destination. Military memorabilia, mostly fading pictures of helicopters and soldiers posed in various tropical settings speak without words from the walls. The "Ballad of the Green Berets" drums through overhead speakers long past their prime. For the men from nearby Wheeler Army Airfield, it's a comfortable place, a haven for war stories and tested manhood. Jared Scott, several days unshaven and comfortably dressed in his favorite aloha shirt and shorts, squints through the gloom. He has taut muscles and broad shoulders. A two-inch splash of white hair over his right temple intrudes into matte black hair. Jared eases himself onto a stool at the bar and nods to the bartender. He gets a friendly smile in return.

"Draft Diamond Head, and some peanuts if you got 'em."

"Coming right up. Want anything from the grill?" The bartender is stuffed into a well-worn bowling shirt embroidered with his name, "Joe." Retired Army, Jared surmises, based on the fading tattoos he sports on both arms.

"Nope, just need a little watering." A Texas twang, softened by several years in the islands, comes through. The bar television flickers with the play-by-play action of the Oakland Raiders as they take on the Kansas City Chiefs. As usual, the game is a week old.

The bartender hauls over the beer, trying not to spill it, despite a noticeable limp. "Here you go, buddy, cold enough to crack the enamel off your teeth."

"A man after my own heart." Jared takes a gulp and nods approval. He glances at the TV image, which at the moment, is nothing more than a writhing mass of silver and black.

"Hey, when you going to get on the satellite feed and watch some real-time football for a change?"

Joe snorts. "Hell, I don't know. They keep saying it's coming, but I'll believe it when I see it. We're just a dot in the ocean out here. In the meantime," he says, gesturing at the TV, "we'll do it the island way — watch last week's game on videotape."

Joe wipes away a wet spot on the bar and checks the TV for the score. "Raiders up by fourteen. Want to make a wager on the outcome?" he asks with a knowing smile. "No way!" They share a laugh.

Jared takes another sip and looks around. His eyes lock on two men in olive drab flight suits. They relax at a table at the far end of the room, one regaling his friend with another bullshit story about flying, women, or drinking, probably all three combined. Their laughter lends a welcoming mood to the otherwise ordinary beer bar. Jared saunters over, a spring in his step. The soldiers don't look up until he reaches the table, a big smile on his face.

"Wayne?" Jared asks the older of the two and then peers at the other man. "And, uh, Jerry isn't it? Jeez, I haven't seen you guys since in-country." He pulls up a chair and joins them without being asked. Wayne and Jerry offer blank stares in return. "Still in, huh? You know, I never figured you guys for lifers." Jared laughs, glancing back and forth between the two. "Hey barkeep, a round for my buds," Jared calls, waving at the bartender. Facing back, he says, "Whatcha drinking, guys?"

Wayne makes eye contact with Jerry, who nods. Without a word, they stand up, pull on their caps and walk toward the door. Jared jumps up, red in the face, and yells after them, "He was dead, goddamn it! I don't care what anybody says, he was...dead!"

Jared hurls the table end over end. Beer bottles and chairs fly as Wayne and Jerry disappear out the door. Other patrons edge towards the exits. The bartender smacks the top of the bar hard with a billy club. "Knock it off, mister, right now!"

"Fuck you! Fuck all of you!"

* * * * *

Vietnam, 1968

The birds are singing.

For this Captain Evans is grateful, very grateful. He wipes sweat out of his eyes with the damp sleeve of his camo uniform and updates the unit's position on his well-worn map, a strain in the gloom of the deep jungle. Satisfied, he takes out his compass, shoots a bearing line and makes a mental note. With a glance over his shoulder, he gives a nod and his platoon rises like green ghosts, seemingly right from the jungle floor.

Painted faces hide their youth and inexperience, most a scant 19-years-old. Oh, their look is menacing enough, all festooned with grenades, Claymore mines, and M-16 rifles. But Evans knows behind the camo paint are raw teenaged boys, not long out of Hometown, USA. Raw recruits more skilled at hot-rodding dad's car around town and chasing high school cheerleaders than the North Vietnamese Army troops in this green hell. No matter, they are learning fast, with a few salty dog NCOs to kick them in the ass.

Evans has a pregnant wife at home, a new company to command when he returns to base camp, and four months remaining on his second tour before rotation. He also has a raging case of jock itch and at least five more days in the bush without treatment. He worries about none of these now. Instead, he carries the focus, fear, and yes, the exhilaration, which comes from lurking deep in bad guy territory. The same unspoken emotions are etched on the faces of every member of the unit.

Evans hand-signals a direction to the point man, Freddy Galinati, a big, good-looking kid from upstate New York. Galinati has the honor and responsibility of leading the unit. He's also likely to be the guy nearest the fan when the shit hits, but, hey, it goes with the territory. The platoon follows him. Slow. Careful. Silent.

Captain Evans permits himself a smile. The birds are still singing.

* * * * *

There aren't any birds singing at the base camp. If there were, they couldn't be heard over the din of landing and departing helicopters, six-by-six trucks hauling God-knows-what to God-knows-where, and the occasional boom of artillery fire going out. The only birds anyone cares about here are the helicopters buzzing overhead, taking grunts to and from the boonies, bringing much anticipated mail, and carrying wounded men to Da Nang for evacuation stateside.

Besides the noise another dominating aspect of the camp is the choking clouds of dust, stirred up by a beehive of vehicles in constant motion. Red grit everywhere — eyes, hair, nose, in the food as well. Relief comes from the frequent rains, a mixed blessing that turns the entire camp into a mucky sea of mud. Throw in the occasional rocket and artillery attacks and you have the recipe for hell in a very small place. Nonetheless, for the grunts patrolling the hills and valleys up against the nearby Laotian border, this is good duty, a place to get laundry done and two hot meals a day. Maybe even a movie some nights if incoming rockets don't drive everyone into the bunkers. Happiness in a combat zone is entirely relative.

Lt. Jared Scott is one of the happy ones today, despite the lackadaisical service at the flight equipment counter in the suffocating heat of the supply tent. Sgt. William "Slick Willie" Wilson, the totally indifferent supply NCO, takes a break from updating his "short timer calendar" to hand over a forty-five caliber Colt pistol and two magazines of ammunition.

Jared takes the ammo and pistol and asks, "What ya got left, Willie?" He racks a round into the chamber of the forty-five, eases the hammer down and slides the weapon into his shoulder holster, adding to the weight of the survival vest he wears over the olive green flight suit.

Willie gives a big grin. "Six days and a wake-up, Lieutenant. Then it's me and the Freedom Bird Utah here. Got a brand new Camaro waiting for me in Frisco." His grin gets bigger.

"Really?" Jared says, amused. "You must be selling a lot of stuff out the back door. Say, it's not too late to go out to Indian country with me. I'll talk to the First Sergeant and get you on as a gunner so you can get some trigger time. Li'l bro Nolan here's going," Jared says, bobbing his head towards the young Private First Class standing quietly at his side.

Willie stutters his reply. "Uh, I think I'm bu-busy that day, thanks anyway," he says, eyes avoiding Jared's.

As they talk, Jared goes through his survival vest to make sure the flares, water bottles, K-Bar knife and extra ammo are all present. He turns on the hand-held radio to ensure the batteries are strong. Satisfied, he zips his vest, and goes through the process again with another pistol and similar survival gear. He hands the equipment over to Nolan after all is checked. Willie pushes some forms over for Nolan to sign.

"Here you go, stud. Sign by the X and remember, it's a loan, not a gift."

Nolan fumbles with the unfamiliar vest as Jared offers advice. Nolan zips up the flight suit to put on the survival vest, and-zips off a handful of chest hair in the process.

"Ye — ouch!"

Jared walks to the waiting Jeep, shaking his head. "God, help us..."

* * * * *

Nolan and Jared sat in the back of a jeep as the driver rolls up to a heavily armed Huey helicopter gunship. Two crewmembers pause in their preparations as Jared makes an announcement.

"Hey, everybody! Want ya to meet my mom's favorite boy, Nolan. He's going to give us shootin' lessons on the M-60 today, so y'all pay attention if we get in a fire fight." Jared, along with everyone but Nolan, grins and chuckles. A slow burn creeps into Nolan's cheeks as he and Jared get out of the jeep.

"Smitty," says Jared, calling up to his crew chief. "How's the bird today?"

Sgt. Smith closes an overhead access panel and looks down at Nolan and Jared, sweat glistening on his bald brown head. "Looking good, sir, looking good. Long as we can keep the parts guys on their toes, she'll stay up and ready, promise you."

Jared says to Nolan, "Smitty here's the best crew chief on the base, maybe even in the whole damned Army. Pretty good door gunner, too."

Smitty steps down and shakes Nolan's hand. "Lovey Smith, glad to meet ya. I'm really into keeping the helo maintained — being a gunner is just another part of the job."

Pointing, Jared continues, "And that handsome fellow there is Warrant Officer Louie Davis, he's our copilot today." Davis, conducting his preflight on the other side of the aircraft, waves hello. "Welcome aboard — I guess we'll call you Texas Two," he says with a laugh.

Jared is nonchalant about it, but the unspoken expectation is that Nolan will take care of business if they get into a fight. To do otherwise would be to endanger the whole crew, an intolerable breach of trust.

With Nolan in trail, Jared walks around the aircraft checking pre-flight items. The helo is visibly worn, obviously a combat vet. The doors are removed to save weight and to facilitate access and there is a liberal amount of mud smeared on the floorboards.

Nolan stops by a series of holes in the metal skin of the airframe. He hesitates, then sticks fingers in some of them. "Hey, Jared, are these, uh, bullet holes?"

Jared glances at the holes. "Yo, Smitty! Those damn woodpeckers been at it again. Just making a mess of the machine."

Smitty, on the other side from Jared and Nolan, booms forth with a belly laugh. "I'll requisition some more of that skeeter, I mean, woodpecker repellent." Jared and Nolan share a smile as Nolan blushes again as they continue the pre-flight. They walk around to the left side mounted door gun.

"Okay, little buddy, this one's yours."

Nolan has a face-crinkling grin on his boyish face as he savors the big M-60 machine gun. He runs his hand along it, as if it were a delicate woman's arm, instead of a cold, deadly piece of steel.

"Aww right!"

"A few rules," says Jared. "Don't shoot at anything unless I give you the word, then short bursts, no more than three seconds each. If you get a jam, sing out and Smitty will clear it for you."

Nolan makes a face. "I can clear it, really. Just 'cause I'm a clerk-typist don't mean I don't stand guard duty twice a week."

Jared looks at Nolan paternalistically and says, "You always were a hard-head. Mom should have stopped with me."

Jared playfully punches Nolan on the shoulder. "Now get your ass on board and get the safety strap on — don't want you flying out the door like Superman. We launch in ten minutes. And, remember, if you knock 'em down and they get back up, it don't count."

They both laugh and Nolan steps aboard, trying to figure out how to fasten his flight helmet chinstrap.

* * * * * *

Under the triple canopy vegetation, the near dusk is perpetual and the humid air lies over the American soldiers like a wet, wool blanket. Freddy Galinati chooses his steps carefully, always alert for punji sticks and booby trap wires. There is no path or trail, he merely walks in a general direction wherever and however possible. Galinati pauses, then starts up a small embankment. Looking for a handhold, he reaches for an exposed root — then freezes. He is eyeball-to-eyeball with six feet of deadly viper lying along a low limb directly ahead. The snake is motionless except for its darting tongue, the gold-flecked eyes staring from the large triangular head. Slowly, Galinati backs away, points out the snake to the troops behind, then glances back at the captain.

Captain Evans holds his fist up, signaling a halt, and the troops sprawl out in a three-hundred sixty degree defensive position. Some adjust gear; others sip water from their canteens. Most just rest and peer into the vegetation.

Per routine, PFC Sanchez, the radioman, lumbers up beside Evans. He crouches into a low profile, and then becomes as motionless as possible. He is the number two priority for snipers. Number one, as Evans is keenly aware, is himself.

"Sanchez, get Top Cover up on the freq. They should be on station by now," the captain says softly.

Sanchez adjusts the frequency on the PRC-25 radio, then covers his mouth and microphone with one hand. "Bravo One-Three, Bravo One-Three, Two-Delta X-Ray, over." He pauses, then adds, "Bravo One-Three, are you up?"

* * * * * *

The Huey pounds along, its rotor blades thrashing the hot and humid air into a welcome breeze for the crew, a rare escape from the oppressive heat. The green rolling hills slide by below, broken by occasional grassy areas and a few villages. The crew scans for anything of interest, but there is nothing to be seen.

Nolan is ecstatic. After two solid months of filing papers and typing reports for 14-hours a day, seven days a week, he feels like he is finally doing something worthwhile — and exciting, to boot. He sights imaginary targets with the M-60 hoping Smitty and the others don't see him pretending. *God, please let there be some targets, anything! There must be some NVA water buffaloes around here somewhere!*

Nolan's reverie is broken by Jared's voice over the intercom. "Hey Nolan, how ya doing back there? Keep your eyes open, we're coming up on station." Jared glances back at Nolan, positioned to his left rear. Nolan tries to look serious and fails, but manages an "OK" hand signal. The radio crackles and they hear, "Bravo One-Three, are you up?"

Jared replies, "Two-Delta X-Ray, Bravo One Three is with you, over."

"Roger, One-Three, standby for Delta X-Ray actual," says Sanchez.

The next voice is Captain Evans. "Bravo One-Three, X-Ray Alpha here. Say status."

Jared responds, his voice modulated by the thumping reverberations of the rotor blades and the whine of the turbine engine behind him. "We're here with you for about the next two point five, loaded wall-to-wall, looking for some fun. Y'all having fun down there? Got some Budweiser iced down in the back. Give me coordinates and I'll airdrop you some."

"Jared, quit screwing around!" Evans snaps, the anger in his voice coming through, even over the scratchy radio. "We stay on the freq too long and the NVA will get a direction finder cut and it'll be raining mortars left and right down here."

"Jeez, okay! Just tryin' to be sociable to my grunt friends. So what can I do for you today?"

Captain Evans replies, "We left LZ Songbird at time one-five last hour. Enroute to, I shackle..." Evans pauses to manipulate an analog encoder with a matrix of numbers and letters to encrypt coordinates. "... lima nine, bravo twelve, alpha six, tango nine at time four five next hour. How copy, over?"

Jared glances over at his copilot, who looks up from manipulating his own shackle device and gives a thumbs up. "We gotcha covered. Bravo Three One out."

"Ya hear that, Nolan?" said Jared. "We got friendly's down below, so make sure you don't pop off any rounds unless I give the word."

Nolan, suddenly impressed with his responsibilities, nods in understanding. He thinks to himself, *Don't want to hit the good guys!*

* * * * * *

In the deep jungle shadows, two figures crouch beside a North Vietnamese Army radioman, an American PRC-25 radio slung over his back. The radioman holds the handset to the ear of the Traitor, who manipulates his own shackle device as he listens. The Traitor's ragged Hawaiian beach shirt blends in surprisingly well with the jungle background surrounding them and his dirty worn jeans would fit well on any college campus in America. Strands of scraggly blond hair escape from under a bush hat. It's the only visible vestige of his former life other than his jungle boots, now unrecognizable from the encrusted mud.

The radio conversation and decryption finishes. The Traitor shows the decrypted coordinates to the NVA officer, a stocky Vietnamese in his thirties and then plots them on the map at hand. After a few minutes of study, the officer stands and gives orders in Vietnamese, seemingly to no one. Dozens of NVA soldiers with their distinctive pith helmets and green cotton uniforms, emerge from the shadows. They assemble in a loose column and move out in a hurry.

The Traitor stands and the NVA officer turns to face him. "Comrade Trazer, I commend you on the correctness of your thinking. You are a true patriot of the Revolution." He offers Trazer a drink from his canteen. Trazer accepts, and returns the canteen after quenching his thirst.

"It is my privilege to serve the People's Army, comrade major. I thank you for your kindness and the opportunity." Trazer puts his hands together as in prayer, and bows to the major, who returns the gesture in response. With a last nod of understanding, they push through the underbrush to get the troops in place for the ambush.

Chapter 2

Jared and his crew fly a lazy pattern along the planned route for Captain Davis and his platoon. The first butt-tightening sign of danger is the burned-out hulk of another Huey, now upside down in a rice paddy. No one makes note and Jared says a silent prayer they won't end up the same. He can only guess the others' thoughts.

Out in front of the Huey, a broad field covered with elephant grass stretches before them. Usually the razor sharp grass is head-high and almost impenetrable, but these fields were napalmed a few months before and the new grass is only waist high. Nothing is amiss and in less than a minute, they will pass the area.

Davis jabs a forefinger ahead and says, "Skipper, check it out, eleven o'clock in the grass field."

A hundred yards ahead, a young NVA soldier jumps up and fires his rifle wildly in the direction of the helicopter.

"Well, howdy do!" says Jared, laughter in his voice. He banks the helo, putting the soldier dead ahead, now fifty yards away with the distance closing fast. At the same time, an NVA sergeant jumps up, runs over to the soldier and flattens him with a powerful blow to the head.

"Did you see that?!" Jared and Davis blurt simultaneously. Jared pounds his leg in amazement as the helo roars overhead the sprawled soldier. Now they can see dozens, maybe more than a hundred NVA soldiers laying low in the grass.

Davis shakes his head in disbelief. "Boy, talk about a dumb shit. What was that idiot thinking? He just gave away their whole unit position."

"Probably a draftee on his first trip south. They're usually more disciplined," Jared grunts, as he pulls the helicopter around in a hard turn. "Smitty, Nolan, you guys ready?"

"Fuckin' A, man! Let's go get 'em!" Nolan gushes.

"Oh, baby! Captain Evans is gonna be buying us drinks the rest of his tour. Talk about saving his ass, big time!" Jared exults.

"Christ, must be a whole company," says Davis, straining to keep the enemy in sight.

Jared completes the turn to line up for a strafing run. The launchers boom, shaking the helo as a salvo of rockets streaks for the field. They explode with vicious efficiency. Pieces of equipment and body parts fly high into the air as the rockets smash the cowering soldiers. The elephant grass is airbrushed with their blood.

The rockets expended, Jared attacks with the mini-guns, multi-barrel Gatlin guns with tremendous firepower. They roar and the grass below churns from the hailstorm of bullets. A few NVA try to run for the tree line, but none make it more than a few feet before they are cut down.

Jared performs another slashing turn to the battlefield. It's up to the door gunners now. There is no need to pick individual targets. The NVA are everywhere trying to flee or hug the ground — every burst of Smitty's and Nolan's guns finds targets.

"Woo-hoo, baby! Set 'em up, knock 'em down!" yells Nolan, hammer fisting the air.

Jared hauls the helicopter around in a figure eight pattern, repeating the attack again and again. He swoops lower on each pass, almost down to the top of the grass itself. Everywhere there are dead or dying NVA, uniforms splotched with blood, body parts missing. It is carnage, the stuff of war.

The mini-guns howl their death songs, then fall silent, first one, then the other.

Jared transmits, "Nolan, Smitty, I'm done, all yours!" The helo charges downhill again.

Nolan and Smitty hose down the area with long bursts from the M-60's.

Suddenly Trazer jumps out of a ditch, AK-47 in hand. With a grimace etched on his face, he shoulders the weapon and draws a bead on the approaching helicopter.

Jared yells, "Smitty, your side, two o'clock!"

Smitty's gun fires three rounds and goes silent. "I'm dry, Lieutenant!"

"Well, he ain't getting away!" Jared looks back at the gunners with a big grin on his face, then pulls his forty-five Colt from his shoulder holster with one hand and flies the helo with the other. He takes aim out of the window as he passes Trazer thirty yards away. For an endless second, they embrace in a deadly stare-down. Trazer shoots, full automatic, the muzzle flashing like a strobe light.

The big Colt bucks in Jared's hand, again, and again, as he attempts to shut down the flashes.

Trazer hits first. The windscreen and the instrument panel explode into shards, Plexiglas and metal fragments fly everywhere. A beehive of bullets savages Davis. His body jerks as the slugs hammer him. "Unghh!" is all he manages to get out before slumping into the seat restraints.

Nolan catches a stinging hail of bullets, slams into the back bulkhead and slides down, his body a mass of punctures gushing bright red blood.

Jared continues to shoot as fast as he can pull the trigger. Finally he connects, a glancing blow on the side of Trazer's head, blowing off half of one ear.

Trazer flinches, but stands his ground and squeezes off another long burst, now at can't-miss range.

Jared takes the brunt of it. Bullets shatter what's left of the windscreen, and one pierces Jared's helmet visor with a snap like the crack of a whip, jerking his head back. Another one hits a hammer blow to his leg and sends his kneeboard flying.

Panic in his voice, Smitty cries out. "Lieutenant, Nolan's hit! Lieutenant?"

Jared is staggered, knocked senseless from a smashing overhand blow. It's Artemis Johnson in the third round of the Golden Gloves tournament rattling his brain again. "Got to hit back or they'll stop, stop the fight," his self-voice says from far away. He tries to swing, but his arms do not answer, and he can see nothing but red. The referee is yelling at him, "Lieutenant!" He feels the wind on his face and is stunned, then terrified to realize where he is — not in control, not flying, not shooting. Pull up! Pull up!

With all his remaining strength Jared yanks on the cyclic control, forcing the helo out of its downward trajectory. He wipes enough blood out of his eyes to find the horizon and points the helo skyward. Dripping red hydraulic fluid and blood are intermixed everywhere, adding to the chaos of the fragmented instruments and windscreen. The helicopter is staggering, barely able to stay airborne.

Smitty, the only one not hit, looks from one bleeding man to the next. There is nothing he can do except plead a loud prayer. "Oh, God! Oh, God, no!"

Jared struggles to keep the helicopter climbing, but it is obvious they are far too damaged to climb over the ridge between their position and the base camp.

"Get the guns overboard, Smitty, the toolbox, ammo, everything!" Jared yells. Smitty slips in the blood and hydraulic fluid as he rushes to comply. He frantically pitches everything not bolted down out the open doors.

"Nolan, get some bandages on Davis, he's hurt bad!" shouts Jared. "Nolan! Answer up!" Jared takes a moment from fighting the controls to glance back over his shoulder. Nolan, bloody from head to foot, lies limp and still on the deck, twisted in a grotesque position.

"Smitty, help Nolan," Jared shouts, his voice shrill.

Smitty scrambles over to tend to Nolan. He rips off one of his gloves and feels for a pulse, but the helo shakes and vibrates so hard it is impossible to tell. He looks at Jared, his face contorted in anguish.

Whack! A protruding tree limb smacks the remnants of the windscreen and jerks Jared's attention forward, just in time for him to wrench the helo enough to dodge more limbs. Then the terrain falls away into a small valley. Looming ahead is an even higher ridge, clearly more than the wounded helo can manage.

Jared snaps a look just as Smitty sees the towering ridge ahead. "Oh, Jesus, sweet Jesus, please, please, please!" he moans.

"Smitty! Get him out! Get him out!"

"What...?" Smitty can't seem to process this command.

"Get Nolan overboard!" screams Jared, his chin trembling. "Do it now or we all die!"

Smitty hesitates, then rushes to disconnect Nolan from the safety strap. He pushes him to the open door on Jared's side. Nolan's helmet comes off. Blood gushes everywhere, and Smitty struggles on the slippery red deck. He finally gets Nolan near the edge, and crosses himself.

Jared, with the ridge fast approaching, glances back and doesn't wait any longer. He rolls the helo on its side and Nolan's body tumbles overboard and falls into the green abyss. Jared and Smitty watch, as if in slow motion. Then Nolan's eyes open wide. A look of horror contorts his face, and Nolan screams an unheard plea: "Jared, no!"

Smitty slumps back against the bulkhead and throws up on himself. Jared jerks his attention forward as they hurtle towards the trees lining the top of the ridge.

"Brace, brace, brace!" Jared throws his free arm in front of his face as the helo smashes into the limbs. For a moment, everything is green and the helo staggers, then they burst through, and the beautiful sight of the base camp is visible a few miles ahead. They are still flying! Smitty cries, heaving sobs of relief. "Thank you Jesus, oh God, thank you sweet Jesus!"

Jared wipes away the blood dripping from under his helmet, and wonders why his leg is covered in red.

Have to get this flight suit washed...wonder if the laundry is open today...

The helo swoops onto the runway, makes a bouncing touchdown, and then spins around a hundred eighty degrees. Dust and dirt fly in all directions it slides to a grinding halt. His consciousness fades, graying the faces and voices of his rescuers. Somewhere the wail of a distant siren comes closer and louder.

An ambulance... I hope everyone's okay...

Chapter 3

Honolulu, 1980

The King-Air twin-engine turboprop adorned with the Island Air logo rolls into the parking area, propeller blades creating a pair of whining horizontal tornadoes. A ground director waves the pilot to the designated spot and makes a cut-throat motion with a hand. A moment later, the engines emit an ebbing moan as the pilot cuts off the fuel flow and the blades gradually spin down. The new quiet is welcome to all standing nearby, even Smitty, who has been around aircraft all of his grown life.

Considerably heavier now, Smitty is stuffed into a gold blazer adorned with the company logo. A poorly knotted tie strains to contain his bulging neck. The ensemble is topped off by a large silver crucifix that swings from a thick chain. It dances like a silent wind chime in the strong breeze. Smitty pauses for the air-stair door to open, then calls into the interior. "Hey, Jared, welcome back. How was the trip?"

Carrying a small suitcase and wearing the white shirt and epaulets of an aircraft captain, Jared appears in the door and makes his way down. "Fine, the plane held up well, and I got everyone where they needed to go," Jared says, fatigue marking his words. "How're things here?" he shouts as they walk towards the dispatch office, competing with the noise of a jumbo jet taking off across the field.

"Outstanding, praise God! I've got you scheduled tomorrow with a bunch of football fans coming in for the Pro Bowl, looking to get down to the Big Island for a few days of fishing. Take 258SR, it's got about a dozen hours left on it before the 100-hour inspection and that'll work out nice."

"They get the radios fixed?"

"Got to go to the avionics shop next week, but we got the shop spare installed, works fine," Smitty stops and faces Jared as they reach the office door. "One more thing, — your student, Lori, was pretty ticked off you stood her up on the flight lesson Tuesday. We've had this talk before, Jared, we can't operate without..."

Jared interrupts apologetically, "Smitty, I know, I know, you are completely right. I will make it up to her, don't worry."

"Okay. I'm counting on you... I can count on you, can't I?" The doubt in his voice is unintended, but comes through loud and clear. Smitty opens the door, and holds it for Jared to enter. "Bye-the-way, your friend Korbler has called a couple of times for you. Said to give him a call back as soon as you could. Please do, he's a damn good customer."

"Korbler, huh?" Jared smiles faintly. "I'll take care of it right away."

Chapter 4

Jared observes the usual things. Wayward tourists, lost since they got off at the wrong bus stop, are wandering around the downtown financial district desperately wanting to shoot happy snapshots in front of something, anything, recognizable as Hawaiian. Sweating, and with fussy kids running amuck, they huddle in small groups attempting to decipher the king of all puzzles, the Honolulu city bus schedule. Waikiki, so near and yet so far!

"Number 16 eastbound, change at Ala Moana." Jared calls out to a knot of lost souls he passes, not breaking stride, or even offering a smile. His destination, the three-man CIA office, hides in plain sight among the low-rise office buildings and palm trees of the Honolulu financial district. Travel agencies, financial planners, and time-share marketing schemers all provide urban camouflage. The lobby directory gives no clues, but Jared knows the way well enough. He ambles down a long hallway on the third floor, escorted by the ever-present piped in Hawaiian music. Unlike the few office workers he encounters, Jared is in island casual mode: faded aloha shirt, well-worn shorts and go-to-hell sandals. Two days growth on his face completes the picture.

At the end of the corridor, he stops at a door labeled, "Industrial Relations, Inc." to ring the doorbell and wave to the lens of a security camera mounted overhead. The buzzer sounds and Jared lets himself in.

The office area, outfitted in government bland, reminds him of the bureaucratic furnishings of his old high school. No one is present. He hears his name through a doorway in the back.

Jared makes his way to the door of John Korbler's windowless office. Nothing has changed since his last visit. The same personal mementos collected by Korbler over the years adorn the desk and walls, memorabilia of a rather small life. Korbler himself continues to age without grace, Jared observes — some of the lines on his face are now old enough to vote. Jared thinks he must be looking at retirement in a few years. Not sure he knows it, but it won't be a great loss to the Company.

As usual, Korbler sports a white dress shirt and a narrow black tie; his paunchy belly tests the strength of the shirt's lower buttons. A wafting fog of cigarette smoke threatens the building's smoke detectors. Korbler seems to be fascinated with his nose. At the moment, he rubs it like its Aladdin's Lamp, as he has done so many times before.

Korbler doesn't get up. "Can't you ever be on time?"

Without waiting for an invitation, Jared flops down in the visitor's chair. "So what's up? I know you didn't invite me up here to lecture me about wearing a watch."

"Got a mission for you if you can get away from work for a few days."

"No problem, they're very understanding down at the flight line."

"I won't waste your time," Korbler says, irritation hanging on his words. "Need for you to go back to 'Nam. Can you handle that?"

Jared leans back in the chair, and pauses while he thinks this over. "Not exactly my favorite place..."

"Well, that's where the bones are."

"Bones?"

"Yeah, bones, remains of some of our Missing-In-Action guys. We got some reliable intel a turncoat American wants to trade for them." Korbler strokes his nose with the back of his knuckles.

"Really?" says Jared. "How'd he get 'em?"

Korbler takes out another a cigarette and fires it up, not waiting for the butt of the last one to cool. He doesn't offer one to Jared.

"The scumbag's name is Trazer. University of Wisconsin student, got real radical and kinda forgot to go to classes, ended up getting drafted in sixty-six when he flunked out. One night he walks away from his firebase up in Quang Tri province, ends up selling his services to the NVA."

He doesn't interrupt, but Jared's eyes narrow.

"Never left 'Nam, mostly deals drugs now from Saigon. In tight with the commies, so he has free access to crash sites where the remains are. Pays a bounty to the local farmers for them, I'd expect."

"Two questions. How much are we paying this asshole, and do you mind if I kill him when done?"

Korbler's face flushes red as he jabs a finger at Jared. "You're not killing anyone. You're just a goddamn courier, and a part-timer at that. So don't do anything stupid." He glares for emphasis, and then leans back into his chair. "Besides, there's hundreds of MIA's, and the families want their boys back. So this could be a long term deal." He plows a nostril with his thumb. "The reason you are needed is because we don't have diplomatic relations, so this is strictly off the books. If the politics ever change, we'll have somebody important go over."

A delightful fantasy of launching over the desk to choke Korbler with his 1950's tie floats through Jared's mind, but he manages to re-focus.

"Okay...so what's my deal?"

"Two thousand, plus twenty dollars a day per diem. And reasonable expenses, of course."

"I am overwhelmed with your generosity, massa. Please tell me it's more than the traitor gets."

Korbler shrugs. "Well,...actually all he wants is a clear U.S. passport. Even though that idiot Jimmy Carter granted amnesty to the draft dodgers, State Department would never allow a passport which supported treason."

"Didn't stop Jane Fonda..."

With a sigh, Korbler asks, "We got a deal?"

After a pause just long enough to create some doubt, Jared says, "Yep."

"Well, good!" Korbler exclaims, his face erupting in a broad smile, "I can stay here and mind the store, busy as hell around here, you know."

Jared glances at the ceiling in anticipation God will send a lightning bolt to fry this liar.

"I'll have your tickets and the visa delivered tomorrow." From the cabinet behind him he pulls a bottle of Scotch and a couple of tall glasses.

"Let's have a drink to seal the deal," says Korbler. "You do like Scotch, don't you?" Korbler adds a handful of ice cubes from the mini-fridge under the cabinet.

Jared shakes his head. "Actually, I can't stand the stuff."

"Really? Guaranteed smoother than a baby's butt," says Korbler, who cranks the bottle in a suggestive swirl. He sniffs another smile from the pour spout. "Well, hope you don't mind if I indulge." He pours himself a couple of fingers of the whiskey without waiting for a reply, then drains half of it, his tongue doing clean up duty on his lips. A look of contentment spreads over his face, as does a blotchy, red patina.

Jared stands up, ready to leave. "Well, I gotta go. Pleasure doing business with you," he says, with a faint hint of sarcasm.

"Hey, uhh, one more thing...Jared, don't take this personal but,...I'm going to need a urinalysis from you before I commit the contract."

Jared stares hard at him, trying to figure if this is a joke. Maybe Korbler has already been hitting the bottle today.

"Langley is putting that requirement on all the contract operatives working the Far East. You know we've gotten our asses burned bad before..."

Jared leans far over the desk to get into Korbler's face.

Swallowing hard, Korbler scrambles back as much as the wall behind allows.

"Jesus, Jared, it's just peeing into a bottle! Takes all of one minute..."

Pausing a moment, Jared straightens up, then reaches down and grabs Korbler's near empty glass of Scotch. In one motion he unzips, pulls out his penis, and fills the glass, rattling the ice cubes. Done, he plops it down the desk in front of Korbler, who falls back in the chair, unable to keep his feet.

"You want a sample? Here's your fucking sample."

Korbler is livid. "You can't treat me like that!"

Jared zips up and strides out the door, nearly knocking over Gaylord, just arriving.

* * * * *

Gaylord is a gangly, youthful newbie agent, long on brains, short on common sense. He strolls into Korbler's office, where Korbler stares at the Scotch flavored urine, wondering what to do with it.

"Hey, boss. Back from lunch, anything going on?"

Korbler pulls at his nose to force his attention away from Jared's gift. "Nothing much, just going over the Vietnam bone run with the courier."

Gaylord slides in the chair recently occupied by Jared. "Is he one of ours? I didn't recognize him."

"Nope, Jared Scott, one of our contract guys. A bit of a prick by any standard. Glad he's just a part timer." Korbler silently mulls over payback options. There's always payback, of course. When and how much are the real questions.

Gaylord digests this, then a frown grows on his face. "Jared Scott? Hey, is he...the guy who, uh, air-dropped his brother in 'Nam?"

Korbler stands. "Yeah, that's him. Only guy I ever met who got a Silver Star and a Dishonorable Discharge on the same tour. Still needs a little discipline, if you ask me." If Gaylord was a peer instead of a new agent, Korbler would unload quite a bit more, but he doesn't want junior to get any lessons on insubordination. "Anyway, you need to get those documents ready for him. No real rush, he's going to be busy for the next few days," Korbler says with a smirk. "Has some anger management issues to work on."

Gaylord stands. "Okay, sure, the docs are just about ready now. Say," he says, gesturing towards the glass of urine sitting on the desk. "Is that Mountain Dew? I love that stuff!"

Korbler turns to leave the room. He hesitates a fraction of a moment, then replies with a faint smile, "Yeah, Jared Scott brought it over. You can have it if you want it, I've hardly touched it."

Gaylord beams, picks up the glass and swirls the ice cubes.

Korbler tries to keep a straight face. "Might need some more ice," he says. 'Could be a little warm..."

Chapter 5

Dr. Robert Sanders peers over the top of his half-frame glasses. "Let's see... 'inappropriate expressions of anger.' Is this your perception of the reason for the referral?" Dr. Sanders is in his forties, a balding, pleasant-looking man wearing an aloha shirt, nice slacks and comfortable loafers. His office has a couple of chairs, bookshelves filled with books, a few tables, and a small corner desk, but is devoid of any personal items other than his framed diplomas hanging inconspicuously on the far wall. Only his well broken-in overstuffed chair speaks anything of his likes or preferences, which is the way he wants it. People don't come to talk about him, so no sense in giving clues or distractions.

Sanders holds a client file and notepad in his lap, which he attends to more out of habit than not. After 20,000 or so counseling sessions, he hungers for a unique challenge when a new client walks in. He rarely gets it. Nonetheless, he tries to reserve judgment until the person has the opportunity to tell his or her story, preferably in a fashion not *too* self-serving. Everyone has windows to their psyches — what you see depends on whether you look in or look out. Sanders, in his patient, low key style, will raise the window shades to which clients grimly cling.

Jared, dressed down in frayed jeans and polo shirt, slouches in the easy chair across the coffee table from Dr. Sanders. He has a Bible in hand, which he flips through randomly. He hesitates so long in answering Dr. Sanders' question, Sanders is about to ask again.

"Yeah." The sullen tone is painfully evident. Dr. Sanders makes notes in his records.

"The intake interview report says you busted up a bar in Aiea, got a whole slew of traffic tickets." He glances over his glasses again. "And something here about being 'really pissed off' at work."

"Yeah."

"Haven't had the same job longer than 18-months...same thing with relationships..."

Jared shifts in his chair, crosses his legs, doesn't respond.

Shuffling through the forms, Dr. Sanders pauses. "This is interesting. Seems you got three women pregnant in one year. All of them members of the choir at the Kailua First Methodist Church." He takes off his glasses and holds them in his lap. "What do you attribute that to, Jared?"

Jared turns his attention to the ceiling. "I don't know, doc. Just like gospel music, I guess."

"Left them all....Do you have issues with religion, Jared? I see you have a Bible."

"Yeah, I carry it with me sometimes. Makes me feel better."

A pause.

"Well then, perhaps you can tell me your favorite passage, and why." Dr. Sanders says, taking a drink from a glass of water at hand.

"I... I don't actually read it much... I just like, I just like to have it with me."

"Kind of like a talisman?"

"What's that?"

"Never mind." Sanders shifts gears in the discussion. "Let me fill in a bit more. Are you currently in a personal relationship with anyone?"

Jared sighs. "No." He mumbles under his breath, "Thank God."

"And may I ask why not? You don't seem to have much difficulty attracting women."

"Getting them is not the problem, getting rid of them is." Jared glances over at the doc, hoping for a nod of understanding. "I'm not good for women, and they're not good for me. I'm just too stupid to face it, I guess."

"Why do you feel a need to 'get rid of them,' as you put it?"

Jared eyeballs the door, the urge to bolt rising within him. His exasperation continues to build. "Jeez, doc, can we talk about something less personal, like wetting the bed or masturbation or whatever else you guys find so fascinating?"

Sanders doesn't answer. Two minutes go by.

"I start to feel, I don't know...trapped, claustrophobic."

Sanders remains silent. Two more minutes go by.

"Scared," Jared says softly.

After making a few more notes, Sanders straightens up and looks straight at Jared. "Well, let's get into it from another angle. Jared, who are you?"

Relieved to change the subject, Jared answers quickly. "I am a pilot, and a damn good one. I work for Island Air Aviation at the airport, mostly charters and flight instruction."

"No, that's *what* you are. I want to know *who* you are."

Hesitation grips Jared for a long, painful moment, as he dreads a trip through the locked doors of his mind. He tries to stare a hole in the floor, big enough to escape through, but it offers no salvation. He takes a tiny emotional step instead. "I'm just an average guy who gets pissed off a lot by the idiots I have to deal with," he says.

"And what do you think is the reason?"

"'Cause they're idiots, aren't you listening?" Jared snaps, his face flushing.

"Okay..." Sanders makes more notes.

Right away Jared regrets his outburst. He looks at the door, desperate to get out.

How much more of this torture!

"What is it you want from people, Jared?"

"I don't know..." He shifts in his seat as if invisible ants are under his clothes. "I just want to be left alone..." He straightens up. "No, I just need...," his voice trails off, then he grips the armrests and regains eye contact. "I got good friends, I get along with most people, I just don't have much patience and sometimes it's easier to not deal with stuff. Look, doc, can you write me an up-chit so I can get on with my life?" He looks imploringly at Sanders.

"I'll be glad to report you have initiated counseling and are making satisfactory progress. Of course, there needs to be follow-on sessions." Sanders punches the call button on his intercom. "Vicki, schedule Mr. Scott for twelve weeks, once a week." He turns to Jared. "Same time good for you?"

Jared doesn't answer, but in an instant, he is on his feet. He storms out of the office, fury in his face. The secretary in the waiting area looks up and says, "Mr. Scott, I'll need for you to sign a couple of..."

Jared doesn't even glance at her as he blitzes the exit. "I ain't signing shit," and he is gone.

Chapter 6

Ho Chi Minh City, 1980

The dilapidated Japanese pickup truck bounces along the pot-holed paved street, forcing its way through the chaos of sidewalk vendors, food carts, touts and ubiquitous squadrons of buzzing motorbikes. To the uninitiated observer, it seems there must be a law requiring every vehicle with a horn to blare every ten feet or ten seconds, whichever comes first. If so, it is the only traffic law drivers obey.

Jared rocks in the passenger seat, beset with an overwhelming case of *deja vu*. The sights, the sounds and smells, especially the smells, roll into the truck through the open windows, borne on waves of fetid air. A couple of three-day R & R excursions were all Jared had in Saigon, then back to the jungle. The memories are vivid, though, and a couple them make him smile.

Best days I ever spent in 'Nam, that's for sure.

A few curse words comprise most of the driver's inventory of English. He flings them out the window with great abandon at various people that block the way, then laughs gleefully and grins at Jared. Everyone on the street ignores the insults, and for that matter, the pickup itself as it bulls its way down the narrow lanes.

Another undistinguished intersection looms before them, but this one has a new feature. Two green-uniformed soldiers block their way, AK assault rifles slung over their shoulders. They take an immediate interest in the pickup and its occupants. One man unslings his rifle, holds up a hand and commands the driver to halt. No longer grinning, the driver coasts to a stop. A jabbering conversation between the driver and the soldier ensues. Jaw set, the soldier looks hard at Jared.

A queasy feeling grows deep in Jared's gut. The last time he saw anyone in these uniforms, they were making every effort to kill him. His heart rate picks up and sweat oozes from his body.

The driver looks over at Jared and makes the universal hand gesture for money. Jared nods his head, albeit with a grimace — some things never change. He pulls a couple of U.S. dollars from his billfold and hands them over.

Flashing a smile, the soldier stuffs away the money. He grins at Jared, then launches into a gibberish rant directed at the driver. The driver shrugs, turns to Jared and says, "More." He and the soldier pause and look at Jared, expectation etched on their faces.

Jared leans over to make full eye contact with the soldier. "Tell him to go fuck himself." There's no need for a translation.

The soldier and Jared lock eyes. Neither blinks. Sweat rolls. From out of sight behind the door comes the unmistakable click of the AK's safety.

Switching from "safe" to "fire?" Or the other way?

The soldier straightens up and waves the driver on.

Jared breathes again after they've gone far enough to ensure they wouldn't be shot in the back while "escaping." Welcome to Ho Chi Minh City!

Continuing through the maze of back streets, Jared wonders, *Does the driver know where the hell he is going?* Then, a more horrifying thought — *What if they are kidnapping me?* He glances at the driver who grimaces like a maniac as he NASCAR's through the narrow streets. With a mental groan, Jared realizes that he is hopelessly disoriented, especially if he has to jump from the truck and make a run for it. He's not carrying any documents to connect him with the CIA, but what if that's been found out? Would anyone even come looking for him?

"Hey GI! You gimme cigarette! You got Mar-boro for me?" An urchin runs alongside the truck, grabbing at Jared's arm through the window. His street mates run in trail, one of them banging on the side of the truck. This sets off the driver, who yanks the wheel hard over, sending a pair of the kids flying into a fruit vendor cart.

"Numba one driver, yeah?" The driver flashes a gold capped grin, earning a weak "thumbs up" gesture from Jared. He wonders what will be next on this obstacle course.

He doesn't have to wait long. They turn into a shabby residential area and stop in front of a walled compound. Roosters roam the streets, chortling their turf claims to each other. Lean, mangy stray dogs slink about, looking for fresh garbage or a slow rooster. A profuse tangle of power lines seems to be the only thing keeping some of the imploding apartment buildings from immediate collapse. The exception is the thick high walls of the compound, crowned with barbwire and imbedded broken glass - a formidable barrier.

Two toughs guard the large, fortified gate. The guards are tall for Vietnamese, each six feet and 180 pounds or more, Jared estimates. There's another difference. Upon closer scrutiny, he notes they are what was called, back in the day, "pinky-poops," the obscene term for the mulatto offspring of black American soldiers and Vietnamese brothel women. Of all of the legacies of the Vietnam War, theirs was perhaps the cruelest. Universally scorned by the Vietnamese, they were brutally ostracized by adults and kids alike, often abandoned by their mothers and forced to live by their own wits. Most fell to crime as a survival skill. The slow learners died on the streets, left to be picked up with the garbage.

One of the guards steps forward and confronts the driver. The other gives Jared a suspicious stare while slipping his Kalashnikov from his shoulder. Jared forces a smile. It is not returned.

After some intense verbal skirmishes with the driver, the guard motions Jared to get out and approach. It's been years, but Jared recognizes the gesture — it's what the Viets use to call a dog.

Well, here's another asshole who needs a lesson on manners, Jared thinks. *This place is full of 'em. Have to save that for another day, though.*

Careful to not make any sudden moves, Jared emerges from the truck, in his hand a small leather folding bag. Sweat streams make waterfalls from his face.

The guards muscle open the squeaky gate, revealing a large courtyard. With one guard in front of Jared and one behind, they troop past a new Toyota Land Cruiser and a bubbling koi fishpond. Jared notes a large back-up generator in a sheltered area to one side of the house. Motion detectors adorn the eves at each corner.

This guy is well equipped. And wealthy.

Ornamental red doors dominate the front of the residence. Groaning air-conditioning units hang out of every window, adorning two stories of gray concrete block construction. The group pauses before the steps, full in the brutal sun. The lead guard claps his hands and waits. The sun cooks through another layer of Jared's flesh. He steals a glance at the guards. They aren't even sweating — unbelievable!

One of the red doors creaks open, or maybe the creaking emanated from the ancient joints of the woman who emerges from the dark interior. Time hasn't been kind to her - a deep wrinkle marks each of the many years of her life, and then some. She has tied her gray-black hair into a knot at the back of her head, helping to balance her stooped stance. Without introduction or eye contact, she says to Jared, "You come with me. Take shoe off."

Jared removes his shoes and steps inside. The delightful coolness of air conditioning sweeps over his body. At once, he is in a better mood as his sweat-soaked shirt starts to dry. The mama-san leads him through a maze of rooms and corridors, occasionally looking back to make sure Jared still follows. He sizes up the house as his eyes adapt to the gloom. Given the shantytown neighborhood, it is surprisingly well appointed, with rosewood furniture, carved artworks, and expensive rugs. Despite the rugs, however, the floor squeaks every step.

A thought pops: *Just like grandma's floors in the old house in Texas.*

Back to the present. Jared is careful to remember the turns in case he has to make a hasty exit. A good habit in case things go bad. Nothing ominous so far, but...

They halt at a spacious living room. The mama-san claps her hands twice and disappears down the corridor.

The dominant feature of the room is a jumbo TV set and a gargantuan sound system, thankfully off, at the moment, since it looks to be able to drown out a Boeing 747. Jared takes in the rest of the room. Everything he can see in the gloom is either red or black. Carved mahogany decorations. Overhead drapes. A bamboo wind chime, bumped by the soft breeze of the ceiling fans, surrenders background music. And the smell — the place reeks of *Phu Quoc* fish sauce. For a moment Jared is transported back a decade, a younger man introduced to an exotic world, populated by natives with breath so bad they could derail a freight train at forty yards just by blowing at it.

Had to take up eating the stuff myself in self-defense!

At first, Jared doesn't see him. The first clue is the ascending and descending glow of a cigarette somewhere deep in the twilight. Trazer nestles into one of several overstuffed lounges, each strewn with embroidered soft pillows. He relaxes, pulls on a locally made cigarette, cirrus clouds of smoke drifting over his head. Black silk pajama robes. Scraggly blond hair and a bandana cover most of his head. A vivid red and green dragon tattoo coils around one arm. Trazer stares off into space, as if in a trance.

Jared, having come halfway around the world for this moment, takes the initiative. He strides over, plants himself in Trazer's space.

"Jared Scott here. You Trazer?"

Trazer looks up as if noticing Jared for the first time. "You got him." He rises and the men size each other up. Neither offers a handshake. "Welcome to my little part of 'Nam."

Even at arm's length, Jared is assaulted by Trazer's body odor, not sweat, but a bone-deep sour reek. A man of the world, Jared knows it for what it is — a heroin funk. Trazer's face is clean shaven, revealing facial furors etched deeper than expected of a man in his thirties. He stares at Jared. The eyes are dead, red-rimmed orbs absent of any hint of a soul.

Looks as if he's doing hard time in a soft jail.

Jared takes a scan of the room and its contents. "You've done well for yourself. Sure beats being ass-deep in a rain-filled foxhole."

"Yeah, the import-export business has been good."

"You here during the war?"

"Yeah."

"Whereabouts?" asks Jared.

"Quang Tri, up near the border."

"Me, too. What years?"

"Sixty-eight, sixty-nine."

"Really?" Jared nods. "Me, too. Army?"

"Yeah."

Jared pauses. "Whose?"

Trazer doesn't answer. The two men stare at each other from a foot apart. Trazer breaks the silence. "Did you come here to reminisce or do business?" He sniffs, turns and saunters over to a large red felt covered pool table. Lying on it is a dirty, lumpy burlap bag. He gestures at it and says, "Here's what you came for."

Jared hesitates, held in place by the sour feeling in the pit of his stomach. His eyeballs are locked, unblinking, on the bag. A dirty, lumpy bag all right, but also an altar of shattered dreams and broken hearts. He edges closer, ready to bolt if starts to move.

"Open it up. I don't want you to buy a pig in a poke...whatever a poke is." Trazer's lips curl in a smile, but there is no humor in them.

Jared reaches, hesitates, then pulls open the sack, revealing a jumble of brown and black bones. Many are shattered, some burned, a few the size of a fingernail. Thank God, there are no skulls. Jared's forehead creases, and he pulls his hand away. He's seen bones like this before, the remains of aircrew who had crashed and burned. Maybe this was someone he knew...

Then the death smell catches his nostrils, and knocks him back. "Whoa, haven't smelled that for a while. You couldn't have washed them?"

"Well, that's extra," Trazer says, a smirk dancing on his face. "No tickie, no washie, that's the way it is here in 'Nam nowadays."

Jared hates him for it. And other things.

"Now, you got something for me?"

Jared, still mesmerized by the bones, pulls a new U.S. passport out of his folding bag and hands it over without looking.

Trazer is quick to grab it. He looks through it and his grin grows ever wider. "Valid without photograph—sweet!" He places it in a robe pocket, then pats it like it is his favorite dog. "A real live 'get out of jail free' card!" he exults. "And for just a shitty bag of stinking bones. Freakin' fools!"

Jared comes out of his retrospective. "You got any proof these aren't just a bunch of water buffalo bones?"

Trazer reaches into the robe's other pocket and extracts a dozen aged dog tags. "Here," he says, holding them out. But as Jared reaches for them, Trazer lets them slide between his fingers. The tags hit the ground with a cold, metallic clatter. "Oh...sorry about that," Trazer offers with the utmost insincerity, still grinning.

Jared glares at him, his hands drawn tight into fists.

"Don't worry, I'll take care of them, Traitor...I mean, Trazer" Jared says, as he reaches down for the tags.

The grin disappears from Trazer's face.

"We both got what we wanted, let's celebrate," Trazer says abruptly. He turns away, holds up a hand, snaps his fingers and gives a command in Vietnamese. Two young Viet teenage girls in lingerie ghost out of the shadows. One carries a hand-held mirror, the other a small mahogany box covered with carved elephants. Trazer grabs the box and sprawls out on one of the lounges. The girls snuggle in around him as he dips a long, painted pinky fingernail into the box, pulls it out piled with white powder. Ignoring the girls and Jared, he pinches off one nostril, puts the powder to his nose. With a noisy snort, it disappears. Trazer stiffens for a moment and his face contorts, then relaxes as the rush passes.

A few minutes later, his eyes open and he appears to come back from wherever his chemically-induced mental orgasm took him. Hands trembling, he chops out a couple of lines on the mirror with a rusty razor. The girls get their own few minutes of nirvana.

"Damn, that's some good shit," Trazer says with a curling smile. "Sure you don't want some?"

"I've got enough problems, thanks," Jared retorts, as Trazer cuddles up with the girls.

"How about a girl? Trazer pulls down the lingerie top of one to expose her small breasts. She doesn't flinch, just stands there. "If you don't like these I got more," Trazer adds in a mock helpful tone.

"Little bit young, aren't they?" A rhetorical question; even in the dim light the girls are barely pubescent. Jared shivers just from sharing the room with them.

"Twenty-five," Trazer says, "...if you add 'em both together!" His giggling laugh echoes across the room.

Jared scoops up the bone bag and heads out. "You are one sick motherfucker," he mutters over his shoulder.

* * * * *

As Jared trudges down the hall, one of the girls leans in to kiss Trazer, inadvertently knocking the bandana from his head. The torn, twisted remains of an ear hide among the strands of his scraggly mane. Trazer backhands her, hard enough to put her down. Without a whimper, she slides back in to hug him.

Trazer ignores her, already thinking about the next snort.

His powder lust is interrupted by the bang of a door opening. A stocky Asian man, almost swallowed by a large white kimono, walks in strutting like a matador entering a bullring. Tattoos cover his arms and neck, and short-cropped hair reveals a sizeable scar on his scalp. The little fingers of each hand are just stubs.

"Who that man?" Fujitta demands, gesturing after Jared.

"Some CIA flunky. A nosy one, at that."

"Is he trouble?"

"Naw, he was just bringing over my new passport." Trazer pulls the little navy blue booklet out of his robe pocket and waves it in the air like it is the Stanley Cup.

"And with this, my *yakusa* friend, we are going to turn our little business arrangement into a very big business arrangement." He pulls the girls close to him. "But first, I'm going to sample some of the merchandise."

Chapter 7

"**D**on't forget to check the sump drain," Jared notes, pointing at the belly of the little plane as yet another wide body jet carrying exhausted and sunburned tourists roars overhead.

"Damn," Lori Konishi says under her breath, blushing. Then she responds to Jared. "I just wanted to show you I could do it all by memory."

Jared, watches her. "Well, you're plenty smart, but it's always better to use the checklist when preflighting the plane. Just too many 'gotchas,' even on this little Cessna. Like water in the gas that didn't get drained out. Darned old engine just won't run on water," Jared shakes his head in mock wonder.

Lori extracts her checklist from her flight bag and finds the proper page. Kneeling underneath the engine compartment, she draws a fuel sample from a drain into a clear plastic cup. She holds it to the sunlight and examines it at length.

"Looks clear," she reports and dumps the sample on the asphalt before putting the cup away. Jared nods in agreement as Lori, now armed with the checklist, continues the aircraft inspection.

"Jared, you take good care of Miss Konishi, you hear?" Smitty calls from a company golf cart as he delivers two elderly women passengers to a charter flight. He and Jared exchange waves and smiles.

"Can do, see you in a couple of hours," Jared offers a thumbs up gesture.

As Smitty continues on his way, Jared adds to Lori, "Smitty is such a great guy, best friend I ever had. The guy is wonderful, will do anything for you."

"Well, that's the kind of friend you need," Lori looks over at Smitty as he helps the ladies from the cart. "He's always been super friendly and helpful to me. Have you known him long?"

"Yeah, we were in Vietnam together. He was my crew chief when I was flying helicopters there."

"Really?" says Lori, untying the tie-down rope from the wing. She glances at Jared. "The way you're talking, did he, like, save your life or something?"

"Not there." An ever-so-slight pause. "Hey, let's keep moving, we got to have the airplane back on time."

"Roger that!" Lori says, saluting smartly, and they laugh at her amateur attempt at aviation lingo.

Using the wing strut as a step, she leans out over the wing to make sure the fuel caps are secured and in the process, stretches her short-shorts and Polo shirt to the max.

That's a seriously fine looking woman, Jared observes, enjoying the view. Tall for an Asian, silky black hair pulled back in a ponytail, a cover-girl face and a smile from here to forever. Not to mention ambitious, smart and a quick learner. Yeah, quite the package.

Jared's brief fantasy is interrupted by a splash of mental ice water. Ghosts of girlfriends past, enough to fill a horror movie, come flying out of memory closets, swirling, screeching, shrieking, claws out, reaching for him!

Start thinking with the brain, moron! Last thing I need is more estrogen complicating my life, I've got enough problems already! Oh, yeah. Don't forget that Lori is also the only child of the newly elected Governor of the State of Hawaii! Better leave well enough alone!

Finished securing the fuel cap, Lori climbs down and consults the checklist again. Satisfied that she is at the last item, she squats down and pulls the chock from under the nose wheel. She stands up, close by Jared, and looks into his face.

"So, Jared, you got a girlfriend?"

Jared is nonplussed. "Boy, you're just full of questions today, aren't you?" He adds, "Naw, I'm just taking it easy, keeping things simple. Besides, I'm not good for women."

Or with them, he adds silently.

"Oh, are you some kind of serial killer or something?" She feigns a slasher movie damsel-in-distress expression.

"No, for God's sake, of course not," Jared replies, not expecting to have to defend himself. "I'm just a very busy guy, and besides, you are my flight student — it'd be kind of unethical, I think. Not sure why, just seems that way." He pauses, looks skyward and scratches his chin a bit. "You *are* semi-cute, though."

Lori snorts the response. "Semi-cute, huh? That's all?"

"I've got a question for *you*, though. Why do you want to learn to fly?"

"Oh, I don't know. It's fun, of course, and I really like the idea of being in control, being responsible for myself," she says, head nodding. "And you get to meet new people..." She glances his way.

Jared ignores the bait. "Well, we got to get down to business. Looks like Dillingham is going to be too windy today, but we can go over to Ford Island and practice there." He gestures in the direction of Pearl Harbor, only a few miles distant.

"Ford Island, in Pearl Harbor?" Lori says, doubt in her voice.

"Yep, it has an old landing strip right in the middle. Navy lets civilian planes use it on the weekends to keep student traffic at a minimum here at the International Airport. Ford's an uncontrolled airfield, so we don't even have to talk to a control tower. You'll like it."

"Okay, just give me a heading. I'm not too good on that map reading stuff yet." They climb into the airplane, one on each side, don their headsets and slam shut the flimsy doors. Without ropes to hold it down the plane rocks gently in the tradewinds, seemingly eager to fly.

Lori snaps open the window on her side, glances about and yells the standard warning: "Clear!" She engages the ignition, the propeller turns and the engine catches with a roar. With a couple of radio calls to Ground Control for authorization, they begin the taxi out.

The little two-place Cessna is dwarfed by the giant airliners around it, like a sardine swimming with whales. With Boeing 747's as bookends, one in front, one in back, they make their way to the runway in use.

"Okay, let's give this guy some more room," Jared says, gesturing at the big Boeing on the taxiway in front of them. "If he powers up we'll tumble like a feather hit by a leaf blower."

"I was more worried about that monster behind us," Lori says, looking worriedly over her shoulder at the half million-pound behemoth bearing down on them.

"Yeah, he could suck us down an intake and not even burp. Comforting thought, huh?"

Lori doesn't answer but makes sure their flashing red anti-collision light is on, as if it will keep the leviathans at bay.

Finally, they reach the long, broad runway. Their whole aircraft vibrates as the 747 ahead of them blasts off for a destination somewhere over the horizon. They are next: Lori runs through the final checks. She looks at Jared, her eyes darting around the cockpit, but he says nothing. At the control tower's direction, they take the runway and pause, a mile and a half of concrete stretching before them.

Jared puts a hand on Lori's forearm for a moment — the muscles are stiff with anticipation.

"Don't worry, you know what to do." She forces a doubtful smile.

"Cessna Four Two Five One X-Ray, cleared for takeoff. Left turn-out approved."

Lori rehearses for a moment, then replies. "Uh, Four Two Five One X-Ray cleared for takeoff." With Jared's nod, Lori pushes the throttle forward. The little engine buzzes like a Vespa motor, more noise than output. They rattle along, reach takeoff speed and the wheels leave the ground, still spinning.

A grin breaks out on Lori's face. She can't help bursting forth with the obvious: "We're flying!"

As they climb to traffic pattern altitude, more scenery comes into view — the beautiful green mountains, the white strips of surf, downtown Honolulu and then the expanse of Pearl Harbor. The control tower turns them towards Pearl and releases them. Lori levels off and pulls the power back to cruise setting.

"Okay, you see the field?" asks Jared.

"Yeah, eleven o'clock, right?"

"That's it, just enter a downwind for the traffic pattern. There's no tower controllers to talk to, just fly the pattern and announce your intentions over the common traffic advisory frequency."

"Got it!"

They near Ford Island, flying over the Navy shipyards and parked ships. Jared gazes at the scene below, picking out the old Battleship Row adjacent to Ford Island, and the gleaming white bridge shape that is the USS Arizona Memorial. Boatloads of tourists churn across the harbor, coming and going to the memorial. Even though he's been here hundreds of times, Jared remains awed by the bloody history of this now peaceful waterway. The airfield nearing brings him back to the present.

"All right," Jared observes, "looks like we've got the landing pattern all to ourselves." Lori nods and maneuvers the little plane around a standard rectangular course, and then descends towards the narrow runway. The glide path is stable, Jared notes to himself, but she's a little rough on the controls. Lori glances at him, but he offers no advice. At this stage, she needs to figure it out herself.

As taught, she says aloud the essential landing checklist items: "Mixture, rich; Carburetor heat, on; Flaps, full; Runway, clear." Jared scrutinizes her performance as the aircraft continues along the flight path, flares and touches down with a small bounce.

"Okay, let's go around, touch and go."

Lori nods, pushes the throttle up and the aircraft surges toward takeoff speed. "Full power; Carburetor heat, off; Flaps, coming up." She manipulates each control as she calls it off. In a short distance, the aircraft is airborne and climbing back to altitude.

Jared says, "Good job. Give me three more just like that."

"You weren't helping on the controls, were you?" Lori says, and gives him a quick look.

"Nope, that was all you. Keep up the good work." Lori beams a toothy smile in response.

They make several more takeoffs and landings as Jared continues the evaluation. "Make this one a full stop and taxi back for takeoff instead of a touch and go."

Lori slows to walking speed after touchdown and pulls the aircraft on to the taxiway. She takes a swig of water from her bottle and bursts forth with a sigh. Jared makes notes on his clipboard.

Halfway to the end of the runway Jared says something Lori has never heard before.

"Let's stop here." Lori looks at him, puzzled, since there's no apparent reason to stop here, far away from anything on the field.

"Is there something wrong with the plane?" she asks as she brings the aircraft to a halt.

"Nope," Jared says, unsnapping his seat belt. He takes off his headset and opens his door. "I'm getting out," he shouts over the engine noise. "Take off, fly a good tight pattern, and come back for a full stop landing."

Lori's eyes get big. "Whoa, whoa, whoa! You're sending me up by myself? Now?"

"Yeah, it's called soloing, and you're ready for it. Just do like you've been doing and you'll be fine. I have the hand-held radio and will be in contact. Happy landings. Bye."

Without waiting for a reply, Jared steps out and slams the door shut. He waves a goodbye and walks over to the side of the taxiway. Lori sits for a moment collecting her thoughts, then swallows hard and powers up to proceed to the end of the runway.

* * * * *

As Jared watches, Lori enters the runway, and lines up. She doesn't key the radio, but in the cockpit she yells aloud: "Focus! Concentration!" She takes a deep breath and applies full power for the takeoff run.

The little plane surges forward. The wheels break contact with the runway and the ground falls away below her. With a grin on her face almost as wide as the wings, she yells: "I'm flying! Solo!"

Lori circles through the pattern. She checks to make sure no other airplanes are competing for the airspace, and that everything is in order. Her belief in herself soars with each passing moment.

Hey! Look at me! She says to herself, to the world.

* * * * *

On the ground, Jared critiques the quality of the pattern flown, and makes a couple of notes. Like all flight instructors who solo a student, he holds his breath, positive, but not certain, all will go well.

Just do what you've been doing. I can see your confidence building by the way you fly the pattern. You wanted responsibility and control — well, here you go!

Handling the crosswind without difficulty, Lori turns on final, dead on for the runway. Jared holds his breath again, but Lori lands like a butterfly with sore feet. Jared bursts out with spontaneous applause.

Darned good, girl, excellent in fact. Of course, she does have a superior flight instructor!

Lori turns around at the far end and taxis back to where Jared stands, her smile flashing. But instead of stopping, she sails on past towards the takeoff runway with nothing more than a wave in explanation.

Jared speaks into the hand-held radio, with just a hint of sarcasm, "Hey Lori, you're supposed to stop for me." Lori turns onto the runway, guns the engine and gets airborne again. "Sorry, I'm having too much fun!" she radios.

"Aw, crap," Jared says to himself, then over the radio he adds, "Lori enough fooling around. Bring it back for a full stop. Now." He doesn't try to hide his irritation.

There's no answer from the cockpit, but the airplane makes a fast low altitude pass down the runway, scattering seagulls and making Jared cringe. He casts a quick look around to see if anyone is witnessing this fiasco.

"I'm sorry, I didn't hear that." Lori radios. "Too much static on the radio." She waves at Jared and blows him a kiss as she swoops by him.

"Bring that airplane back right now, young lady. No shit!" Jared demands in his sternest voice, face reddening.

"Not until you tell me I'm REALLY cute, not just *semi*-cute."

"Look, Lori," Jared says, calming himself, trying the reasonable person approach. "We don't have time to play grade-school games. Just come back, land and pick me up, okay?"

"Really, REALLY cute!"

Jared is seething again. "Alright, really, REALLY cute. Now get that damn airplane back on the ground." Such insubordination!

"Sure, I'll be right there. By the way, *you* are semi-cute yourself," she adds. "But I do have one more request..."

* * * * *

Lori buzzes along the *Kalanianaole Highway, queen of the road* in her bright yellow Volkswagen Beetle. She leans back, head rocking as she sends the lyrics to Born to be Wild flying out of the sunroof.

> *Like a true nature's child,*
> *I was born, born to be wild,*
> *I can climb so high,*
> *I never wanna die!*
> *Born to be wild...*

Listening to the music, she thinks, *Wild enough to steal an airplane if that was how to get Jared to notice her!*

She smiles and glances at her watch. *Need to stop by the drycleaners before I get home, want to allow plenty of time to get dolled up and to the party at Father's.* Fortunately traffic towards Manoa is light, a rare blessing, so she's making good time.

Lori takes a moment to beep the horn and launch a *shaka* wave to a bride and groom disembarking a limo at one of the palatial compounds that line the beach. The couple return the gesture, all grins, radiating happiness. *Beautiful dress, girl, you should be happy! Got to be a Vera Wang, for sure. One day....*

It's been a while since she's been in such a good mood. Her exploited-women rescue movement, *Freedom Network*, takes a lot of her time and effort and more recently, Rocky's campaign has become all consuming. Zero social or recreational appointments on her personal calendar. Hard to accept for someone not yet thirty, even if self-imposed. Taking flight lessons was a little rebellion against no one in particular, time for herself instead of everyone else. That was pretty much in character, since rebellion had been a constant theme in her life.

Lori allows her thoughts to drift back to Jared...again. Pale blue eyes, black as ink hair except for the white splash, strong enough to pick her up with one arm. And his hands! Big, twice the size of hers, long muscular fingers, and most surprising, exceptionally smooth and soft palms. Best of all, he had hair on his knuckles! Not like these island boys that are hot for her. What is it about hairy knuckles that is such a turn on? She twirls a strand of her hair, just behind the ear. More head rocking. The smile on her face begins to show teeth as she contemplates an intimate moment.

"*Oh, shit!*" Lori yelps her standard exclamation when the blue lights come on behind her. She breaks her gaze on the rearview mirror to glance at the speedometer — oops! Her stomach does a flip-flop. Oh, boy, Father's going to be mad!

Lori gives an acknowledgement wave and slows the car. She cuts onto the service road, then turns the engine off in the Ralphs' shopping center parking lot. The police car, a black Olds 442, rolls in and stops behind her, but the little stick-on blue light keeps flashing. In Hawaii, most police officers use their own cars, attaching the roof bubble gum machine when on duty. Even more incongruous: a gaily colored baby seat is left to guard the interior as the police officer steps out. He extracts his uniform hat and dons it, adjusting it carefully.

Lori checks the area. Sure enough, a half-dozen shoppers have paused to watch her misfortune. She groans and turns away in the hope no one will recognize her. She really does not need such negative publicity at this moment.

Her HPD tormentor takes his time, filling out some forms as he strolls towards her car window. Lori checks him out in the side-view mirror: smartly creased black uniform, shiny shoes, the badge and nametag all perfectly placed. An impressive amount of cop stuff is hooked neatly on his belt. Obviously a perfectionist. Great, just great!

He stops at her window. Lori musters her most luminescent smile and shines it at him.

"Why, hello Officer..." she checks out his name tag, "...Wong." She gives him the once-over. A scraggly little caterpillar of a mustache crawls on his upper lip. She checks his hands. No hair on *those* knuckles. Or even the arms. How old is this kid? Twelve? "Might I help you with something, sir?"

"License, registration and proof of insurance, ma'am."

No "Good Morning," or "How you doing?" Not a good start. Lori fumbles through the glove box, which triggers a cascade of documents, maps and assorted trash. A growing sense of alarm churns her stomach. Sweat pops out on her brow. Where is that registration stuff!

Officer Wong taps his pen on his clipboard, looks at his watch.

"Here it is!" Lori exclaims, fishing a plastic folder from the mess on the floorboard. She flashes a hopeful smile at Wong as she hands it over. Then another fear grips her. Was it all current? She racks her brain—did she ever send in the paperwork for the registration? The insurance card? She was so busy...

Wong scribbles. Lori frets. She can't get another ticket! They will suspend her license for sure. She is already on the SR program, the state issued insurance you end up with when no commercial company will take you, at about five times the usual cost. Which Father is blessedly paying. Uhhh, make that past tense, since Rocky made it clear she'd be walking if she got another ticket. Something about "finally growing up." Just not fair!

"Forty-seven in a thirty-five zone, Ma'am. Do you have an emergency somewhere?"

Lori sees an opportunity. "Well, officer," she says, shifting to a serious, concerned expression," actually there's an important meeting down at the campaign headquarters I'm late for. Getting the inauguration put together, you know." She nods her head with a little frown, clues as to the seriousness of the obligation. No response from Wong. His face is an impassive and unsympathetic mask, which brings a flash of anger from Lori. Hasn't this dumb ass put it together yet? He's got my license with "Konishi" on it, three bumper stickers scream "KONISHI FOR GOVERNOR" and I'm on TV all the time! What does it take for the boy cop to get it? Is he nursing a grudge about Japan and that Nanking thing back in the war? Hell, the Americans even forgave Pearl Harbor. Move on, junior!

Lori decides on a charm offensive. She tilts her head a bit and gives Wong the doe eye treatment, with a few fluttering blinks thrown in for good measure. "I bet your family would really like to be front row center for the inauguration, yeah?"

Wong's eyes, never round, narrow to slits. Lori hears him take a deep breath, and let it out slowly.

Uh, oh! Overplayed my hand!

Wong sticks the clipboard under Lori's nose. "Sign by the 'X,' which is a promise to appear. If you do not appear at the hearing date mailed to you," he drones on like Robbie the Robot, "a warrant will be issued for your arrest."

Lori see's his upper lip quiver as he tries to suppress a smile. She conjures a glare with enough hate to stop a witch's heart. Snatching the clipboard, she scrawls an unrecognizable signature and shoves it back to him. Wong rips off a copy of the ticket and hands it to Lori. He bends over so he is eye level with her, leans close.

"Have a nice day." With that and a crooked smile, he turns and in a moment is back in his car. Ten seconds later, he pulls into traffic and is gone. Lori watches him depart, still lasering an "I hate you" scowl after him.

"*Chinese asshole!*" she spits, and punishes the steering wheel with a hammer fist.

Chapter 8

As daylight fades, Jared wheels the rumbling Corvette convertible up the winding narrow road marking the uppermost edge of Tantalus Mountain. Houses are far between up here. They cling daringly to the precipitous terrain, too steep for safe construction in most places.

However, Jared notes great views of Honolulu and the southern coast of the island reward the eye, whenever he can catch a glimpse. More important at the moment is to stay on the road and to not kiss a guardrail on the one side or the rocky wall on the other. Even the Corvette is hard pressed to track on such a torturous road.

Spotting a small parking area, Jared yanks the wheel and whips into the space, barely stopping in time. He turns off the engine and waits a moment for the dust to settle. Unfolding himself from the little cockpit, he strolls over to the low stone wall and props a foot on it. He is treated to a God's eye view — Diamond Head crater dominating the leftmost land mass, then the multitudes of hotels of Waikiki, and the accompanying white froth of the surf. The downtown area is next, marked by a proliferation of excessively large bank buildings, then the Punchbowl Crater rises above the works of man. The headstones of the Veterans cemetery are just visible in the dusk, dotting the green lawn that forms the crater floor. Last is the great expanse of the naval base at Pearl Harbor, close by Honolulu International Airport, with tiny jets swooping in and out.

A soft breeze carries up a few faint sounds from far below, but otherwise, only the metallic ticking of the Corvette's cooling engine breaks the silence.

Yeah, it's not Texas, but it's the next best thing. Not that he is keen for the scorching heat of a Texas summer, or dead-end construction work while trying to figure out his next life move. Living in Hawaii isn't without challenges, but things could definitely be worse. Sometimes, when the darkness threatens him, he has to remind himself that this really is paradise. Even his punishing karma somehow allows him a flying job in Hawaii and not condemnation to a bleak existence of selling shoes to sweaty fat women at Sears — or worse. Visualizing his escape from high-heel hell always makes him feel better, if but for a moment.

Then thoughts of his mother come back. Along with the hurtful reality that his self-worth account is running on empty.

Just wish you were here, Mom, so I could show you around this beautiful island. I wonder what you are doing now, way back on the farm. An empty house don't make for good company. And an empty heart can't forgive. Not even a little.

Jared has moments of hate for Nolan, even though he realizes that he can't hate Nolan without hating himself. Someone that Jared *can* hate is his father, the one who abandoned them to a life of near destitution. Jared's only memory of him is that of a tall man with a scratchy face who left in a big red pick-up truck one day in the hazy past. Jared's mother, big with child, cried for days.

They stayed on the little farm, but the fields were rented for a pittance for others to plant. A hard life, little cash income, homemade toys under the Christmas tree. His mother struggled each day to keep the little family together. Everyone scratched out what they could to keep the place going and the chores were never ending.

It was during one of those morning chores that Jared's fascination with aviation began. He was driving their creaky old Ford tractor along a dirt track bordering one of their outlying fields, helping a neighbor locate a cow that had jumped the fence the night before. It was just after sun-up, with dusky shadows still lurking in the hollows. Jared was zoned out, just swaying with the motion of the tractor, half-awake.

The only warning he got was a split second of feeling, rather than hearing, a reverberating thump-thump-thump. Then, *ba-boom!* The Army helicopter roared overhead, less than thirty feet above, assaulting him with a raging tornado of propeller downwash. Jared's favorite hat vanished into the maelstrom as he was blasted head to foot with stinging sand. He jerked his head up and saw a big, green mechanical monster with Army markings rapidly getting smaller as it sped away, kicking up dust devils behind it.

Then the pilot banked sharply to one side and Jared could see him, wearing a white helmet with a green visor. He was looking back over his shoulder at Jared, and then he grinned, a big wide-mouth grin — the son-of-a-bitch had done it on purpose! In that instant Jared decided, by God, he was going to be the one doing the thumping someday, not driving some broke-down tractor chasing stupid cows for the rest of his life. And unlike most of his other endeavors, this one he had pretty much accomplished, with an unwitting push from Mary Lou Simpkins, or more to the point, her father.

He still smiled when he thought of her. Mary Lou was a sweet young thing in his senior class, eager to please star football players at Waco Central High. She was for-sure a *lot* of fun, but, as it turned out, also quite inconveniently fertile. Jared found this out when she got herself all worked up about not fitting into her senior prom dress. He didn't have to be a weatherman to see storm clouds brewing.

The next day Jared was down at the local Army recruiter's office, trying to put as much distance as possible between him and a shotgun-toting daddy who was exceedingly lacking a sense of humor. In a stroke of good fortune, the Army only required a high school diploma to go to flight school in those days, so with hasty goodbye's to Mom and Nolan, Jared was soon on a Greyhound bus headed east. Destination: the great Army helicopter training base at Fort Rucker, Alabama. It certainly wouldn't be the last time he'd look for a way out of an emotional situation, if necessary by the back door.

Jared's reverie was broken by the sound of a large white van laboring up the incline. The side of the van was adorned with a colorful picture of a Hawaiian granny with a big smile on her face. Beside granny is a fancy logo inscribed in large letters with the words "Mama Tutu's Catering and Events — Honolulu's Finest."

One look is enough to remind Jared it's time to trade sightseeing for chow, never a hard decision for him. He climbs back in the Vette and follows the van as it struggles up the winding road.

The broad driveway forms a spur to the left. Jared checks the address against what he has recorded on a notepad — *yep, this must be it.* The caterer thinks so, too. He heads up the narrow incline that soon opens into a broad parking area, where he stops the van alongside four other similar vehicles.

Jared takes a moment to admire the impressive house dominating the drive and car park. *Very nice, very nice indeed.* He doesn't know much about real estate, except he can't afford any in Hawaii, but he knows that in these days of inflated housing prices, this is prime property indeed.

A valet is waiting as Jared pulls up to the front door. Leaving the motor running he hops out, dressed in his finest safari shirt, with linen slacks and tasseled loafers. Except for his tousled hair, a product of driven with the top down, he cuts a fine figure - lean, tall, and well-muscled without being ostentatious.

"Good evening, sir," the young valet says, with a smile.

"Howdy, pardner, how you doing?" asks Jared, slipping into his Texas accent.

The valet is entranced with the car, which continues to rumble, almost alive. "Four-fifty-four, right?" the valet asks, impressed. "Don't see too many of these in the islands."

"Just look for them at the gas stations — they can't pass one without stopping for a drink," Jared replies, shaking his head in a sad way. With the Arab oil embargo a recent memory, everyone has gas and economy on their minds. "I'm trading it in for a skateboard as soon as I get a chance." They both laugh. The valet climbs in as Jared walks toward the front doors, momentarily wincing and glancing back as the valet gives the gears a good grinding.

"Sorry!" yells the chagrined valet, who then finds the right gear position and heads off for the parking area. Jared keeps him in sight long enough to make sure he doesn't drive off a cliff or something. Satisfied there's no threat of immediate destruction, Jared approaches the tall, imposing mahogany doors. Before he can knock, they open and Lori Konishi appears, wearing a long, clingy tropical print dress and a smile warm enough to melt an iceberg. A plumaria behind one ear holds back a portion of the long, glossy black hair that frames her face. This is the first time Jared has seen Lori in anything other than casual clothes, ponytail and no make-up. Now, with her all decked out, Jared appreciates that she is *really* good looking, and not, as he joked, semi-cute. Flat out beautiful, in fact.

"I thought I heard your car."

"Aloha, y'all, as they say in southern Hawaii," Jared responds, returning the smile. "Well, don't you look nice, all dressed up," he adds, giving her a greeting hug.

"Aloha yourself. Sorry I had to twist your arm to get you up here."

"Well, if I had known you lived in a castle, I'd have found my way up sooner," Jared says, looking around as if noticing the estate for the first time.

"Oh, I have an apartment down near the UH Manoa campus. This is Father's place." She ushers him through the doorway. "Anyway, you don't have to take your shoes off, we're not that down home."

"Okay, thanks. I didn't want to make a *malihini* mistake."

Lori closes the door behind them. "You've been here way long enough to be a *kama aina*, so you can turn in your newcomer's club card. Anyway, welcome to the festivities," she said as they make their way through the foyer and enter the living room. A warm buzz of conversation and laughter surround them as the well-dressed guests mix and mingle with smooth expertise.

Jared, more than a little awestruck, pauses a moment to take in the scene. The living room alone is larger than his entire apartment. Elegantly decorated, the magnificent room presents a tasteful blend of contemporary Americana accented with island and Japanese carvings and artwork. The chairs and sofas are all white, as is the carpet. The most spectacular element of the room, however, is a two-story glass wall. Laid out below is all of Honolulu, lights gleaming and overhead stars emerging as twilight deepens.

Worthy of a freaking movie star, Jared thinks, then does a double-take as he glances around the room.

"Hey, uh, Lori," Jared says softly. He nods toward the decorative but rarely used fireplace where several guests are gathered. "Isn't that Jack Lord?"

"Oh, yeah. You want to meet him?"

"No... I mean, maybe later. I don't want to bother him," Jared says, trying not to sound too impressed by the presence of the biggest guy on TV. At least in Hawaii, that's for sure, maybe everywhere. It's easy to lose perspective out here in the middle of the Pacific Ocean, far from mainstream America.

"He's a really nice guy, don't worry, he's used to it." Lori takes a couple of glasses of wine from the waiter circulating among the guests, and hands one of them to Jared. Jared scans for more celebrities, and picks out the Mayor of Honolulu, Frank Fasi, chatting up a young blonde.

"So you gave this up to live down by the campus?"

"Yeah, it's just hard to commute from way up here. I wanted some more privacy, too, I'm almost thirty now. It's time." Jared doesn't ask her to elaborate, but mentally files the information away.

"Are you still taking classes? I mean, you finished your undergrad, right?" Jared says, still trying to figure out who he is dealing with. Sure, she's a beautiful woman who is also a passable flight student, but what's she really all about? As Jared knows from painful experience, women (and men for that matter) that come from money are often screwed up in significant ways. Maybe even as much as him. One nutcase in any relationship is more than enough...

"No, I was enrolled in the Masters in Social Work program, but I got bored with it. I just want to do something on a big scale, not just being a caseworker or something. Not that there's anything wrong with case workers, of course," she adds. "At the moment, I'm helping with Father's campaign and working on the human sex traffic problem."

Before Jared can respond, Lori takes him by the hand and leads him out toward the lanai and garden. "But let's not talk about that now. Let's go outside where it's not quite as noisy."

They walk out on the adjoining lanai, which so far has escaped the notice of the other guests in the living room. By now, it is fully dark and Lori and Jared stop and gaze at the lights of Honolulu laid out below them, the party noise now just background music. They stand together silently for several minutes.

A cool breeze wafts along Lori's bare shoulders and brings a shiver.

"Japanese weather," she intones. "A little nip in the air." A giggle follows. Jared looks at her sharply. *Is this some kind of test?* He decides to play it safe. "Beautiful view, isn't it?"

"The best," Lori says simply. She pauses, then turns to face Jared. "So tell me about yourself. You said you were in the Army, and that you're from Texas. How did you end up way out here in Hawaii?"

Jared smiles. He's unpacked this bag many times before, or at least part of it. Some things aren't coming out into the sunshine, however, not now, not ever.

"Well, let's see. I grew up on a farm, 'cept we called it a ranch, outside of Waco. The usual thing out there, Budweiser, pick-up trucks, cowboy hats and Friday night football. In other words, America as God meant it to be." He gives a crooked smile to let her know he's not taking this too seriously, although deep down he might believe it. Lori gives a little nod and her own smile of understanding.

"But then I got the urge to go learn how to fly, and the circumstances all lined up," Jared continues, neglecting to mention the motivation provided by Mary Lou's dad and his wedding plans. "So off I go to Ft. Rucker in Alabama, and sure enough, they can teach cowboys how to fly. In fact, they put me in the Air Cavalry, I thought that was appropriate. But I did learn it's a damn sight harder to fly a helicopter than to ride a horse. Especially when someone's shooting at you."

"So you got shot at? Really?" Her head tilts to one side, a subliminal invitation Jared notes.

"Well, I did two tours in Vietnam, kinda goes with the turf. Anyway, got out, decided to try college awhile, so I spent a couple of years at UT Austin before I figured out I was just spinnin' my wheels."

Jared put the best possible face on it. The Dishonorable Discharge he got when he was thrown out of the Army meant no VA benefits, so going to school was a real financial challenge, a manageable one were it not for other issues revolving around getting along with others. This all came to a head one day in his political science class when the pinko candy-ass professor claimed North Vietnamese Army soldiers were the "good guys" in the recent war in south-east Asia. Jared snatched him up by his lapels and asked him to please reconsider, politely informing him, nose-to-nose, that he didn't know what the fuck he was talking about. Somehow the university construed this as "threatening behavior" and invited him to leave and not come back. About the only positive thing Jared cared to remember about his time as a student was that he twice won the Golden Gloves state championship in the light heavyweight division. Unfortunately, he'd had more fights outside the ring than in, not exactly the way to build a career.

"After that, I just got in the Vette and drove mostly, did some pick-up work in the oil fields, was a lifeguard, did some flight instruction. Just trying things out to see what I liked."

Actually, his employers of the moment got tired of trying to figure out which Jared was going to show up for work — the gregarious happy guy, or the sullen, truculent malcontent with little self-control. Little wonder that his average job lasted not even a year.

"So, Jared, you never answered my question — how'd you end up in Hawaii?"

Jared takes a sip of wine. Even though he's not much of a wine drinker, he appreciates it is a top quality vintage.

"Well, here's where Smitty comes in. He calls me up right out of the blue and offers me a job at *Island Air*, flight instruction and charters. Still haven't figured out how he found me," Jared adds, almost to himself. "Hey, I'm ready for a change in scenery, and it's a flying job, so why not? Been here ever since."

Jared omits the job offer included the opportunity to fly confidential charters for "the Company," mostly regular courier duties with an occasional "special mission" thrown in to keep things interesting. Jared had laughed out loud when Smitty advised him of the latter. "Smitty, in case you don't remember, I didn't leave the Army on the best of terms. Ain't no way I'm getting a security clearance!"

"You'll be getting a questionnaire in the mail in a couple of days," Smitty responded. "Just fill it out. And answer everything straight-up honest — they're going to check, you know." So Jared dutifully answered all the questions for the background check, including the incredibly tedious listing of every address he'd had in the last ten years, along with the name and address of every employer he'd ever had. He'd been *very* tempted many times to chuck it all, but a flying job in Hawaii? Those didn't come around every day!

Six weeks later Jared received an advance paycheck in the mail, along with a plane ticket to Honolulu courtesy of *Island Air*. Apparently, as long as you weren't a drug abuser or a drunk, and you could fly a plane, the CIA didn't really care about your other shortcomings.

Jared looked at Lori's beautiful face and says, "So why'd you invite me up here?"

Lori turns to him with a coy look, then hands him an envelope she has been carrying. Perplexed, Jared takes and opens it, extracting a plain white card. He holds it up to the faint light from inside the house and reads: "Dear Jared. You're fired."

"Okay...I don't get it," he says.

"Remember what you told me? You couldn't go out with me because I was your flight student. Well, I just fired you as my flight instructor!" With that, Lori pulled him close planted a wet and intimate kiss on a very surprised Jared. Their tongues dance, with Jared having to play catch up. Finally, she pulls away and leans her head on Jared's shoulder.

Jared somewhat regains his composure. "Well! Now that we are acquainted...you are one good kisser!" Lori giggles and leans back to look up into his eyes.

"I got all 'A's in kissing school!"

"Lori! So here you are. I'm about to do some presentations, need your help."

Lori snaps around to find her father, Rocky Konishi, standing close by with a stern gaze etched on his face. Pulling back from the oh-so-enjoyable clinch of seconds before, Lori blushes brightly enough to cast shadows. Jared wipes his face to remove any tell-tale lipstick evidence. In the dim light, Jared channels Mary Lou's dad's image onto Rocky for a disconcerting moment.

Glancing at Jared, Rocky continues, ice water in his tone, "And your friend is invited, too."

Rocky, a Japanese-American in his late fifties, is dressed in a Tori Richards aloha shirt, expensive slacks, and loafers. He walks with a slight limp and shows his age, but otherwise appears to be in good shape, fit and tanned. He has an air of quiet self-confidence making him seem larger than his rather small stature.

"Oh, umm, Jared, let me introduce you to my father. Jared, this is Rocky Konishi..." Rocky and Jared exchange handshakes.

"Jared Scott, a pleasure to meet you, sir," Jared offers.

"Saburo Konishi, please call me 'Rocky.' A pleasure to meet you as well." A little warmth finds his way into the words.

Lori continues, "Jared's my flight instructor, the one I told you about."

"Really? Looked like you were the one giving lessons..." Rocky manages a small smile while Lori and Jared blush even more.

"Anyway, come on in soon, these are some very important people to the campaign." Rocky turns away and disappears into the house. Lori and Jared watch him leave, then look at each other and burst into giggling laughter.

Chapter 9

Hong Kong, 1980

"So then I had to pantomime, 'I need Imodium, *now!*' The pharmacist was laughing so hard he nearly crapped *his* pants!" The twenty-something blonde throws back her head and brays a horselaugh so loud the few patrons left in the small dark bar look over to see what's so funny. The man with the woman joins in her laughter and they exchange a high five slap, both red-faced with mirth and alcohol.

"Could have been worse, at least you had a change of clothes. All of us ex-pats got stories like that. Trust me, you'll have more the longer you stay," the man says, laughing again. They are at that point where *every* statement or comment is followed by laughter.

"Well, I wanted to get out of Nebraska, and by God, I'm sure as shit out of Nebraska now." The woman slaps the bar top for emphasis, looking around at the Chinese signs and décor that dominate the narrow barroom. She is girl-next-door pretty, no doubt always having to watch her weight, but graced with the full breasts that come with plumpness. Her blonde hair catches the eye first and she really stands out in brown eye, black hair Hong Kong

"Say, thanks for the travel information and thanks for looking me up. You can't believe how tired I am of talking baby talk at the language institute."

"Teaching English to locals is kind of like regressing to second grade, I guess," the man says, commiserating with her in a considerate tone.

"It's very stressful," the woman says, getting serious for a moment. "They have to recite perfectly for their stage exams, and if they don't do well, I'm the one who gets yelled at. I'm frazzled, and I'm only three months into it." Teaching English to young Chinese is a government sponsored project that prompted many English language schools to pop up all over Hong Kong and mainland China. The students have to pass a national competency exam or the schools won't get paid, thus the pressure to do well is intense. The teacher's only qualifying skill: be a native English speaker.

"You going to stick it out?" the man says with concern, leaning in towards her.

The woman gives a derisive snort. "Like I have a choice! If I left now, I'd have to pay my own way back, that's about two thousand dollars... plus it's pretty sketchy that the institute would send me any back pay." Her tone makes it clear that she's had these thoughts before, like many of the teachers who preceded her. She takes another gulp of her drink.

"Oh, I guess I'll do the year," she says with resignation. "I just didn't know it would be so...isolated, you know." She wipes away the beginnings of a tear.

The man doesn't say anything, but rubs her back to console her. His sleeve rides up, exposing a green and red tattoo.

"I'm just a little stressed out, I guess. Never thought I'd be homesick for Nebraska!" At this, she brightens and laughs at the absurdity, which brings a smile to flirt with her face.

The man glances around and says, "Well, if you are up for it, I do have some "stress release herbs" we could do. Really potent stuff, it'll wow you." The man smiles and nods in a knowing way.

"Grass?" the woman says, "That'd be great. I haven't turned on since I got here, and I'm down to my last two Valium. The other instructors are such dweebs, it's unbelievable what mice they are," she says, the dismissive attitude dripping from her words.

"But we can't do it here, can we?" she says, looking around.

"Oh, I know the owner," the man says. "There's a private room in the back."

"Well, just a couple of hits, then I got to get back to the housing facility. You're sure this is good stuff?"

Trazer stands and offers a hand to help the unsteady young woman to her feet, then whispers to her. "Don't worry, baby, I guarantee an experience you'll never forget..."

* * * * *

They spread the blanket in a shallow basin at the top of the huge sand dune, using a gym bag to hold one corner against the ever present trade winds. The last rays of the sun are gone and it is dark, except for the explosion of silver twinkling stars decorating the black heavens.

Lori and Jared sit down facing the surf, not talking, just taking in all sensations. The ocean, always restless on the windward side, splashes and froths at the shoreline, never giving up its quest to devour the island. The soft roar of the waves competes with the sea oats rustling around them, together a symphony of white noise. The smell of sea salt, lofted by the warm breeze, climbs the dune to their nesting site. Far away down the coast is civilization, but here, they are in their own world. His arm cradles her shoulders, and she twines the fingers of one hand with his.

Lori is content, a rare calmness enveloping her.

"It's so peaceful, isn't it? This must be what heaven is like," Lori muses.

"I hope so. Of course, it wouldn't be heaven if you weren't there, too."

Lori leans her head to his shoulder. "Well, aren't you Mr. Sweetie?"

"Naw. You may have gotten all 'A's' at kissing school, but I'm just lucky I didn't flunk out of charm school. That was my best line."

"Oh, I'm sure you got plenty more," Lori intones. "Not that you need them."

"Jest tryin' ta get by the bestus I can, Ma'am." Jared replies in a fake hillbilly accent. They both laugh, savoring the moment.

Jared digs through the gym bag and extracts a bottle of wine and a couple of glasses. With a twist and a yank of the corkscrew the bottle pops open. Jared pours as Lori holds the glasses.

"Doesn't quite meet the high standards of Boone's Farm, but it'll have to do," Jared jokes as he takes his glass. "We should have a toast."

"You go ahead, I don't think I know any. I'm not much of a drinker."

"Well, I've been around a bar or two in my time." Jared says with false modesty. "How about this?" He raises his glass and Lori follows. "Born of the Irish in me."

> *Here's to a long life and merry fun.*
> *A quick death and an easy one.*
> *A pretty girl and a handsome son.*
> *And forgiveness,*
> *May we need none.*

They clink glasses. "Cheers!"

* * * * *

They finish the wine and the wind abates to a soft breeze, but the sky is still brilliant with stars. They lay back, cuddled together, lost to their silent thoughts as they gaze upward. For the hundredth time, Lori wonders which of the stars is *Sofu?* And *Sobo?* She knows for sure they will be close together, wherever they are. Grandfather and Grandmother always were.

Her mind drifts back to her grandparent's farm, clinging to the high slopes of the Kauai central mountains. So isolated, only a steep, treacherous footpath reached it. Three hours of hard hiking from the nearest road, first through the pineapple fields, then the sugar cane, and finally a long journey through the rain forest. As a little girl walking with Mother and Father, it seemed to take forever, but eventually the unpainted wooden farmhouse would come into view. *Sofu* and *Sobo* would be sitting on the front porch waiting for them. *Sofu* would get up and ring the big bell on the rail, while *Sobo* pumped a pitcher full of the best tasting water in the world. Then everyone would stand and bow repeatedly to each other, which Lori always thought was crazy. No one did that in Honolulu. But this was, she realized even then, a reserved and formal family, to include her own parents.

None of that formality existed with Jared. He was as down-home and informal as could be imagined. And a heck of a hunk of a man. A few rough edges, but she could work on that. She snuggled closer.

"Is it too cool for you?" He asked.

"No, I was just having some warming thoughts." A soft giggle. If he only knew!

Her mind goes to her childhood, summers on the farm and the country lifestyle. Lori mostly had to entertain herself during those long summer days — there were no neighborhood kids around, no neighbors at all, in fact. She did not see this as a problem. She climbed trees, chased butterflies, read and re-read all the books she loved. Then in the cool of the evening, *Sobo* and *Sofu* would light the paper sky lanterns. Then the grown-ups would begin telling stories, in Japanese of course, of growing up in Japan, and of ancestors going back hundreds of years. It was another world.

And then it all came crashing down — literally. Lori was twelve, she and her parents were at home in Honolulu. It was a school night, and everyone was asleep. It wasn't a big earthquake, not as earthquakes sometimes are — just enough to rattle the dishes and set dogs to barking. But it was enough to bring a landslide in Kauai. And in the middle of it was the farm and her grandparents. They never found them, and hardly a trace of the farmhouse was uncovered. It was as if they never existed.

A year later more bad news, terrible news. Keiko, her mother, was diagnosed with pancreatic cancer. Bright, vivacious Keiko, always a country girl at heart, gracious and loving, was consumed by the disease. In six months, the cancer physically destroyed her. In nine months she was gone, another star in heaven. Lori and Father were devastated beyond words. It took two years, but they gradually came out of the depression that enveloped them. But Keiko was always close in their thoughts.

Lori noticed it one day when they were getting out of the car. Her Father, always so fit and spry, moved a little slower — not much, and no one else would have noticed. But Lori did. And it scared her. Badly. Because, ever so slightly, she had glimpsed her father's mortality. One day, in her whole family going back a thousand years, there would be only one. Her. It was terrifying. From that day on, she looked at the world differently. And she looked at the night sky a lot.

"Oh, look!" Lori says, pointing skyward. "It's a satellite."

"Where?"

"Right there, just to the left of Orion's belt. Look for the movement."

"Okay, got it." Jared studies it for a moment. "Don't you think it's a jet?

"No, it moves too fast, and the lights will flash if it is a plane. I took an astronomy course at the university and we got pretty good at spotting them."

Jared groaned. "So in addition to all your other skills and talents, you're an astronomer?"

Lori laughs. "Well, all you need is a dark night and good vision, no big thing!"

"You're too modest. Okay, are we supposed to make a wish, like with a falling star?"

"Never thought about it, but why not?"

"I guess we keep 'em secret, too."

"Yeah," she says. "That would be traditional." They close their eyes, silent for a few moments.

"I hope your wish comes true," Jared says.

"I hope *your* wish comes true, too." Lori replies.

They caress each other, Lori's head resting on Jared's arm. He brushes her forehead with a light kiss and runs his hand along her back. She squeezes closer and leaves a trail of kisses from Jared's neck to behind his ear. Her hand slips under his shirt. Their lips meet and nibble, then they clasp each other with passionate hunger.

Lori strokes Jared's cool, smooth skin, feeling the firm muscles underneath as he releases the buttons of her blouse. A nipple peeks out, taut against the breeze. She slides her hand downward, inside the waistband of his shorts.

"Mmmm," she whispers. "I think you're ready."

He doesn't say anything. He doesn't have to.

Her hand explores further. "Oh, you're *really* ready!" She giggles. "I think my wish is going to come true."

His breath is close against her ear. "What a coincidence...I think mine is, too."

Chapter 10

R ocky is as relaxed and unwound as he can remember in a long, long time. The sails and sky are above him, the blue water all around, and the beautiful panorama of Honolulu and the Ko'olau mountains rise in the distance. The small waves slap at the sides of the boat, trying to slow it, but the sleek forty-eight foot yacht pushes them aside, staying true to its course. The never-ending trade winds fill the sails and cool the crew and passengers. Rocky takes it all in. He is a very happy man.

Lori appears from the teak lined interior, a sumptuous display of woodwork and functionality. Balancing against the rocking of the boat, she brings drinks for Jared and Rocky. They sprawl in the cockpit while a crewman steers the boat. Another crewman tends to the sails and prepares the fishing poles mounted on the stern. Behind their blank expressions, the crew cast surreptitious glances at Lori, barely clad in an immodest bikini. Her tanned skin is slick with suntan lotion and stylish sunglasses complete the picture.

Relieved to be away from the relentless pressures of campaigning, running his company, and media sharks, Rocky meditates. Out here, it is just him and the sea, even if others are aboard — no phones, no interminable meetings, no pressing decisions.

This is what we work for, he muses, *then we don't take time to enjoy it. Most of my life is behind me, I should be thinking seriously of retiring, selling the company, maybe sailing around the world before I get too old. Oh, yeah, one little thing — I went ahead and got myself elected Governor of Hawaii!*

"Thanks, Lori, you make a great first mate," says Rocky, smiling as he reaches for the proffered drink.

"Yeah, but I don't do windows!" she says, sassy as always.

Jared joins in. "Or floors either, I suppose?" They all laugh. Good feelings flow from one to the other, like liquid sunshine karma.

Rocky is perched on the high side of the boat as it leans with the wind, looking over the scene like a benevolent monarch from his throne. He's not dressed like a king, however, turned out in shorts, an old Filipino shirt and a floppy expedition hat to keep some of the sun off. Jared is much the same, wearing colorful surfer jams, a stained cotton shirt any respectable wife would soon trash, and a baseball cap in constant danger of blowing away.

Rocky soaks it all in: wind on his face, rush of the water and taut, well-trimmed sails. "My Lord, beautiful today, isn't it? Another day in paradise!" he says, a phrase said with sarcasm most places—but not in Hawaii, and certainly not by Rocky Konishi.

"Hey, lucky you live Hawaii, eh?" Lori adds with a grin.

"So Rocky," Jared says, stretched across the low side of the cockpit. "All of this is going to be yours. Being the governor, I mean." Jared's hand makes a broad sweep across the horizon.

As usual, Rocky is without ego. "Well, of course, it's not mine, it's the people of Hawaii this belongs to—I know it sounds corny, but I really believe that."

"I know you do, I think that's why you've been so successful," Jared replies as Lori settles in beside him. Rocky is a keen observer of people and can distinguish sincerity from flattery in an instant. It reinforces a positive opinion that has taken root regarding Jared. At dinner last week, he was prepared to dislike the man, especially given the circumstances of their first meeting. The results of the background check Rocky obtained didn't help. One doesn't get far in politics and business without access to resources that speed the "getting to know" process quite a bit. However, somewhat to his surprise, he and Jared got on immediately. Unlike many of his generation, Jared was respectful in a polite but not deferential way, he was easy to talk to, laughed at Rocky's jokes and was full of humorous stories. While he didn't dwell on his military service, Jared didn't avoid it either. Of course, he didn't mention why he was no longer in the Army, and, of course, Rocky didn't ask about what he already knew. For now, Rocky was of the mindset that Lori had made a good choice in boyfriends— for a change. She certainly had a spotty success record in that regard.

"Okay, Rocky," Jared says with a grin. "Can I be, like the Commissioner of Beer or something?"

Rocky grins back. "Actually I had you in mind for Minister of Mai-Tai's!" They all share a laugh, each with a mind-picture of Jared promoting Mai-Tai's at the inauguration, or something equally ridiculous.

Jared turns serious for a moment. "All kidding aside, what *are* you going to do? And I apologize, I haven't paid much attention to politics, I'm kind of a know-nothing in that regard. Maybe Lori will tutor me a little." He flashes a sweet smile at Lori.

"Well, I guess I should share that with you, in case Lori persuades you to work some for the election committee." Jared launches a quizzical look at Lori, but her expression gives no hints.

Rocky continues, "First, I am the luckiest man in the world..."

"Yeah, I saw the name of the boat when we got in." *Rots 'o Ruck* was painted prominently across the stern, and virtually everyone in Hawaii knew to whom it belonged.

"I came to this wonderful country with only a few dollars in my pocket and a suitcase full of dreams. As you know, my family in Japan was lost during the war, so I started out as a construction worker, just pick-up jobs mostly, whatever I could get, going to college at the same time at night. Then the best thing that ever happened to me – I met Keiko, the woman that would be your mother, Lori."

Lori looks out in the distance, touched by the image in her mind.

"After I got my college degree, even though it took six years, I got married, worked my way into construction management – not easy to do, you know the Portuguese got that about wrapped up in Hawaii. But statehood that changed everything – construction work exploded and my company just took off - for about fifteen years we couldn't do anything wrong, except – and here's the irony - pave over the whole state."

Lori sings the words softly. "Paved paradise, put up a parking lot..."

Rocky gives a dismissive wave of his hand. "Yeah, that's about it. Here's another irony – too many Japanese moving to the islands, buying up so much real estate the locals can't afford to buy a home. You know most kids here don't move out of their parents house until their mid-thirties 'cause they can't afford the inflated prices. It's a travesty, just completely unacceptable. So that's why I want to be governor, to stop this crazy overdevelopment, and to go to Japan and convince them to stop running the housing prices up to the stratosphere. I figure I must have some credibility since I'm a developer and Japanese." He laughs heartily. Jared and Lori nod their heads as well in agreement.

"Well, it must have worked," Jared interjects. "You won the election. Of course, being a damn good businessman didn't hurt!"

"Yeah, fiscal sanity is always a plus. Kind of rare in Hawaii, unfortunately."

"So, Father, are you getting excited about the inauguration?" Lori asks. "Only a couple of weeks away now. I still can hardly believe it."

"Well, actually I am. It's such a validation of my beliefs and all that we have worked for in the last three years. I still hardly believe it – never in my wildest dreams, especially when I stepped off that ship that brought me here, could I imagine I might be the governor of the most beautiful state in America." He shakes his head in disbelief.

"My only wish is that Keiko was here to share it with us." He turns his head away to stare out to sea. Jared and Lori remain respectfully quiet.

Suddenly there is a *snap* sound, and one of the fishing reels shrieks as it unwinds at a blistering pace. Jared jumps up and takes the rod from the holder and jerks it back to set the hook.

"Hey!" Jared shouts. "We got something! Feels like a good one." His face is a happy grimace as he sets himself to the contest. He repeatedly leans back against the pull of the powerful fish, bringing it a few feet closer with each tug. Then he loses yards of line as the unseen foe charges away from the boat. Lori and Rocky can do little other than offer encouragement as Jared matches his endurance against that of the sea creature. The bend-and-pull cycle goes on, ten, twenty, thirty times and more. Dripping sweat everywhere, Jared's forearm muscles bulge with strain.

"What is it, a shark?" Rocky asks, looking over the side.

Leaning against the pull of the rod, Jared grunts out an answer: "Don't know yet, but we will in a minute."

Jared makes one more strong pull and one of the crewmen yanks hard on the gaff. A multi-hued four-foot long fish is heaved over the transom. Desperate to escape back to its realm, the fish tries to beat the boat deck into submission, sending blood from the gaff wound flying.

"Oh!" Rocky says. "It's a mahi!"

"Yeah, and a big one too – maybe twenty five pounds." Jared adds, out of breath from the exertion of the fight. They all stare at it as the flapping of its tail slows. Oxygen depletion sets in and the life ebbs from its body.

Lori says, "That's a mahi-mahi? Sure looks different on a plate!" They all laugh.

"Gosh, it's beautiful!" Lori says excitedly. "Look at the colors – it's changing like a chameleon."

The fish with a big square head is indeed changing colors, its skin a living prism.

Jared says, "Yeah, it changes colors as it dies – I guess it's the fish version of your life passing in front of you."

Lori's face crinkles as she absorbs this information. "Oh, so sad!"

The fish gives a last kick and the gills slow and stop. As they watch, the rainbow hues fade to a drab gray, disappearing into the shadows of the sinking sun. Rocky, Lori, and Jared are all lost to their thoughts as the *Rots 'O Ruck* turns for the Ali Wai boat harbor and sails into a Thomas Kinkade sunset.

Chapter 11

As always before going live, Mike Flocca, is a nervous wreck. In two minutes Channel 9 News will kick off, ready or not, and Mike knows it had better be ready — or else. His title, News Director, implies he is the local god of current events. In reality, he is not much more than a convenient whipping boy for the two prima donnas now embroiled in yet another bitching contest.

Linda and Dave are ridiculously good looking, even for TV people. Linda is in her late twenties, long, softly curling honey blonde hair draped across her tanned shoulders. Her high cheekbones are evidence of her former life as a model, as are her long legs and thin frame. Her co-anchor, Dave, is a little older, just as tanned, with short, dirty blonde hair and a square jaw, and blue eyes that gleam as if backlit. Of course, they both have perfect white teeth to complete the picture. Small wonder the staff at KGMB call them Barbie and Ken, sometimes to their faces. Mike calls them a lot of other things, mostly under his breath.

Dave is in his face again, his voice shrill. "Mike, that light rack simply *must* be moved. I cannot read copy with that glare, and I will not tolerate such adverse working conditions, *do you understand?*" He jabs a finger towards Mike, close enough to be inside Mike's "personal space."

Linda, her own pressure cooker about to pop, crowds in front of Dave, "That is *totally* unacceptable. Moving it there would cast a shadow from my nose — I don't need a 'Betsy Big Nose' image going out over the air. I make my living by how I look, and I'm not putting that in jeopardy, got it?" *Well, no pretense of being a real journalist, at least.*

"For Christ's sake, people, can we just get through this newscast and *then* sit down and make some decisions," Mike pleads. "We can't move the lights now anyway, we're...," he glances at the wall clock..., "Oh, my God, sixty seconds from live! Please?!"

His voice shrill enough to break glass, Dave snarls, "Okay, Mr. Director Man, but if I flub even *one* word I'm shoving a grievance up you and Goldilocks' snouts so far you'll be sneezing confetti all week!" He stomps off to his seat.

Linda gushes a torrent of obscenities and heads for her side of the set. They settle into their chairs as the camera crews take aim.

The set is by design, "non-mainland," rejecting expansive desks and a crew of diligent newshounds scurrying about in the background. Instead, Dave and Linda sit in comfortable straight back rattan chairs with a small table in between for papers and water glasses. With both of them in aloha attire the set looks more like an afternoon talk show than a newsroom, which is exactly the intent. The informality also helps to tone down the prima donna drama — at least that's what Mike hopes.

Mike sweats through the count down, "...four, three..." the "two" and "one" are cued by hand signals. Dave, his voice now three octaves lower and flashing his trademark grin, starts the dialogue. "Aloha, ladies and gentlemen, Dave and Linda with you here tonight, hoping you are all having another great day in paradise."

Linda takes her turn at the teleprompter. "But our first story is a reminder that not everyone is so lucky to live Hawaii. For this disturbing report that fortunately has a ray of hope, let's go live to the State Capitol where Jenni Lee has the story for us. Over to you, Jenni."

Jenni Lee is an attractive Korean girl, working hard to get off the reporter beat and into the newsroom and some regular hours.

"Thanks Linda, hello everyone. National news down here at the capital today, but not the usual political developments in this election season. Instead, Lori Konishi, daughter of Rocky Konishi, our Governor-Elect, was feted today by none other than Jimmy Carter, President of the United States. President Carter was in town for a campaign rally, but spent much of the afternoon honoring Lori for her volunteer work in developing "Freedom Network," a rescue operation combating forced prostitution and human trafficking. We sat down with Lori during a rare quiet moment to better understand what Freedom Network is all about."

The video coverage switches to a large office, sparingly furnished with inexpensive tables and chairs. The viewers can see telephones, scattered about on the tables that are the main functional feature. A large poster decorates the back wall displaying the words "Freedom Network" emblazoned at the bottom. Two large hands, one held out in the "stop" posture, and the other, beckoning, complete the artwork. Volunteers, most of them local women, answer phones and hustle about.

"So Lori, you are the daughter of the man who just got elected as the first Japanese-American governor of Hawaii in history. How did you find time to develop the Freedom Network? Tell us all about it." Jenni holds the microphone for Lori, who appears anxious to talk about her creation.

"There is a scourge out there, Jenni, horrible crimes are going on every day, right here in Hawaii and across the Pacific hardly anyone knows about, and even fewer care about. That scourge is sexual slavery, the buying and selling of young women and girls."

Passion rises in Lori's voice. "Especially in the Philippines, Korea, Singapore, Taiwan, Hong Kong, and even here, women are sold into slavery by their parents, lured away by promises of "modeling" jobs or just plain kidnapped. The police have done very little about this. They always say, 'We don't have the money or resources to investigate.' Well, Freedom Network has gotten beyond that. These criminal rings need two things to succeed — girls and customers. What we have done is to infiltrate the customer side, sometimes with bribes if necessary, to gain the confidence of the girls and plan escapes for them, then we provide new identities and safe houses until we can get them back to their families - or to new families, if need be. So far, we have rescued over a thousand girls and women, but that's really only a drop in the bucket. That's why I am so thrilled by President Carter's initiative."

"Yes." Jenni says, turning to look at the camera, "That's the exciting news today. Here's a clip of President Carter awarding a Presidential Citation recognizing you for your achievement in setting up and developing Freedom Network."

The viewers see President Carter handing over a framed gold certificate to Lori. He then shakes her hand as Jared stands on stage beside her, pushing imaginary pebbles with his shoe.

"Mr. President," Lori says, beaming a smile at him, "on behalf of all the volunteers at Freedom Network, thank you *so much*, for your support. We love you!" She gives him an impromptu hug, making the Secret Service agents nearby visibly tense. The President and Lori wave and grin as the audience cheers.

The camera turns back to Jenni and Lori.

Lori continues for the camera. "The very best part is that, based on Freedom Network's efforts, Congress has authorized monies for the police departments in all of those trafficking hotspots to create integrated anti-slavery units — and, even better, there's funding for at least one Freedom Network employee to work with all of them to provide oversight and to keep them on task. We are going to bust up these rings," Lori says with conviction.

Jenni wraps up, "We should also add an important provision of the program is that rescued girls and women will get automatic refugee status in the United States, provided they testify against the traffickers. Altogether a wonderful day for women's rights here and abroad."

Lori can't resist — she grins and motions her hand in the "shaka, brah" wave of victory.

Jenni beams a smile and wraps up. "This is Jenni Lee, reporting live from the State Capital. Back to you, Linda."

* * * * *

Jared appears at the door of the Freedom Network headquarters, which is buzzing with calls and activity in the aftermath of the newscast. He dodges a couple of bustling staffers scooting about and walks over to sit by Lori. She is on the phone taking notes at a furious pace.

"Yes, yes. Of course. We will absolutely check that out. I'm going to put you on with a caseworker who will get the details for the investigators. All anonymous. Thank you *so* much for calling us." She forwards the call, sighs, and gives Jared a smile, which jumps off her face. Jared puts down a couple of bags of Chinese food on the table between them.

"How's it going?" Jared asks, already knowing the answer.

"It's just crazy! Stuff we never had a clue about is coming in, from all over. It's really disturbing what is out there."

"Really?" Jared asks, poking through the bag contents. "You wanted the fried rice, right?"

"What I want, Jared, doesn't come in a little paper bag. This is what I want," Lori says, sweeping her hand around to indicate the volunteers hard at work.

Jared pauses from rummaging in the bag. *Stepped on it again, knucklehead!* He hesitates, trying to formulate the right answer. Noting her disapproving glare, he decides to go with apologetic.

"I applaud your passion, Babe. I wish..."

A young man with wild looking hair, a Freedom Network worker, walks up and interrupts, unaware of the "oops" in progress.

"Hi Lori. Great job on TV, and congratulations." Without waiting for a response, he turns to Jared. "Hey Jared, saw you in the newspaper article, that profile of Lori and the award. Still giving her the flight lessons?"

Jared, a little flustered by the change of topic, but happy to go with it, says, "Actually, we just..."

A big local gal in an expansive muu-muu shouts from across the room, "Excuse me, Lori, caller on line four is asking for you by name."

Lori nods, picks up the receiver and punches button four. "This is Lori."

She listens for about a minute, gets a pained expression, then hangs up abruptly.

"That was weird. Scary, actually."

"What was it?" Jared asks, careful to be more sensitive to Lori's feelings this time.

Lori pauses, then shakes her head slowly in a this-can't-be-true motion.

She reaches over and grips Jared's hand tightly. "I guess you'd call it a death threat..."

Chapter 12

K orbler rips a page of paper off the classified teletype, reads it, and then leans back in his chair and stares blankly at the ceiling. *Damn it!* First his bitch ex-wife notifies him she is going back to court to double the alimony, and now Langley drops a hot rock in his lap. *Wonderful! Doesn't Operations know the reason I'm parked in this beautiful backwater is precisely because I can't be trusted with anything important? Low profile, under the radar, three more years and I can cross the finish line and retire. Dear God, I can't do a winter in Afghanistan helping the Mujahedeen fight the Russians, much less* three *winters. Which is certainly what's going to happen if this gets screwed up.*

I should just kill myself now — the .45 is in the drawer.

Korbler slides open the desk drawer, pulls out the big Colt automatic. He tries to remove the magazine to check the load — it won't move. *Shit! Haven't changed the rounds in, oh, maybe ten years — rusted tight. Jeez, I'm not even competent to kill myself.* He slams the drawer shut.

I could just drink myself to death, that'd be more fun, anyway. Korbler opens the cabinet behind him and pulls out the bottle of Scotch — it is only half-full. He plops it on the desk in and stares at it.

The worst part is I'm going to have to depend on that prick Jared Scott. Maybe I should kill him first, then myself — a classic murder-suicide. This thought actually brings a smile to Korbler's face.

No! I'll set him up with my ex-wife — That dickhead will screw anything. Korbler imagines the whining, crying, psycho-shrew of an ex-wife bitching out Jared as he dances around, post-coitus, trying to get into his pants after being accused of some imagined slight. Then he relishes mental images of

Jared receiving an endless barrage of threatening phone calls, letters and messages, maybe even a frivolous lawsuit or two. *A fate worse than death! And I'll have to stay around to enjoy it — beautiful!* This is funny beyond words and Korbler starts giggling like a teenaged girl, halfway to tears.

Gaylord sticks his head in the door to see what all the laughter is about. "Uhh, you okay, boss?" A look of scorn flashes across his face as he spies the Scotch. Korbler, still in a laugh spasm, barely notices. Gaylord eases cautiously into a chair.

Korbler regains some self control, gives his nose a good rubdown. "Yeah, fine, just letting off a little steam. Hey, guess what? You're always wanting to go out on a cowboy mission, right?"

"Well, yeah, I mean, of course...depending on what it is..."

"Jesus Christ, Gaylord, how many times have I told you, always volunteer first, *then* ask what for!" Korbler cranks up another of many cigarettes. "Anyway, I'll spare you the suspense. Need for you and Jared Scott to take one of the King Airs down to Jakarta and pick up a couple of VIPs and drop 'em off at Subic Bay, Philippines. Navy will take care of them from there. It's a night vision goggles thing, in and out, no lights, no radios, no shutdown. Should be an easy flight. Scott's good at it, just don't let him do something stupid, like throw you out of the airplane..." At this, Korbler laughs again and only stops when a cigarette induced hack takes his breath.

"Just a pickup? Who are these guys anyway, some of ours?"

Giving a nostril yet another fingering, Korbler answers. "Well in this case, VIP means very important politicians. Remember when the Indonesians invaded East Timor a couple of years ago and set about killing off all the resistance? Did a pretty good job, must've killed about twenty thousand or more, starved to death about three times that many. Anyway, several high-ranking Indonesian military and government officials secretly defected to us, and have been hiding out in our embassy. The deal is if we get them out, they testify at the next United Nations General Assembly about what's going on. Somebody at State is engineering all this, but we can't afford to have our fingerprints on it because technically, we are buddies with the Indonesians as long as they stay anti-communist."

Gaylord leans back in his chair digesting this information. As he does his crossed leg starts bouncing faster. "So... what airfield? They don't have many, so they're pretty busy — but this sounds like a low profile deal."

Korbler shuffles around some glossy photos on his desk. He doesn't look up. "Actually, it's a road, but not bad at all – straight, good pavement, no telephone poles, experienced ground crew to turn you. They'll mark the landing area and give an all-clear signal to get you in. Going to create a power failure in the area to keep the authorities busy, plus stage a couple of accidents to keep the road closed, the usual thing. A piece of cake."

Korbler hopes it is not obvious he is doing a sales job. He looks up at Gaylord with a half-smile on his face and with just the slightest tinge of doubt in his voice, he asks, "You're good for it, right?"

If needed to close the deal, always challenge manhood.

Gaylord doesn't hesitate. "Hell yeah, I am!"

Korbler smiles with relief — he won't have to go himself — "Great, find Jared and get him up here and briefed. Take the King Air with the long-range tanks and porta-potty, it's a long way between fuel stops. Also, have 'em load pillows and blankets, there's plenty of room in the cabin for our passengers to stretch out."

Korbler takes pleasure in the look of dismay on Gaylord's face when he adds, "Get on it, this is a rush job. You need to be on the way tonight."

* * * * * *

Lights from the instruments softly illuminate Jared's face as he peers through the windscreen into the black night. Several minutes of intense concentration go by.

He grunts to Gaylord, "We're here," and he turns down the aircraft instrument panel lights, pulls a set of night vision goggles onto his face and tightens them down. Feeling like a useless appendage, Gaylord sits beside him in the co-pilot seat, wondering how close they are to those invisible plane-killer mountains he knows are there.

Not having NVG's like Jared, Gaylord sees only absolutely terrifying blackness. The plane bucks hard from a burst of turbulence. Gaylord grabs his penis and clenches tightly, horrified his bladder wants to flush from fear. Now!

Piece of cake, huh? That rat bastard, Korbler!

Jared is busy lowering flaps and flipping switches, and a lot more bewildering pilot stuff as Gaylord watches helplessly. The plane lurches, the engines roar and Jared wrestles with the controls. Then he exhales audibly, and raises the night vision goggles.

"Are we going to land now?" Gaylord asks, completely lost in space somewhere.

Jared doesn't answer, but gives him a "you fucking idiot" look Gaylord correctly interprets, to his chagrin.

Someone unseen throws open the aircraft door, and a tall, lanky man with very short red hair scrambles through, dimly illuminated by the subdued cabin lights. He wears a black polo shirt, blue jeans and what looks to be a nice pair of knock-off Adidas. Jared beckons him forward and he scuttles awkwardly to the cockpit, bent half-over in deference to the low overhead of the cabin.

"Hey Skipper, Jack Jackson, Marine Security Guard OIC. I'm escorting tonight." He extends his hand to Jared for a handshake, but Jared ignores it and looks back to the open door.

"Where's our guys? Let's go!"

Two figures fly through the door like sacks of potatoes, thunking against the far bulkhead. Whoever is assisting them is evidently highly motivated. The door slams shut and Jackson yells to the struggling passengers, "Strap in and hold on!"

Gaylord's eyes, now better adjusted to the dark, can see two small pick-up trucks and several men, some armed, positioned around the aircraft in the faint starlight. Beyond them is a slender road arrowing through pineapple fields.

Jared wheels the turboprop out of the turning area and onto the road. He pulls the NVG's back over his eyes, then pushes the throttles up to the max. The engines reach redline and the aircraft shakes and rattles.

"Here we go. Stay clear of the controls!" Jared warns. Gaylord jerks back as if the throttle quadrant is full of cobras.

Jackson scrambles to get into his seat. The aircraft accelerates down the road, with Jared peering through electronically assisted eyes.

Suddenly, dead ahead down the road appears two pairs of headlights, side-by-side, both accompanied by flashing red lights. They are rapidly getting brighter as the airplane and cars close the distance between them.

"Oh, shit!" says Gaylord. He doesn't need the NVG's to know he only has seconds to live. A tiny little component of Gaylord's autonomic nervous system sends an emergency message to his sphincter, telling it to stand by for action.

"You can say that again," Jared responds without humor.

"Ohhh, shit," says Gaylord. "What are you going to do?" Gaylord yells above the screaming engines, looking frantically at Jared for salvation.

"I don't know!"

Suddenly Jared throws off the night vision goggles and with one motion sweeps on all the plane's fiercely brilliant landing lights. They are spotlights thrust into the eyes of the car drivers, who jerk the steering wheels hard to avoid them.

Both cars plow into the fields, one on each side of the road, as the plane roars overhead, just barely off the ground. As Gaylord looks back, one car flips over, throwing a figure violently into the dark; the other car slams into a stump, jerking to a halt in a cloud of dust, red lights still flashing.

The plane reaches into the black sky. Gaylord, wondering what it will cost to buy Jared's silence, duck walks to the lavatory to clean up an excretory accident.

Chapter 13

Trazer wakes up early, masturbates to completion, and smokes two cigarettes before getting out of bed. He considers another hands-on session, but he has too much on his mind for that kind of focus. He has a lot to do today, a lot indeed. He smiles in the bedroom twilight, savoring his thoughts.

* * * * *

"Okay, so that's one hundred twelve dollars and forty one cents, including the fuel charge. Put in on your account?" Jane, the all-purpose secretary at Island Air Aviation, is a pleasant, middle-aged transplant from California, well versed in taking care of the administrative side of the business. On this Sunday morning, the office is quiet, just a lone student winding up a solo flight.

"Yeah, and I'm going to need to get on the schedule Tuesday afternoon, after five." The flight student is a college student at Kapiolani Community College fortunate enough to have a small inheritance to devote to flying activities. So far, it has been a very positive experience. Jane figures that is about to change as soon as she catches sight of the maniac.

The lanky, unkempt intruder with half an ear missing flings open the front door and steams in. One look is enough to determine he is not in search of a softball game, despite the metal softball bat in his hands. He beelines it for the counter where Jane and the student turn to stare. In mid-stride, he yells, "Where's Lori Konishi?"

The student looks at Jane in bewilderment, puzzlement all over his face. Jane finds words first. "Who are...?"

"The new governor's daughter, the one breaking my rice bowl!" The man reaches the counter and the student, heeding the bat and the snarling tone, clears out of the way.

Jane, flustered, attempts to provide something, anything, to calm this scary individual. He leans over the counter, bloodshot eyes locked on her. She doesn't know what he is on, but he is obviously whacked out of his mind on something.

"Oh, uh, she's not here today, she usually..." Jane remembers she shouldn't give out student information. "...and, uh, who are you?"

"Jared Scott?" he demands. Jane's confusion jumps to the next level. She inches backward to put some distance between her and the red-faced crazy. She glances at the flight student to make sure he is still there in case she needs help, but he looks as if he's about to cry.

"Jared Scott! Where is Jared Scott?" The intruder froths at the mouth. Jane is afraid his head may explode at any moment.

"Well, I can check his schedule, it's pretty irregular," she says, backing away from the counter ever so slightly. "Right now, he's on a trip for a couple of days. Were you looking for a charter, or...?" she adds hopefully, trying to find something positive to address. It is a useless effort.

"Here's a message for them: Payback's a mother-fucker!" With that, he swings the softball bat like a lumberjack on steroids swings an ax, smashing to pieces the typewriter that sits on the counter.

Jane screams and dodges back into the corner. The student, eyes big in disbelief, tries to retreat, but trips and falls over backward. The madman, swinging with both hands, smashes the telephones, lamps, and a glass display case. Jane scrambles to the student, grabs him and pulls him into the bathroom. She locks the door, not at all confident it will withstand the lunatic's assault. She pulls back the privacy curtain from the window ever so slightly and takes a peek. The intruder continues his rampage.

Is the phone still working? That may be our only chance!

He runs out of frangible targets. He pauses to catch his breath, looks around. *Now it's our turn for his wrath!*

Jane's knees get weak, and for a moment, she thinks she might collapse. She takes a last look, a scream poised if he heads their way.

But with a mighty swing the intruder hurls the metal bat through the front plate glass window. The window explodes into fragments, a shower of tinkling shards attacking the cars parked just outside.

Sweating and breathing heavily, he kicks open the door and disappears beyond.

* * * * *

"Lori, would you like some cheesecake? It's an old family recipe and I guarantee that you will like it!" The aged but impeccably dressed Margaret Chen is beaming a smile so bright it seems she has a halo.

Lori makes a dismissive wave of her hand. "Oh, Margaret, I really shouldn't. I can hardly fit in my clothes as it is."

"Oh, go ahead! You've got something to celebrate, so why not?"

Lori gives in. Cheesecake is a temptation that rarely escapes her. "Well," she says with a smile, "maybe a little one." Margaret serves it up, then scans expectantly around the table. "Anyone ready for seconds?"

Lucy, a well-fed bleached blond on the wrong side of forty makes a comment that the rest of the women endorse: "Honey, if I eat another bite I won't be able to waddle out the door!" They all laugh, their mood lubricated by the champagne served with lunch.

"Just want to make sure everyone is on a good sugar high when it comes time to write some checks, right Lori?" Margaret plays her role as hostess to the max, which Lori deeply appreciates.

"What was it like, meeting Rosalynn Carter?" an attractive woman at the far end of the table asks, more interested in the First Lady than the President. "She seems so reserved when you see her on TV. Is she just being polite, do you think, or is that the way she really is?"

Lori dabs a crumb of cheesecake from her lip. "Oh, she couldn't have been nicer! She was just so sincere in her interest and knew lots of facts about Freedom Network. Wanted more information, too. We must have talked for forty-five minutes backstage waiting for the ceremony. One of the staffers told me that Rosalynn was really the person responsible for the Network being singled out for the prize. The funny thing is, and I'm really embarrassed by this," Lori blushes, but continues, "her Georgia accent was so thick I had to ask her to repeat herself half the time because I just couldn't quite understand what she was saying!"

The ladies laugh so hard the table shakes. "Not da island kine, eh?" one of the ladies says with a giggle.

Margaret joins in the laughter, then announces: "Okay, on that happy note I'll have the coffee out in just a moment, and Lori will have a chance to bring you up to speed on the Freedom Network and how you can help. Who wants decaf?"

"Margaret, can I freshen up a bit before we get started?" asks Lori.

"Oh, sure. Use my bedroom bathroom, honey, it's right through the door here," Margaret says, pointing. Lori slides from her chair and makes her way to the ornate bathroom. A small collection of pictures of

Margaret's grandkids adorn the counter and Lori is careful to not splash water on them as she cleans up.

They are really cute kids, hope I have some like that!

Lori steps out of the bathroom and into the large master bedroom. It is lavishly appointed, suitable for an interior design magazine. She pauses for a moment to take it all in. Her gaze falls on the dresser and then on a little gleaming object. It is a solid silver rhinoceros, engraved with the official seal of Kenya. Lori picks it up and stares at it, turning it over in her hands, feeling its contours and the cool smoothness of the metal. A familiar feeling wells up in her – a mixture of fear and thrill.

It started with taking things from friends when at a sleep-over or home visit – nothing really valuable, usually just make-up items, a piece of clothing, or some costume jewelry. Lori never tried to sell any of them, not that she needed money with such a wealthy father. And she never took cash. Only rarely did any of her friends ask if she knew where a missing item might be, and if they suspected a theft, they never mentioned it.

Lori was not so lucky when she graduated to shoplifting as a teenager. Twice she had been detained by store detectives and both times Rocky had to come down and pick her up. Needless to say, he wasn't happy. The result was the first of many conflicts over most of that decade, not only over the thefts, but over an assortment of issues. Maybe her actions were due to the early loss of her mother, Keiko, and to the lack of love she felt from her father - at least that's what the psychologist said, many sessions later. But Lori knew it was simpler than that, just a character flaw deep in her psyche that would never heal.

Over the years Lori controlled her theft urges — mostly. Or at least she learned enough to escape detection. In any event, as far as Rocky knew, the psychologists had "cured" her years ago.

Really and truly I don't want to disappoint Father.

She slips the rhino into her purse anyway. The clasp snaps with a satisfying click.

"Lori?" Startled, Lori turns to face Margaret. She stands at the door, a puzzled look on her face. "Did you find everything okay?"

"Oh, yes – I was just touching up my lipstick. Are we ready to go?"

"Yes, all set."

"Well then! Let's go raise some money," Lori replies, chin held high as she leaves the bedroom. Margaret quietly follows, the smile gone from her face.

* * * * * *

Warm and mellow from the Scotch, Korbler sits at his desk, content to do nothing in the empty office. With practice, he can zone out so no thoughts at all circulate through his brain, his personal version of nirvana. The trick is to think about not thinking, a conundrum that would have stopped less adept slackers, but after sustained practice, Korbler has determined there is a magic elixir in the Scotch, which can take him there.

Ah, the Scotch!

The phone rings, intruding upon Korbler's efforts at mind paralysis. The fog lifts marginally and after many rings, he picks up the receiver. "Korbler," he croaks.

"Hey, boss, Gaylord here."

"About time. Where are you?"

"At the airport, just got in." Gaylord's tone is noticeably downbeat.

"Good," says Korbler, "Saw the message our customers got delivered to the Philippines. Good work."

"Yeah, that part went well," says Gaylord, hesitating. "But we had a little trouble at Subic Bay, so I came back commercial."

Korbler sits up straight. "Commercial? The airplane didn't get wrecked, did it? I thought the flight was routine."

"Well, *I* wouldn't call it routine," Gaylord says in a moment of unfiltered honesty. "Scared the shit out of me."

Korbler laughs out loud. "Well, welcome to the big-boy's club, sport! So anyway, you and Scott need pickup at the airport?"

"Well," Gaylord hesitates, "not exactly. Jared's still in the Philippines, and will be for a few more days. He's kind of... in custody, house arrest I guess, until we pay to have all the commodes in the Subic Bay Officer's Club replaced."

"The what?" says Korbler, unable to process this data. "I thought you said... commodes?"

"Yeah." Gaylord says, his tone subdued. "We got into Subic, no problem, made the delivery, then went over to the Officer's Club to, you know, celebrate a little. Anyway, Jared couldn't have been nicer—full of funny stories, told me all about growing up in Texas, lots of stuff—did you know he ran a crab fishing boat up in Alaska?"

"No. Get to the point." Korbler's pleasant mood has turned surly and he is only a nanosecond away from full-on seething.

That goddamn Jared Scott!

"Well, we're just sitting at the bar, drinking some San Miguel's, pretty low key, then I come back from the bathroom, and Jared's got his Bible out, reading some passages. Next thing I know, he's doing shots and pounding down Boilermakers, and I mean really putting them down. Then he gets this kinda blank stare in his eyes, goes to the bathroom, and he comes back carrying a toilet! Drops it right in the middle of the dance floor, goes back and rips out another one, brings it in, throws it down with the other one, just keeps doing it, everybody's screaming at him, manager's going nuts, Jared just keeps piling 'em up, never says a freakin' word."

"Then the M.P.'s get there, and I figure, oh boy! Fight's on! But Jared seems like he comes out of his trance, now he's embarrassed by the whole deal. So anyway, the Navy's got him locked in a BOQ bedroom till we pay up."

Korbler jumps to his feet. "Jesus freaking Christ, Gaylord! Why do you think I sent you along? I give you one simple mission, just one cowboy to wrangle and you dick it up. Nice going!"

Korbler has bailed many agents out of "unfortunate" situations. He's relieved it isn't worse, but he can't pass up the opportunity to chastise the young agent.

"I know, sir, I'm really sorry, it's just he was so nice and then..., then he went berserk, and I didn't know what to do. He's a heck of a strong guy, you know," Gaylord says, a little defensively.

"So what's the tab?" Korbler says with a sigh.

"Well, it's uh, they said, maybe get it done for... five thousand dollars," Gaylord stammers.

Korbler emits a dismissive snort. He can take it out of operations funds and no one will know or care. Still, he can't resist screwing with Gaylord — he's such an easy target, and Korbler wouldn't dare confront Jared like this.

"And tell me why it shouldn't come out of your pay?"

Korbler can almost hear Gaylord gulp through the phone. Five thousand dollars is six month's pay for a junior agent.

"Gee, boss, that's uh, a lot, isn't it? I mean, nobody got hurt or anything," he adds plaintively.

Korbler mellows a bit. "Go home and get some rest. We'll talk about it tomorrow when you come in."

"Sure, chief, sounds like a plan," Gaylord says, relieved somewhat. Korbler visualizes him wiping the sweat off his brow. "Uh, what about Jared, he's still, you know..."

"He can just cool his heels till tomorrow, then I'll work on it. Do him good to spend some more time reflecting on his behavior," says Korbler, with a smile Gaylord can't see.

Don't even have TVs in those BOQ rooms, and hopefully the air conditioning will go out as well. Yep, Mr. Jared Scott can just keep his ass parked in Subic for a little while longer, the prick.

Korbler hangs up without a goodbye. He splashes another dose of Scotch into his glass and settles back in his chair.

Now to think about not thinking...

Chapter 14

The incessant ringing drills through the final layer of dense fog surrounding his brain. One eye opens, assisting the transition from semi-asleep dreaming to semi-awake thinking. This is a major accomplishment for Jared's jet-lagged skull, at the moment, full of mush.

Jeez, why didn't I remember to unplug the alarm clock when I got home!

It finally sinks in that the noise is someone leaning on his doorbell with the vigor of a New York cabbie honking his way through rush hour traffic.

"Hey, knock it off, will ya!" he tries to yell, but it's a mere rattle. A pillow thrown in the direction of the noise is also ineffective. Sighing, Jared rolls out of the bed and stands up. Head swimming, he finds himself a moment later sitting back on the bed.

Let's try that again, much slower this time.

Gripping the bedstead, Jared gets up again and manages to pull on a pair of sun-washed jeans. Lurching his way to the front door, he notes from the sunlight streaming into the living room it seems to be broad daylight, not zero-dark-thirty like it feels to his biorhythm-challenged body.

Still the ringing! He fumbles with the latch.

This better not be a Jehovah's Witnesses calling!

He gets the door open and Lori bursts in, a human tornado. Jared can't tell if she's exasperated, angry or both, but she's clearly upset, pacing madly, talking gibberish at warp speed. Jared eases the door shut, not sure what's happening.

"Lori...it's a good thing it's you because...why didn't you use your key?"

"'Cause it's at my apartment and there's way too many news media there," she says, spitting out the words. She throws her purse on the couch and faces him, her tone charged with anger.

"Jared! Where have you been? I've been trying to reach you for days!"

Jared settles onto the sofa, but Lori continues standing, arms crossed, foot tapping.

Aw, man, she's missed a period! What the hell's the matter with these gals? Don't they know how to douche? Here we go...

"I was on a mission, I mean...a trip, out of the country. Way out of the country. I told you, remember? I just got back late last night, parked the airplane and came home and crashed."

"You left me a message you'd be gone a couple of days, not almost a week!"

Never fails, sooner or later they gotta possess you, always seems to be after they get preggers. Must be the hormones or something.

It's always worse when they come over — if it was at her apartment I could just bolt, hopefully before things are being thrown.

He instinctively glances around. Lori is between him and the front door. No escape. His anger flares. "Lori!" Jared snaps. "What are you so pissed off about? Is this about, your, uh, ..."

Lori takes a deep breath, and takes Jared's hand in hers and says, "Jared, you've got to help me with Father. I need..." She struggles to finish her sentence.

What the hell? I know she's had some head-butting with her father, but I thought that was long past. A relapse?

"Jesus, Lori," Jared says, not trying to hide his exasperation, "you're almost thirty years old. I thought you got past any issues with your dad way back."

Lori pulls Jared to his feet and looks up at him, her brow crinkling. "Jared, don't you know? Father has been arrested...it's murder!"

"For, for *what!*" He pushes her to arm length and shakes his head no. "That can't be right..." He pauses a moment to catch his breath, and squeezes Lori's hands tight.

"Don't worry, baby, there's no way the Governor-elect is going to go down for this, it's got to be political shit, I'm sure of it. Or one hell of a screw-up on somebody's part."

Lori's eyes glisten with tears and her face contorts in anguish. "Jared, Jared...you don't understand. I saw it happen. It was murder."

Chapter 15

It is late on a Friday afternoon. Lori takes a moment to catch her breath and grab a cup of coffee. Rocky's campaign headquarters is winding down, not because there is nothing to do, but because he has ordered anyone not handling critical action items to go home, rest and relax. With the general election complete, the campaign committees race to transform themselves into a governance role. In politics, only the losers get a respite from the grueling year of campaigning — for the winners, the sixteen-hour days go on unabated. But no one complains, because for most of them it is happy work, the culmination of years of hopes, dreams and wishes.

Compared to the worker-bees, Rocky seems serene. Although he has plenty to do and an endless list of people who want to see him, he takes it all in stride, never too busy to talk to staffers and volunteers.

Lori is not so calm, juggling a blizzard of details and deadlines. Her short-term goal is simple: get enough tasks completed so she can spend some quality time with Jared when he returns from his trip to Indonesia.

Yes...quality time! Delicious anticipation flies through her mind, a welcome distraction from the necessary but tedious campaign work.

For Lori, the campaign was a life-altering event. A political novice, she immersed herself with her usual vigor and determination and became a real asset to her father and his campaign. She found she had a natural flair for producing and organizing events, and learned the ropes quickly. When Rocky told her he was surprised she took to politics so well, she reminded him she almost single-handedly put together the Freedom Network.

How ironic, Father joined *me* on stage to get an award and praise from the President of the United States.

Rocky was very proud of her and told her often, which meant a very great deal to her. She spent much of her early twenties rebelling against what she perceived as his cool, distant and emotionally withdrawn persona — in other words, a typical Japanese father. That was in the past. As the inauguration loomed they had never been closer. Rocky even told her he loved her, a verbalization unthinkable a few years ago.

Lori finished her coffee and trooped into Rocky's glass-walled office.

"Ready for another round?" She asked, plopping a list of inauguration ball attendees on the desk. It's another step towards gridlock in the traffic jam of competing papers decorating the desktop landscape.

Rocky leans back in his leather and chrome executive chair. "Yeah, I suppose so. We've got to get these in the mail by Monday or they might not get delivered in time." A faint hint of fatigue weighs upon his words.

Lori stands beside him, looking over his shoulder and scribbling notes. With reading glasses perched on his nose, Rocky scrutinizes the inauguration party lists, absentmindedly scratching his brow.

Lori glances up as a burly, shaved-head Asian man approaches the office. He pauses at the entryway and then steps inside. The man says nothing, but holds Rocky in a burning stare, his multi-colored tattooed arms crossed tightly over his chest.

A little sketchy looking, but nothing unusual. Campaign workers often drop by to lobby for a state job. Rocky refers them to his Chief of Staff, but he always takes time to chat with them first, regardless of the time or duties that must be set aside.

"Can I help you?" Lori offers. The man ignores her, walks slowly up to the desk where Rocky sits. He stands in silence and continues the hard look.

Rocky's jaw slackens as his gaze shifts up into the face of the intruder. For a long moment, the stranger clinches Rocky in a visual choke-hold.

"*Anata no shimobe ga modette mairimashita,*" the intruder growls.

With great deliberation, Rocky takes off his reading glasses and places them on the desk. He rises, never taking his eyes off the face of the inked apparition in front of him.

Lori scans the intruder, bewildered by his actions. She looks at her father and is shocked. *His normally ruddy face is white as a sheet of paper!* For a moment, she scarcely recognizes him.

"Lori, close the office and send everyone home. Do it now," Rocky says. She recognizes the "don't ask questions, just do it," tone from her childhood days. She blinks for a second, looks at the tattooed visitor and decides not to argue. Glancing over her shoulder as she shuts the door, she leaves the two men facing off.

The stranger flops into the seat across the desk from Rocky, both visible in the glass-walled office to Lori and the others. *This is not the usual community volunteer looking for a job with the Parks and Recreation Department!* Lori runs alternate possibilities through her mind and comes up blank.

Rocky and the stranger talk in Japanese, but the glass walls mute enough of the conversation so Lori can't make out what they are saying. In moments, however, the body language signals an increasingly intense argument.

"Who's the tatt freak talking to your dad?" asks one of the staffers who stops by with some expenditure requests for approval. Lori doesn't answer, but both of them gaze at the unfolding scene for a few moments.

"Is he missing some fingers?" asks the staffer.

"Tell everybody to leave, go home now," Lori says, still not sure what to do, but it seems appropriate. By now a half dozen workers have stopped what they are doing. They watch as the dialogue becomes louder and the tone harsher.

The burly intruder leans forward, and with a hateful sneer on his face, strikes the desktop in slow motion with his clenched fist.

Lori jabs a couple of buttons on the intercom and says, "Security, Lori Konishi. Get up to Rocky's office, wiki-wiki, we got somebody here causing big problems. Hurry!"

Lori looks up in time to see her father open the desk drawer. He grabs a revolver from it and jumps to his feet. Rocky, arm outstretched in front of him, takes dead aim at the stranger and pulls the trigger. *Bang!*

The stranger's face blossoms shock and surprise, then contorts in pain. Again: *Bang!*

A staffer down the hall screams.

The arms of the intruder flail spasmodically.

Bang! A bullet explodes through his up-stretched palms and hits him in the throat as hard as a Nolan Ryan fastball. He tries to yell, but his words are a gurgle.

Bang! Bang! Bang! The man jerks as the bullets smash him. Crimson mist is airbrushed repeatedly on the glass wall near him. His chair tips over backwards, propelled by the lead hammers slamming into his contorted body.

Lori screams, the sound of her terror even louder than the gunshots. She runs into the office, followed by the staffer. Her first impression is the acrid smell of gunpowder from the gun, forming a haze cloud throughout the room. Her next is revulsion as she sees the gurgling, bright red blood flowing from the stranger's multiple wounds. A shocked expression is frozen on his face, his eyes open wide, seeing nothing.

Rocky lowers the revolver and drops it to the floor. It lands with a clunk. Campaign workers cluster to stare in disbelief through the glass office walls, jabbering questions, some turning away from the blood.

An obese security guard shows up at the door, out of breath and sweating. He stops and stares with the rest of the growing crowd.

"Call the paramedics!" Lori yells to anyone listening.

Several workers run for the phones, others cry, hugging each other. The scene rapidly descends into anarchy.

"Oh, God! Oh, my God! The governor has killed someone!" screams an unidentified worker. Others shout and dial phones in a panic.

Lori steps away from the rapidly growing red puddle and backs over to her father's side. Rocky seems to emerge from his daze, at least a little.

"Lori," he says softly, "please forgive me..." He takes a yellowed piece of paper from the desktop and gives it to her. "Take this...take it." Not comprehending, but obedient in a crisis, she accepts it.

Just then, the campaign center doors almost fly off the hinges as cops, medics and passers-by come bursting in. Instantly it is chaos squared, shouts, screams and crying competing with the paramedic's desperate commands. Everyone is yelling, but no one is sure what to do. Several people are knocked down as the crowd surges, their cries for help unheeded.

Finally the cops take charge and a phalanx of police hustle the blank-faced Rocky out of the building and into a squad car, with Lori fighting her way in as well. The car, lights flashing and siren blaring, launches from the parking lot. No one in the car has a clue where to go.

* * * * * *

Lori sits on a well-worn metal and plastic chair in a bare bones interview room in the Honolulu Police Department headquarters. *Looks just like those you see on TV,* she thinks wearily. She is frazzled to the max and struggles to hold up her head, exhausted from crying and stress.

The detective sitting across from her is considerate, but makes it clear he has a job to do, and is one of those annoyingly meticulous types often found in bureaucracies. Now that the adrenaline has worn off, Lori is approaching her limit of the detective's persistence and thoroughness. It doesn't help that they often have to repeat themselves to hear one another over the clamor of shouts and questions from news crews milling about in the area. The police have their hands full trying to corral them back into the lobby, much less conducting an investigation.

"Can I go now? I've told you everything, twice over," Lori pleads. She has already thrown up once and her bowels are increasingly in distress.

The detective says, "Actually, there's a few more things. Shouldn't take..."

Lori stands up abruptly. "I'm done," she says, nostrils flaring. "Where's my father?" Without waiting for an answer, she strides out of the room and charges down the hallway, the detective trying but failing to keep up with her.

"Ms. Konishi! Would you please just..."

Lori's search mission is rewarded by her discovery of a large interview room. Through a glass window in the door, she sees Rocky with two plainclothes detectives facing him across a wooden table.

Lori bursts into the room, blowing past the "in use" sign and surprising the two detectives. They turn towards Lori, puzzlement etched on their faces. Rocky sits across the table but does not react to the intrusion.

"Where's his lawyer?" Lori says angrily.

Detective One, the younger of the two, says, "He didn't say he wanted one. In fact, he hasn't said anything at all. But you can't..."

"Well, *I've* got something to say: Get the fuck out of here and don't come back until there are lawyers sitting on either side of him," Lori snarls. "Got it?"

Detective One looks at Detective Two. He shrugs and they get up and leave as Lori's hot glare follows.

Through all of this Rocky has not moved or spoken. As the door closes, Lori bends down to hold him. Rocky stares straight ahead, unresponsive to her embrace.

"Father, Father... Always..." She sobs, still hugging him.

He doesn't respond, does not react in any way. Her tears wet his face.

Chapter 16

The trade winds blow softly through the jalousie windows, bringing coolness to what would otherwise be an unpleasantly warm day. The Ala Wai canal and the distant mountains provide a view, not a million dollar view, but pleasant nonetheless. Jared brings Lori a hot cup of tea and then settles in beside her on the sofa. She takes a sip as Jared studies her face. The dark circles under her eyes are overly evident, and she looks thinner than the last time he saw her.

Jared's apartment is Hawaiian middle class, right out of the bachelor catalogue: comfortable, not pretentious, with pictures of airplanes and army memorabilia for decorations. The furnishings tend heavily toward Oriental kitsch picked up on various trips around the Pacific, no consistency, just whatever Jared came across that he fancied. Several times, Lori mentioned she could have it completely redecorated, courtesy of daddy, as a payment for Jared's volunteer work on the campaign. Jared always rejected such notions. He didn't say it, but the thought was always there: *First they want to make the apartment over, then they want to make me over – nope, not falling for it!*

Lori takes another sip of the tea, and resumes her narrative. "Anyway, after I answered about a million questions for the cops, I had to go into hiding so I could get some peace or I was going to have a nervous breakdown. I don't know who's worse, the cops with their stupid questions, or the news media with theirs. I never knew the TV guys were such jerks, sticking those bright lights and cameras in your face and asking the same questions over and over." Her voice drips disgust.

"What about the gun, Lori? Could it have been the intruder's? Maybe he was there to attack your father."

Lori laughs with false amusement. "Oh, it was Father's gun all right. The ironic thing is he got it from the police! Actually, they gave it to him for his personal protection as soon as he was elected, it's a standard procedure. All the judges have them too."

Jared shakes his head, emphasizing his lack of understanding. "Yeah, I guess that was too easy. But what's your father's story? He must have an explanation for all this."

Lori sighs and slumps visibly. "That's the part of all this that kills me, Jared. I thought father and I finally had a great relationship, not just good, but great, that we could really confide in each other. But he won't tell me anything, not a thing. He's almost catatonic. He sits silently with his eyes closed for long periods and won't respond whenever I talk to him. Same thing with the lawyers, he just tells them he's guilty and won't offer one word of explanation."

She sighs again. "Refuses bail, I think to avoid to having to deal with people. Mostly he just sits in the cell and writes for hours, then destroys it without showing it to anyone."

Jared tries to get his mind around this information. "Really? Man, that is weird. Have the doctors had a chance to look at him? Maybe he's still in shock or something."

"No," Lori replies. "It's not shock, the best they can say is it's severe depression. But he won't take medication for it, and believe me I've pleaded with him."

Jared thinks over what Lori has told him. "Didn't you say Rocky gave you a piece of paper? What kind of paper? Do you still have it?"

"Oh, yeah," Lori says, reaching into her purse. "It's right here."

"All right, maybe now we'll be getting somewhere." Jared says, sitting up straight. He feels a surge of excitement as Lori hands over a brown piece of weathered paper. It is about five by eight inches in size, frayed and worn in places and stained to various degrees over its entirety. Jared studies it intently for a minute or so, then puts it down and looks up, hoping disappointment is not evident on his face.

"Well, hell, the damn thing's all in Japanese. Or Chinese, maybe."

"Oh, it's Japanese," Lori responds.

"Well, what does it say?"

"Uhh, I'm not too sure. It's all technical writing, obviously handwritten, but I'm not familiar with a lot of the characters and style. I'm much better with spoken Japanese, you know." She adds the latter a bit defensively.

"About all I can make out for sure is this part," she says, pointing to some characters near the center of the page. "It says something about fuel, and then just a little bit later there are some numbers that don't make any sense."

"That's it? Your dad killed someone over a set of fuel figures?" Jared says, and instantly regrets it. He waves his hands in visual apology. "Hey, babe, I'm sorry. That was a stupid thing to say. I guess I was expecting a treasure map or something. I'm still not thinking too clear," he continued. "Coffee hasn't kicked in yet, I guess."

The hurt look flashes across Lori's face and fades quickly, but Jared reminds himself to try to keep his foot out of his mouth in the future.

Jared resumes, "Well, this doesn't give us a lot to work with, does it? Which brings up a big question, Lori. You know I'd do anything in the world to help you. And Rocky, too, for that matter. But this is police business, solving crimes is way out of my league. I'm not even a private investigator, for crying out loud. You really ought to give this to the cops and let them check it out."

"What, and let that son-of-a-bitch Ralston get his hands on it!" Lori explodes. "No way, for sure, not until I know what it means."

Jared belatedly remembers Rocky and the District Attorney, Richard Ralston, are bitter political enemies, their animosity going back years. Ralston had filed charges against Rocky accusing him of a fraudulent land deal just as Rocky was first becoming active in politics. The validity of the charges was suspicious, especially after they were thrown out of court for lack of evidence. Rocky replied with a counter suit, alleging malicious prosecution, but later dropped it.

One thing certain, Ralston had his eyes on the Governor's mansion and he regarded Rocky is a dangerous political threat to his eventual campaign for that office.

"Yeah, I guess I see your point," he says. They sit in silence for a few moments.

Lori looks at Jared, hope writ large across her face. "But you can find out what it says, can't you? You've got ...connections, yeah?"

Jared looks at her sharply. He's never mentioned anything about his part time job, simply explaining he often had to pick up and deliver aircraft bought and sold by various companies. This explained his absences and a lifestyle considerably better off than a typical flight instructor. Maybe her dad really did have him checked out. For all his worldliness, Jared wasn't too familiar as to how the wealthy operated.

Trying not to sound evasive, he says, "But your dad has access to tons of legal help, you could go to them with this, couldn't you?"

"Jared, are you going to help me or not?" Lori says harshly, the words ringing with accusation. Her face reddens and she jumps to her feet. "I come to you practically begging and it sounds like you're trying to pawn me off on someone, anyone, else."

Her hands clench and find her hips.

"Are you going to throw me overboard like you usually do when someone really needs you?"

The stinging challenge rocks Jared back for a moment. He slowly stands up and stares into Lori's eyes, then takes her hands in his. A long moment passes as Lori's words echo in his mind.

"Lori, Lori...of course I'll help you."

Lori buries her head on Jared's chest, and sobs with relief. Jared hugs her at length, sighs, glad she doesn't see the expression on his face.

Chapter 17

It's just past rush-hour at the Columbia Inn coffee shop on Kapiolani street. From the faces in the booths, it's clear this is a locals' place, and a popular one. Jared, seated at the counter, scans the entrance between sips of Coca-Cola.

Lt. Henry Fong enters, looks around and sees Jared's wave. He strides over and they exchange grins and shake hands. Fong is a Chinese-American in his early forties, fit and trim in his black HPD uniform.

"Henry! You looking good, brah. Catching any?"

They pause as the waitress wipes up for them and slides each a menu.

"Slaying 'em," Fong says, adding a chuckle. "Me and my cousin, Larry, spent three days trolling the Big Island, brought back a thousand dollar ahi, man."

"No way! A thousand dollars!" Jared is impressed. "That'll pay for a lot of gas."

"Yeah, the crew at the fish market said that's the biggest ahi they've seen so far this year. Probably auctioned at close to three grand. Too bad we're getting only wholesale price."

Fong picks up the menu, consults it briefly. A plump local waitress appears, notepad in hand.

"What can I get for you and your handsome friend, Lieutenant?" She gives them both a flirtatious smile.

"Spam omelet, black coffee," Fong says.

"I'll have steak and eggs, darlin', and some more ice for my Coke," Jared adds. He winks at the waitress, who blushes and gets flustered.

She scurries off to the kitchen, glancing over her shoulder at Jared before disappearing through the swinging doors.

"So, what you been up to? Just down here hanging out?" Fong inquires.

Jared glances around to see who might be close enough to overhear, then speaks confidentially to Fong.

"Well, I need a little info on the Konishi case, ol' buddy."

The waitress drops off a coffee and a glass of ice. Fong cools his coffee with a swirling spoon and waits until she's well away. He looks sideways at Jared for a moment then laughs and shakes his head.

"Yeah, you and every reporter in America. I've had calls from as far away as Maine and I'm not even directly involved in the case."

"No, this is legit. I need to find out what the investigation has turned up so far, motive, that sort of thing."

Fong hesitates for a long moment, an edge to his voice when he replies. "Hey, brah, easy now, you're talking some heavy stuff. I could lose my lieutenant bars for even discussing this with you."

Jared calls up every bit of sincerity he can muster. "Henry, I know what I'm asking for, and I promise you it's for a good reason. And, if I remember right, you got those bars because of that tip I gave you about the fishing trawler loaded with heroin – you said so yourself."

Because he flew airplanes all over the Pacific, Jared kept an ear open for who was moving what and where. Most was bullshit bar talk, but occasionally the whiskey would reveal a little too much, or maybe an illicit business proposition was put on the table. Jared passed along some of these tidbits to the appropriate government agencies. Sometimes a guy might need a favor returned. Like now.

Fong shakes his head slowly back and forth. "Jared, you can't screw me on this one, brah. My ass is hanging out just being here. You know the chief's put the clamp down, no leaks. If anything I say gets out into the newspapers or on TV, well..."

"I understand completely, Henry. You got my word on it."

Fong pauses, looks around. "We can't talk here. Tell you what, I'll pick you up on the corner of Kapiolani and Lau in about an hour. I'll be in the Impala."

* * * * * *

Sprawled on a bench overlooking a busy sidewalk park, Jared absorbs the vibrancy and energy that resonates in the heart of Waikiki. As usual, the streets and beaches are awash with its lifeblood tourists. They are every size and age, from hundreds of countries, all attracted to this Disneyland of the Pacific. For the most part, this little piece of Polynesia delivers. Even though Honolulu is a small city and the island of Oahu can easily be circumnavigated on a day trip, for those who seek all the fun that starts with "s," i.e., sunbathing, sailing, snorkeling, scuba diving, surfing, sightseeing, there's not a better place on earth. Add another "s" –safe. Hawaii has a reputation that can't be bought. It is widely regarded as a place to go and do most anything without being harmed. Unless perhaps you are a Japanese tourist meeting the new governor.

All this winds through Jared's mind as he passes time waiting for Fong to return. Local teens play a raucous two-on-two basketball game on a nearby court. Offshore, amateurs from the mid-west make laughable attempts at surfing on Waikiki's gentle waves. And tourists swarm everywhere, most of them decked out in elaborate aloha attire purchased in the last few days. It's a gigantic outdoor costume party where everybody decides to wear the same thing. No wonder the locals sometimes have "tacky tourist" parties where they dress like tourists dressing like them.

Whack! An errant basketball hits Jared a glancing blow in the back.

"Hey, a little help!" A chorus from the teenagers, a demand, not a request.

Jared stares hard at them and without a word throws the ball back. The tall, bushy haired one says something Jared can't hear and the other players chortle with laughter. The Beast, always sleeping lightly, has awakened and is pacing the cage. The door is there, ready to be flung open.

Be cool, steady up. It's just stupid kids who think they own the beach. Nothing personal. It takes a few minutes of determined effort, but Jared talks the Beast back into the dark. Gradually his breathing and blood pressure turns to normal. He feels good, almost contented. A minor battle with himself, won. The tropical breeze soothes him. It's easy to be mellow in the islands.

A yell. Thunk! The basketball hits Jared square in the back of the head. At first, he doesn't move, then he hears laughter from the players. That's all it takes. The Beast roars within and the lock is off the gate. Someone's skull is about to be cracked, and Jared doesn't care, not one bit, if it is the local teens' or his own. He grabs the ball and marches to the court. A tall skinny kid, brown as a nut, steps forward, a malicious grin on his face.

"Hey *haole* – why you keep getting in way? You stupid, maybe?"

Jared torpedoes the ball at him, a double hand pass which hits the kid in the chest so hard it knocks him on his ass. He lies stunned for a moment, then scrambles to get up.

"Oh, want beef, eh?" The biggest teen, a six foot, two hundred pound Samoan advances toward Jared, a snarl on his face and hate in his eyes.

The others circle left and right. Jared clenches his fists, ready to take and deliver punishment, to spill blood and break bones.

A gold Impala screeches to a halt at the curb, horn blaring. Lt. Fong steps out, billy club in hand. The ruffians glance at the black HPD uniform and flee over the wall that separates them from the beach. They sprint away, zigzagging around sunbathers and beached surfboards.

"What was that all about?" Fong asks, watching the teens disappear down the strand.

Breathing heavily, adrenaline still raging through his body, Jared blurts a response. "Ah, nothing. Just some punks looking for trouble. No problem, it was just four of them. I got a little excited, but I'm okay." He takes a deep breath, holds it a moment, and lets it go. "Actually, I feel pretty good now. Needed to let out some tension that builds up. Haven't been able to get to the gym lately." Jared manages a grin, his face cooling in the soft trade wind.

Fong eyeballs him up and down. "Jared," he says, shaking his head, "sometimes I worry about you. I really do." He checks to make sure the punks have split. "Let's get out of here before we draw a crowd."

Jared and Fong jump into the Impala and pull away, careful to avoid a flock of jaywalkers. They head up Kapiolani, make a couple of turns and arrive at the First Chinese Church of Christ. The tree shaded parking lot beckons, empty, save a flock of squawking blackbirds. Fong wheels around so that the car faces the exit and kills the engine. He hands over a thickly stuffed envelope without a word. Jared hesitates, not sure what to expect, then peeks into it.

"Let's make it quick, I need to have those documents back before the shift change," Fong directs, scanning the street and sidewalk. "And don't get sticky fingers, it's all accountable."

"No problem, partner. Let's start with what I heard on TV – name's Fujitta, right? And is this guy really *yakusa*? Japanese mafia?"

"Oh yeah, up to his eyeballs. Check out those coroner photos." Fong gestures at some color glossies as Jared extracts them from the envelope.

Jared finds the eight by ten inch pictures and examines them. With clinical precision, they portray a naked, middle-aged Asian man stretched out on an autopsy table. His body is a riot of color, almost completely covered in elaborate *Samurai* tattoos. Some are ripped and torn by bullet wounds, but the blood has been washed away. Another series of pictures are close-ups of Fujitta's hands. Both little fingers have been chopped off.

"What's with the tatts and missing fingers? This guy looks like he belongs in a circus."

Fong chuckles, then glances at Jared. "The tattoos are the colors of the crime family Fujitta was in, and he cut off the fingers to prove his loyalty and dedication to the head *obuyan*. Or it could have been an act of atonement if he pissed the guy off."

"Yeah, well, he probably wasn't a piano player."

Fong waves to the church gardener, a stooped and aged Chinese man arriving with an armload of yard tools. The Lieutenant adds a friendly smile. The gardener nods, his face expressionless, and goes to work trimming the hedges.

Jared rummages deeper into the envelope. He finds another photo of Fujitta, this one where he was very much alive. He laughs and holds it up for Fong to see. "Check out the threads – quite the dresser. Looks like he's seen too many *Untouchables* episodes." Decked out in a black suit, black shirt, and white tie, Fujitta sports an aggressive frown under a snappy fedora. He stands in front of a big black Lincoln Continental, which looks very much out of place with the quaint Japanese buildings in the background.

"I know, looks ridiculous to us, but these are pretty tough customers. We haven't got any US arrests on Fujitta, as far as we know, he's never been here before. He's been locked up a couple of times in Japan, mostly on gunrunning charges, amphetamine manufacture and distribution."

Jared nods as he mulls this over. "Is that what you think Fujitta was here for? And what's his tie with Rocky Konishi?"

To Jared's surprise, Fong produces a cigarette and heats it up.

"When did you start smoking?

"Again? Today" He blows a cloud out the window. "It's pretty much guesswork right now. Makes sense Fujitta was in town on mob business - the DA's office is working that angle. Their theory is that Fujitta and Mr. Konishi were cooking up some scheme, maybe laundering drug money through some of Rocky's construction companies."

Jared groans aloud. "Ah, that's a crock and you know it."

Fong shrugs. "Hey, you know those guys over at the DA's office had been waiting years for opportunity like this. They're going over it hard, trying to tie those two together looking to build a case for first-degree, I think."

"Oh, Jesus, Henry! They'll be lucky to get the grand jury to buy manslaughter." He stuffs the photos back into the envelope.

"I don't know, Jared, I'm not directly involved in the case. I am sure they think there's a connection between Fujitta and Mr. Konishi. But so far, there's no evidence they've ever met or communicated. The only thing they seem to have in common is they were both Japanese by birth. It doesn't seem likely they met, however. They're from different regions, Fujitta is older and served in the Japanese Navy during the war, while Mr. Konishi was too young and left Japan for good a couple years after the war was over. There must be some link, though. A governor-elect doesn't shoot an unarmed man full of holes after knowing him only ten minutes, even if the guy is *yakusa.*"

Jared can't argue with that logic. He recalls the comment Fujitta initially made in Japanese to Rocky. Evidently Lori has not told the police about it.

The inventory of Fujitta's belongings catches Jared eye. He scans it carefully — no guns, drugs or incriminating documents. No mention of any stained and aged papers like the one given to Lori. Or perhaps Fong was withholding some key info.

Which makes it more important than ever to find out what is on that *intriguing piece of paper.*

Chapter 18

"**J**ared! Jared! Wake up! You're having a nightmare!"

"Hunh...what..."

Lori snaps on the reading light, and Jared squints against the sudden glare. "I guess I was dreaming," he gasps.

"That was more than dreaming, honey," Lori says, wiping his brow. "You're soaked with sweat, and your heart feels like it's beating a hundred miles an hour."

Jared's breathing slows.

"I fell into a well, and everything I tried to grab onto broke, and I started to fall faster and deeper...it's okay now...I'm...okay..." He covers his eyes with his arm as Lori snuggles in beside him and rubs his chest gently.

A long moment passes.

"Jared?"

"What?"

"I'm a good listener..."

Pause.

"Really? Did my snoring bother you?"

"Oh, please. You know what I'm talking about."

Long pause.

"When you're inside me I want to be inside you. It's a girl thing, I guess." She snuggles in a little closer. Jared tenses.

"You're not going to say the "L" word, are you?"

"Is that so bad?"

Jared reaches up and turns off the light. "Goodnight, Lori. Sweet dreams."

Lori doesn't reply, but hugs him in a tight embrace. A couple of minutes go by.

Jared turns on the light, and gets out of bed. He pulls on his jeans and grabs his shirt.

Lori sits up in bed, pulling the sheets around her. "Where are you going?"

"Home. Out. Somewhere." He pulls on the bedroom doorknob, but it won't open.

"Jared...please..."

Jared yanks on the knob, his jaw clenching harder with each tug.

"It sticks sometimes, just lift a little when..."

Jared gives a mighty jerk and the knob comes off in his hand. He hurls it to the floor.

Wham! He smashes his fist through a door panel.

"Jared! Oh, Jared!

Red-faced, gasping for breath, he glares at the door, daring it to fight back.

His vision grays. The strength disappears from his legs. Then blackness.

* * * * * *

There is roaring in his ears. Somewhere through the foggy sound comes something familiar, comforting. He knows he has heard it before... *Mother? Mom? Are you there? Is it time for school?"*

He feels his body convulse, and he wants to sit up, but all energy is drained from him. His breath is scary hard and fast.

"Jared, Jared...just breathe into the bag, relax now, relax. You're doing good, just slow it down, okay?" Lori rubs his chest with one hand and keeps the paper bag over his mouth with the other. The rapid rise and fall of his chest slows.

Jared opens his wet eyes. He is crying gently and doesn't know why.

* * * * * *

Jared fires up the Corvette, then puts the top down as he waits for it to warm up. With four hundred fifty four cubic inches, even at idle the grumbling exhaust is loud enough to make the irritated neighbors aware he's coming or going. Of course, the gleaming white body with the blue sash on the stern is distinct enough to confirm who it is, should anyone glance out of a window. Little wonder he is seldom invited for tea and cookies.

This throbbing horsepower is wasted as Jared, along with about a hundred thousand other motorists, percolate the jammed roadway, losing a race with the snails in the median greenway.

People often asked him why he kept such a high-speed fuel hog on a tiny island, especially since the Arabs belatedly made the islands part of the recent gas embargo. There was no rational reason, except it was Jared's gift to himself after he got thrown out of the Army. The car was the only thing of value he owned. Girlfriends come and go, he mused, but although the Vette could be temperamental and expensive, at least it didn't keep him up all night bitching about something that he couldn't - or wouldn't - change.

Forty-five minutes after launch, he has covered the six miles to the Manoa Campus of the University of Hawaii and traded the problem of stop and go for the problem of no stop at all, i.e., not being able to find a parking place in the university parking lot. Paying the entry fee didn't mean there were actually any parking spots available, as new visitors to the campus soon learn, especially here at the East-West institute.

Situated halfway between North America and the Orient, Hawaii was perfectly placed to find common ground among the vastly different cultures bordering the broad Pacific, a challenge the university addressed with the creation of a research institute aptly named the East-West Center.

Jared's patience diminished with each circuit around the parking area. The sun is fully up, and even with the cooling trade winds, it is still sweaty hot. Finally, he spots someone leaving and makes a play for the spot, cutting off a lady who was closer but less aggressive. She blows her horn and leans out her window, "Hey, asshole!" she bellows.

Jared doesn't even look her way as he strides away, just flips her the bird and keeps walking. He finds a directory at the bottom of the entry stairs to the big modern building and searches until he finds what he is looking for — the office of Professor Raymond Tanaka. A few flights of stairs and a couple of corridors later, he is at Tanaka's door, which is open to let the breeze flow through.

Dr. Tanaka, a Japanese linguist and cultural historian, is almost lost in the clutter of his office. Piles of papers are stacked wherever there is room, on shelves, chairs, and most of the floor. Hundreds of books add to the fire hazard, crammed onto the bookcases covering two walls. Banners with Japanese writing advertising lush, mountainous destinations, or exotic festivals decorate what little wall space remains. An old typewriter and decidedly clunky black phone adorn the desktop, almost lost under the layers of papers and publications.

Jared knocks on the doorframe and announces himself with a big smile. "Hey, howdy, neighbor! It's Jared Scott..."

Professor Tanaka looks, up, takes a moment to focus behind his thick rimless glasses, then returns Jared's broad smile. "Well, indeed it is! Come right in young man." He stands, still beaming, and grabs Jared's extended hand. Using both hands he shakes Jared's vigorously.

Tanaka is a small man in his early sixties, with a careful, cultured manner and world-class dandruff. He wears a button-down shirt, rare for Hawaii, somewhat offset by the casualness of the sandals with socks he sports. Clearing a stack of papers off the visitor's chair, he waves Jared to it.

"So, you still have the Corvette? Since you moved, I never see you on the street," Tanaka says.

Jared settles back in the chair — he knows this is going to be a lengthy conversation. "Yeah, still got it. That's why I moved, couldn't afford to commute over the Pali every day. That four-fifty-four is a thirsty beast!"

They both laugh. Jared pauses, then takes a more serious tone. "Are you still chairman of the Japanese Studies department here?"

"Would you like some tea? I've got it brewed up right here," Tanaka says, indicating a small, ornamental teapot. He doesn't wait for an answer, but pours a cup for himself and one for Jared. Jared accepts, but ignores it.

Tanaka continues, "Yes, for a couple of more years. Then I'm going to take that cruise I told you about." This brings an unmistakable gleam of anticipation to his face.

"Lucky you! If I win the lottery I'll join you," Jared says, faking a happy face. "Anyway, this isn't entirely a social call. I have a small professional favor that I'm hoping you might do for me if it's not too much of an imposition." He opens his Bible and carefully removes the document Rocky had given to Lori from between its pages. He pushes it gently across the desktop to Tanaka. "I was wondering if you could translate this for me..."

Tanaka adjusts his glasses and peers intently at the document for several moments. Then he picks it up and holds it up to the light for a better look. "Well, most of these characters are semi-legible at best and many are totally blurred. Some naval references. I'm guessing it could be from a workbook of some sort. Doesn't look like a routine entry, it's noting some unclear problems."

"Okay...well...hmmm. Do you think you can tell me anything about its age or origination? Looks like it's about a hundred years old to me."

Tanaka sits back in his chair and puts the paper on the desk in front of them "Well, if you want to be precise I can have some of my friends over at document research and restoration have a look at it. But I can tell you, it's a high-quality linen reserved for important documents," he answered, rubbing the paper between a finger and thumb.

Jared leaned forward and pointed at a particular part of the document. "Yeah, that'd be great to get it thoroughly examined. What about this part right here, Dr. Tanaka? I was told this may be some kind of fuel planning, maybe. What do you think?"

Tanaka takes a second look at the document and he answers without looking up. "Well, there is a reference to fuel, but I'd say the numbers are geographical coordinates, then there's a bit of flowery talk about struggle and heaven." He looks up from the paper. "Japanese can be frustratingly imprecise, you know. Where did you get this, anyway?"

"Coordinates? Really? Can you write them down for me?" Jared feels a stir of excitement with the mention of something that he can readily understand.

Tanaka takes out a pad and inscribes what he can decipher. He gives the translation to Jared, who places it inside the Bible.

"I really appreciate this, Dr. Tanaka, I really do, please let me know the moment the document exam guys are finished," he says sincerely. "I owe you a flight to any of the islands. Just let me know. Whenever, wherever." He starts to get up and make his escape.

Tanaka holds up his hand in a stop gesture, then pulls a book-thick manuscript from a desk drawer.

"Before you go, I must share with you my latest *haiku* addition, a special sentiment. I did the calligraphy and illustrations as well." Tanaka opens the volume and points out several of the poems and illustrations. His voice softens and he is soon cooing over his work, which is professional quality, even to an untrained eye. Jared reluctantly sits back down and pretends to look interested.

"This one is a favorite," Tanaka says, enthusiasm growing in his tone. "Now, believe it or not, it came to me one morning when I awoke in, how should I say it, an aroused state. Must've been a very special dream." He smiles and chuckles with a hint of embarrassment. "Well, of course, at my age that's worth commemorating, so I grabbed the notepad I keep near the bedstead and..."

Jared rolls his eyes and then sneaks a peek at his watch. He groans silently to himself.

Nothing is free, even if it doesn't cost cash. Lesson learned – never let a professor get between you and the door...

* * * * * *

The car has no markings, but it's obvious at a glance it's an unmarked police vehicle — a full size sedan with high performance tires, a couple of extra antennae sprouting from the roof and no visible upgrades or options. The windows are darkened, but the driver's side is down and an arm the size of a ham-hock rests on the window frame.

Yep, might as well write HPD all over it in big letters.

Jared wheels the Corvette into a guest parking spot and shuts down. Before he can get out, he sees Lori emerge from her apartment, lock it up and head down the walk. Reaching the HPD car, she leans toward the passenger side window and says something to an occupant, then points to Jared and the Corvette. The sedan starts up as Lori proceeds across the parking area, waving at Jared as she approaches.

"Who are your friends?" Jared says, nodding towards the unmarked car. "Oh, just HPD doing its job. Mostly keeping the gawkers and press off my doorstep. But now they got the private security at the gate, so that's not a problem anymore and not many people know I live here anyway. They all think I'm at the Tantalus Mountain home. It's only for a few more days, I'm guessing."

Jared opens the door for her, a dated bit of decorum drilled into him by his mother long ago. "Is being out in public a problem? I know you are sick of being cooped up, but aren't you afraid of getting hounded?"

"Not as long as I'm dressed like this," she indicates the big floppy sunhat and large sunglasses. "And, of course, stay away from the mall and expensive restaurants." Thank God they haven't figured out where *you* live yet."

Jared exits the parking lot, with the unmarked car following a half-block in trail. "Yeah, that's why we should visit here, or my place only after dark." He shakes his head in disgust. "I feel like I'm on the run from the law or have done something despicable. I can't imagine how bad it is for you. Anyway, where we going? I know you said you wanted to get out of the house."

Lori leans back against the headrest. "Oh, Jared, I don't know. The moon would be nice, I don't think anyone knows me there. For now just drive."

In silence they head east, or "Koko Head," as the locals would say, along the Kalanianole Highway, green mountains to the left, blue ocean to the right. Under usual circumstances, they would have been captured by the beauty of it all, but not today.

Jared finally breaks into Lori's private reverie. "Anything from Rocky? Has he, uhh, come forth with anything helpful?"

"No, and I don't want to talk about him. I'm in the 'mad at him' stage. You know that mindset widows sometime get when a husband dies and leaves them alone and lonely? Well, that's where I am at the moment. I don't know who needs a shrink more, me or him." This brings a faint fleeting smile to her face.

"O--kay," Jared replies, not quite sure how to respond. He decides to change the subject. "I did speak to that friend of mine I told you about, you know, the HPD guy." Jared is careful not to reveal a name. "Gave me what the cops know about Fujitta. He's a bad actor, for sure, up to his ass in all kinds of Japanese mafia stuff. Not clear at all why he would come visit Rocky, though, he--"

"Let's talk about something else, okay? I can't deal with this shit anymore."

Jared looks over at her, but her face is lost in the sunglasses and hat. *Boy, she's in a mood! Not that it isn't completely understandable, just never saw this side of her before. Usually they get like this 'cause of something I've done. Can't be the door – can it? I had that repaired already, so...?*

Jared runs through a mental checklist of other grievances he's likely guilty of. This absorbs him for ten minutes or more, but there are too many choices to know for which to apologize. *I was really getting to like her, too. Why don't they come with an operating manual so trouble-shooting isn't such a chore! Or at least a decent warranty?*

Lori gives a big sigh and looks at him.

Oh boy, here it comes! I can never think fast enough to figure out an escape plan.

"How about tell me a story."

"A what?" Jared says, glancing at her, not sure he heard right.

"A story, something that has nothing to do with the here and now. Maybe, how'd you get this thing," she said, patting the Corvette dashboard.

Jared, relieved he is not about to be castigated or castrated for some real or imagined sins, quickly warms to the task.

"Well, a friend of mine convinced me to go to Alaska with him and crew on a crab boat. Imagine, a West Texas wrangler boy, doing blue water fishin'!" Jared marvels, shaking his head in disbelief.

"I guess you could say you were a fish out of water, but that'd be mixing metaphors, yeah?" Lori manages a smile.

"It was an incredible experience. When we got on the crabs, that's Alaskan King Crabs, the one's about three feet across, we hauled the traps up and down as fast as we could, day or night, rest and sleep be damned. I went thirty hours without sitting down or eating anything because we were getting paid on shares — the more we hauled out, the more we got. I made $26,000 in one day!"

"In *one* day?" Lori asks, doubt in her voice.

"Yup, and that with only an eighth of a share. The captain, he's sitting up there driving the boat, and he's making a fifty percent share! So, me and my buddy, we figure we got this thing scoped out, so when the season's over and we cash out and buy our own boat. Get it crewed up when the next season starts, and off we go. Would you believe it, that was the year the crabs migrated, I don't know where, but we didn't catch squat the whole freakin' summer! Ended up losing the boat and a lot more, only thing I got to show for it is the Corvette. It was a great experience, though, wouldn't change it for nothing."

"I'm glad you kept it. It fits you."

"You want some shave ice? I'm ready for one," Jared says, pointing to an ocean-side park just ahead with a shave ice truck parked in it. He pulls over into the parking area and backs carefully into a spot, close by the guardrail, with the beach and ocean just beyond. The unmarked car pulls into the common area and shuts down as well, as Jared and Lori extricate themselves from the low-slung car body.

"Carwash, Mister?" A young, local-looking teenager holding a carwash sign accosts them on the way to the shave ice truck. "It's for Punahou High School student government. Only three dollars."

They stop. "Punahou, huh?" Jared says, impressed. "You must be a real smart guy to get in there."

"And rich," Lori adds *soto voce*.

"What's your name, kid?" Jared asks, looking through his billfold.

"Barry. Barry Obama."

"Okay, Barry, tell you what. The car doesn't need washing, but here's three dollars for you. Good luck on your fundraiser. What are you going to do with the money?"

"We're going to Washington DC, going to the Capital, the White House, get to meet senators and everything." His face beams excitement.

"So what are you planning to be when you grow up?" Lori asks, offering an encouraging smile.

"I'm going to be President," Barry says, looking at each in turn, "of the United States."

"Well, good luck on that one," Jared says, shaking his head. "If it happens I want my three dollars back. With interest!"

They all laugh. Barry goes to intercept the next potential donor and Lori and Jared stand in line for the shave ice.

"Nice kid, but he's going to have to change that name if he expects to get anywhere in politics," Jared says. "What flavors for you?"

"Strawberry and banana."

Jared places their order, and they watch as the machine slowly scrapes the numerous thin layers of ice, the basis for this Hawaiian favorite. A few splashes of liquid flavor and their patience is rewarded. Jared notices a couple of young women in skintight bikinis coming up from the ocean. "Water must be cold today," he says with a grin.

Lori punches him on the arm.

"Jared! Don't be a pig!"

"Oink, Oink" Lori punches him again as he playfully tries to defend himself. They both laugh.

Icy treats in hand, they stroll back towards the car. Suddenly Jared stiffens, then drops his shave ice. The Beast is raging, charging out of the cage. Jared follows, like a fighter fired from a carrier catapult. Their target is the scraggly surfer dude sitting on the back deck of the Corvette, smoking a reefer and serenely contemplating the quality of the waves, his surfboard leaning against the side of the car.

Jared slams a hammer fist into the surfer dude's back, right between the shoulder blades. The impact resonates like a baseball bat hitting a hanging side of beef. The beach bum flies over the guardrail and lands face-first in the hot beach sand. The wind is knocked completely out of him and he can do little more than gasp and squirm.

"You want to sit on something, you little son-of-a-bitch? Here's something for you to sit on!" Jared takes the surfboard high over his head and smashes it down on the guardrail, splintering the board into fiberglass shards. Everyone on the beach stares, aghast, as Jared leaps over the rail.

Lori runs to catch him. "Jared! No! No! Stop!"

Jared, his face crimson red, reaches the punk and grabs him by the hair.

"Maybe you'd like to eat some lunch while you think about respecting other people's property," he screams, and rams the terrified guy's head into the sand. With a vice grip on the back of his neck, Jared shoves him forward, digging a bloody furrow with his face.

Lori pulls at Jared, but she is a child straining against an angry bull.

Finally, the two cops from the unmarked car plunge into the fray and wrestle Jared away from his whimpering victim.

"Get his keys and follow us to the substation until he cools off," one of them yells to Lori. "Quick, if the uniforms get here he's going to the county jail!"

Lori throws a hundred dollar bill that she keeps for emergencies at the near-dead surfer and jumps in the Vette. She follows the unmarked car to the substation, sobbing all the way.

Chapter 19

T he glass specialist guides the replacement countertop into place, then lets it drop the last inch with a thunk. "Okay," he says, looking up, "That's the last one."

"Great, and thanks again for coming and getting the repairs done so quick," Jared says.

"No problem, glad to," the repairman says, gathering up his equipment. "Say, did they find the guy yet, the one who busted up the place?"

"No, but he better hope the cops find him before I do." Jared says flatly. The repairman glances at Jared's face. There is no trace of a jesting smile.

Jared holds the door open for the repairman, shaking his hand and adding a couple more "thanks" as the guy exits. Then he returns to his task, working a plotter on an aviation chart. He shakes his head and sighs, just as Smitty comes in the door.

"Hello, Smitty," Jared says, looking up. "Come here a sec, would ya? Got a question for you."

Smitty lumbers over, looking around. He is sweating visibly, as usual. "Hey, they did a nice job with the glass. Get the lettering up and its good as new."

Jared tosses the plotter down on the chart. "How 'bout plotting these coordinates and see what you get." He reads off the translated numbers given to him by Tanaka: "Twenty-two, fifteen point five, north; One-fifty-nine, thirty-nine point zero, west."

"All right...got it," Smitty said, marking the intersecting lines. "Looks like about two miles off the Kauai north shore," he says, looking over at Jared curiously. "What is it, a new fishing hole?"

"Maybe. Or maybe I'm missing something." Jared stares at the chart for several moments. "We still got that charter to Princeville tomorrow afternoon?"

"Yeah, but I told..."

"Let me have it, would ya? I'll do it for free, just a little help towards the office insurance deductable." Jared flashes a grin at Smitty, melting any opposition.

"Well, since you put it like that..."

"Thanks, and I'll need a couple of days off, too..."

* * * * * *

Lori sprawls near him, but far enough away so they can cool the post-coital glow. It's the ultimate in mental and physical relaxation, therapeutic in fact. At least that's the way Lori sees it. Especially now.

He turns to her and props himself on an elbow. Her eyes open momentarily as he gently brushes her raven black hair from her rosy cheeks. She gives a contented sigh. Total relaxation.

"That was nice," she says with a smile.

"That was great, baby, outstanding. As always." He leans close and gives her a gentle kiss on the cheek. "Thanks for calling me"

He rolls away and takes an unfocussed look at the ceiling. "I have to say I was kinda shocked to hear from you, what with, well, what's going on with your father." He looks over at her. "I haven't asked a single thing about that have I? For the record. I mean, it's a little awkward, me working for the TV station."

Lori opens her eyes, but for a moment doesn't say anything. "Oh Mike, forget about that. I trust you or I wouldn't have invited you over."

"Anytime, Baby, anytime." He glances at his watch. "Well, all good things have to come to an end. I've got pick up the boys for soccer practice, and then get down to the station for the evening broadcast. If I can work with a big grin on my face." He shines a wicked smile at her. "I'm just going to jump in the shower, be right back. Don't move."

Mike Flocca eases out of bed and in a moment is testing the water temperature in the shower. Lori still relaxes, but her thoughts return to the present. Like most of her boyfriends, Mike has three important characteristics: He is at least ten years older than she; he is *Haole*, the mildly racist term for Caucasian; and he is safely married.

Jared is an exception, one that she is ready to give her heart to. But not until she finds out who he really is.

This crazy behavior, like with the surfer punk yesterday. What kind of insanity was that? The nightmares? And why can't he open up to me, let me be close to him? He's just not trying—and I'm worth working for.

Her way to punish him was to invite Mike over to get reacquainted. Not that Jared would know about it, she'd certainly never tell. And it wasn't for better sex—Jared was, somewhat improbably, incredibly thoughtful and giving in bed, the best ever. No complaints there!

She hears the shower cease.

No, illicit sex was her therapy—a refuge she took when things were going badly in her life. She gives a sigh only she hears.

Boy, oh boy, things are sure not going well in my life right now!

* * * * * *

Ten minutes after take-off from Honolulu International, Jared levels the Twin Beech at the assigned altitude and clicks on the autopilot.

"How's everyone doing back there?" he asks over the intercom, glancing over his shoulder at the half-dozen people behind him.

"Great!" they answer in unison, dazzled by the breathtaking mountain and beach scenery passing by them, only a few thousand feet below. They babble happily as they point out scenic sights along the coast of Oahu, camera shutters clicking with the intensity of horny cicadas on a summer's evening.

Jared says a small, silent prayer for smooth air and an uneventful trip. He isn't worried about the safety of the aircraft, but he doesn't want to have to put up with problems from the "PIB's," shoptalk for the People In Back. Jared doesn't fly many passenger flights, preferring cargo runs and aircraft ferries, because passengers are frequently too much of a pain in the ass. As everyone at Island Air knows, Jared has a low threshold for idiots, even if they are paying customers.

He remembers ruefully the time when a mai-tai soaked mainlander passed out on a flight back from the Big Island. Jared didn't care about that, he'd been there himself often enough. But when the asshole peed his pants—and the airplane seat, etc., in the process—Jared got a little upset and goose-stepped him across the parking ramp when they landed, then launched him head-first into the drainage canal.

The owner of Island Air happened to be watching from his office and came bursting out the door like a pit bull guarding a doublewide. The only thing that saved Jared was the applause of the other passengers, including, Jared recalls with a smirk, the drunk's wife.

Fortunately, the sunny extrovert is at the controls today. *Just don't pee on my plane!*

The twenty-minute flight goes quickly, and the green mountains of Kauai soon emerge from the horizon. "Okay, folks, I've got a special treat for you," Jared says as he begins his descent. "Since we are a bit ahead of schedule I'm going to give you a little sightseeing tour of the Na Pali coast before landing at Princeville"

Jared goes on to extol the fabulous beach and mountain scenery passing off to the side of the plane. He levels off about a thousand feet above the water, and consults his annotated chart.

Coming up pretty quick now. He banks the airplane into a gentle turn that allows him to view the scene below him better. Nothing...just deep blue water sprinkled with whitecaps. Not a boat or a buoy or reef or a tiny island or... anything.

Jared reverses course for another pass to see if there is anything remarkable in sight on the rugged coast two miles distant. The scene is dramatic, sheer green cliffs dropping into the sea, backed up by verdant valleys and fronted by gleaming white beaches.

A beautiful vista, but nothing to provide any clues as to the significance of the coordinates. If that's even what they are...

"Well, that's about all we've got time for today," Jared says over the intercom, trying to mask the disappointment creeping into his words.

Chapter 20

The big twin pulls onto the ramp and coasts to a stop. The ramp attendant chocks the aircraft's nose wheel, then signals for engine shutdown. Jared chops the throttles back to the idle/cutoff detent, and the engines whine down as the attendant opens the air-stair door. Holding their hats and sunglasses against the stiffly blowing trade winds, the passengers file out, cheerfully assisted by the attendant.

Jared appears in the door after the passengers disembark and shares a grin with the ramp attendant, an island born teenager.

"Hey, Captain Scott, welcome back. How long are you in Princeville today?"

Jared passes down suitcases from the interior of the airplane. "We're scheduled out at four," Jared says. "Top off both tanks, I want to leave sooner if the passengers are all here."

"You got it, sir, truck's already on the way."

Jared makes his way into the office, which also serves as the terminal for private aircraft operations. The décor is island themed, but the artwork adorning the walls hardly competes with the real mountains and beaches seen from any window. The rattan chairs and sofas are inviting, but Jared passes them by. Instead, he steps into the flight planning alcove, picks up the phone and closes the clearance for the flight just completed. He updates the weather and files the return trip authorization on request.

With the administrative details completed, Jared checks the time and mentally relaxes. A couple of employees bustle about, and a taxi driver is rounding up luggage for the tourists that just arrived, Jared, trying but failing to look serious, eases up to the dispatch counter. A middle-aged lady sits behind a desk, a big local gal in a kaleidoscope muumuu the size of a circus tent.

"Hey, Lulu! How ya doing?"

Lulu looks up from her paperwork and her eyes and grin get big when she recognizes Jared. "Mo betta, now you come see me! You bring me orchids again?"

Jared lapses into passable pidgin. "Aww, not this trip. Besides, I come all time with flowers, your old man get mad! Chase me around with stick, yeah?"

Lulu laughs so loud her body shakes like a California earthquake. "No problem! I give Felix da stink-eye, he sit down, be quiet." She laughs again, even louder than the first time.

Jared leans on the counter, easily visualizing Felix obeying Lulu's orders. "You know, somehow I believe it!" He turns and looks around the waiting area. "Say, are the passengers for my return flight here yet?"

"Naw, no see yet. Hey, you come sit, talk to Lulu." She drags a chair over from another desk.

Ordinarily Jared would have been tempted to just kill time reading a newspaper, but he spotted something that piqued his interest. Almost lost in the muumuu's riot of color is a campaign button proclaiming, "ROCKY," and in smaller letters, "For Governor."

Jared ambles around the counter and settles into the offered chair.

"You want Coke, yeah?" Lulu slides a small ice chest from beneath the desk and fishes out a frosty Coke in a traditional glass bottle. She expertly pops the bottle cap and makes a ringer tossing it across the room into the trashcan.

Jared accepts his favorite drink and takes a long swig. "Where do you get these things? Nobody in the islands has Coke in bottles anymore, especially the small ones."

"Good connections," Lulu says, nodding her head in a knowing way.

Jared props his feet on a step stool and relaxes. "Must be with Rocky Konishi's campaign, I see you are still wearing the button."

The smile vanishes from Lulu's face. "Yes, for da support. Mr. Rocky is great man, not killer. I know him all my life."

"You're somehow related, right?

"No, no, not Mr. Rocky, but wife Keiko is first cousin. Everybody Kauai cousin!" This brings forth another laughter earthquake, complete with aftershocks.

"Mr. Rocky lucky, lucky man, you know. Grow up in Hiroshima, then *boom*, everybody gone to da sky." Her hands make a passable rendition of an ascending mushroom cloud. "But him and other kids in forest, collect wood—not go up in cloud that day."

Jared nods in agreement. "You're right, he's had incredible luck. Well, up to recently, I guess."

Lulu continues, a natural talk-story gal in the Hawaiian style. "All family gone, parents die Hiroshima, big brother killed in war. Somehow Keiko's parents find out and sponsor him come here. Live w' dem high up mountain." Lulu makes a gesture towards the lush green mountains visible through the windows. "His name Saburo then, but family all call him Rocky, I think 'cuz his head so hard." More laughs.

"I just kidding, you know! Mr. Rocky got more brains than Lulu got pounds! That make him smartest man in islands." This revelation provokes a gale of laughter and enough jiggles to move needles on seismographs throughout the Pacific. Jared wonders how much more punishment her already creaking chair can handle.

"Then, wonerful t'ing—Rocky fall in love with farmer daughter—that be Keiko, but no joke dis time! Move to Honolulu." She says the latter dismissively. "I say 'Keiko, you *lolo*, girl—great big city eat you country kids up!' But Rocky go college, start construction business, make money—all work out. Smart man!"

Jared drains his drink and eyeballs the lobby—still no sign of the passengers. He turns back to her and nods, which is all the encouragement Lulu needs.

"But Rocky all time want more. He ambybit...no, how you say it?"

"Ambitious?" Jared offers.

"That it! First off, city council. Then Congressman, three times! Look! Got one picture here!" She opens a desk drawer and withdraws some yellowing campaign literature. Featured is a noticeably younger Rocky Konishi, beaming a smile from behind his desk in his Congressional office in Washington D.C.

"Sure looks the part," Jared observes.

Lulu's expression darkens. "But then Keiko pass away. Very sad! Rocky give up politics for few years, no can smile for pictures, I think. But last year decide to run for Governor—and win! Big news, first Japanese-American governor in Hawaii, maybe whole USA! We very happy, you know, big heart!" She pats her chest firmly, sending forth visible shockwaves in all directions. "But now, what to happen? Can be governor in jail, same time?" she adds hopefully.

"Jeez, Lulu, I don't know—who does? He's offered to resign, that's what the TV says, anyway. But for some reason it's on hold until they can get some legal research done." Jared throws up his hands in exasperation. "All I'm sure of is it's gonna be a month of Sundays before they figure it all out, and a lot of lawyers are going to be very, very rich."

Jared glances at the sound of a small commotion at the front door. "Great talking to you, Lulu. Got to get to work, looks like the four o'clock passengers arrived."

"Here's the manifest," Lulu replies, sliding a clipboard across the counter.

Jared glances at the manifest and does some quick math. He ambles over to a pile of luggage, presided over by a short gal with sassy red hair. Jared sizes her up: cute but not quite beautiful, late twenties, lots of freckles. Somehow she has managed to zip the short-shorts that threaten blood circulation below the waist, offset by a loose fitting purple T-shirt with a large Japanese character on it. A pair of high-class flip-flops adorn her feet. Despite the casual appearance, she has a compact out and is touching up her makeup as Jared approaches.

"Howdy, ma'am. I'm Captain Scott, and I believe you are scheduled for the four o'clock charter with me to Honolulu."

She ceases with the makeup, apparently satisfied with the results for the moment. Thus composed, she reaches out and shakes Jared's hand, offering up a big smile. "I'm your gal, and those are my parents over there." She points to a middle-aged couple in the lounge chairs nearby. "I'm Betty." She says, holding on to Jared's hand far longer than appropriate.

"Great," Jared says, retrieving his hand. "I'm going to check the weather and then we'll load up." He gestures towards the luggage at hand. "This all the bags?" He says.

"Well, this is my stuff. My parent's stuff is over there." Betty points to several suitcases near where her parents sit.

Jared can't keep the disbelief from creeping into his voice. "This here is just for you?" he says, looking at a half dozen suitcases and hat bags.

"Uhh, yes," Betty says, a bit defensively, shooting Jared a frown. "This is my wardrobe. I'm a performer. I've been at Charo's dinner theater over at Hanalei Bay for the last couple of weeks. It's not going to be a problem, is it?"

Jared, with a bit of a strain, picks up one of larger suitcases. "Looks like I'm going to have to weigh everything..."

He walks over to the counter, picks up a portable scale and brings it back. "Okay, here you go," he says, placing it on the floor in front of Betty.

Betty glares at the scale, then at Jared. "You're kidding, right? You expect me to jump on the scales right here in front of God and everybody? Betty sweeps her arm around to indicate any breathing organisms. "And announce how much I weigh? Right!"

Jared scratches at his chin and smiles bemusedly. "Well, Ma'am, it's not my rule, it's actually a law... a law of physics. Darned ol' airplane won't fly if it's too heavy. Just can't reason with it."

Betty's face reddens to match her hair. "That's ridiculous! You can put twice this much in a limo."

Jared refrains from stating the obvious: *Lady, this ain't no limo.* Instead, he mulls a list of options. He ceases with the chin scratching, then taps his head with a finger to let out an idea. "Tell you what, Betty, how 'bout you and your parents weigh yourselves and give me the combined weight? That way you can keep it in the family."

Betty's expression brightens. "Well, I guess that would work..."

"Great, and I'll need one of you to sit up front with me in the copilot seat to make sure we have the weight well distributed."

"Oh, I can do that!" says Betty. "I've never gotten to do that before."

"Excellent, let's get started then," says Jared, picking up a couple of the bags.

* * * * *

The aircraft roars down the runway, unsticks from the asphalt, and turns for the coast. In the cockpit, Jared is comfortable in the left seat. Like a kid at Christmas, Betty bounces around in the right seat. Even though she has to stretch to see over the instrument panel, she proudly wears the headset with a boom mike that Jared gave her. Her parents, in the passenger seats behind her, are treated to a big grin when she turns around to wave. Her mom snaps a picture as Betty makes steering motions as if flying the plane. They all have a good laugh.

Jared establishes a climb speed and power setting, then fiddles with secondary duties as Betty takes it all in. With everything satisfactory for the moment, Jared leans back, one hand casually on the yoke.

"So, uhh, Jared, you really know what all these thingamabobs do?" she says, giving a wave to the multitudes of controls, instruments and gauges.

Jared glances at her to make sure she's not yanking his chain. Not a hundred percent sure, he gives a safe answer "Well, yeah, the FAA kinda likes for us to know about 'em; it also keeps the passengers from getting too nervous."

Betty makes a happy face. "Whoa, far out, dude! Very cool!"

They cross the verdant shoreline and continue to climb, punching holes in a few puffies. Jared takes a moment to look down at the crashing surf, that division of land and water. "You know, I've made this trip a thousand times, but I never get tired of the view."

"I can see why, it's unbelievable." Betty says, catching the blue and green vista.

"Yep, best view of any office in the world." He pulls back on the power. "Okay, we are at fifty-five hundred, Oahu on the nose. Let me get George turned on..." Jared levels out, leans forward to click on the autopilot and takes his hands off the controls.

Betty eyes the yoke, which is moving by itself, then glances at Jared. "Aren't you supposed to have your hands on that steering wheel thingy? And who is George?"

Jared settles back, folding his arms. "George is the autopilot – all autopilots are named George for some reason. One of those quaint aviation customs, I guess. Don't worry, he flies better than I do. Never complains, either."

"Well! Good – I guess. I just don't trust machines." She shifts from side to side in her seat. "Or anything I don't understand, I suppose." She settles down facing Jared, and gives him the eyeball once-over. "So, I guess I better understand you a little bit better." She offers a flirtatious smile. "How long you been a pilot?"

"Since I was nineteen. Got started flying Army helicopters."

"The Army let you fly helicopters as a teenager?" Her face gushes disbelief. "What are they, nuts?!!"

Jared laughs as he looks over at her. "Not as nuts as me and the rest of us Warrant Officers! It's a wonder any of us are still alive."

Betty shakes her head. "I guess I'm old-fashioned – I like airline pilots to have lots of gray hair. But you got the white splash going," she says, nodding at Jared's temple. "Is that, like, uhh, a genetic thing?"

Jared responds nonchalantly. "Naw, a AK – 47 round bounced off my skull there. Grew out white ever since. I guess I could dye it, but why bother?"

"No, no, I didn't mean that – it looks fine, distinctive even." Betty pauses, looks him over again. "What's an AK...whatever?"

Jared abruptly flashes a hand at Betty in a stop mode. He fingers a button on the yoke with the other. "Island Air fifty-two-thirty-one looking for the traffic," he says to a far away and unseen air traffic controller. He peers through the windscreen, scanning the horizon.

Still looking out the windscreen Jared says, "It's a magic wand – reach out and touch someone with it and you change their lives forever." He chuckles at his private joke; Betty is blank-faced.

"Fifty-two-thirty-one has the traffic, no factor," Jared says, keying the radio button again. A dot of an airplane passes overhead by a comfortable margin.

"So what about you? You said you were performing at Charo's – is that a long-term gig for you?"

"Not really, just a couple of weeks. Mostly I work on the mainland, just play some local venues to give me a reason to come back and visit my parents and friends for a while." She gestures to her parents, who now doze slack-jawed in the back. "I grew up on Oahu, Aiea High School – go Dolphins! Woo hoo!" She waves her arms and pumps her fist like a cheerleader. Jared grimaces as the headset rattles his eardrums with the shout.

"Could have fooled me – I don't hear a trace of pidgin." Jared notes.

Betty gives a snort. "Not in my house! I'd be down on my hands and knees scrubbing floors if I brought any of that home! Nothing against those that talk local, of course," she adds, involuntarily glancing over her shoulder.

"So, how long have you been an entertainer? And what kind?"

"Oh, just about forever, professionally since I graduated high school. Mostly as a singer – I'm too uncoordinated to dance! I look like a drunk camel trying to wear high heels." She hoots and Jared chuckles at the image.

"What kind of singing? Like rock, or..."

"It's kind of my own style – difficult to explain – some rock, some blues, even some classic fifties stuff. Mostly I write my own, though." She brightens. "Hey you want to come see me? I'm going to be in town for a few more weeks."

"Well sure, why not?" Jared says, flashing a grin. "Are you at one of the hotels, or..."

"Actually, I'm at the Hula Hut, out by the airport."

Jared snaps her a look, vertical creases dividing his forehead. "The Hula Hut? Isn't that a... strip club?"

There's a bit of weariness in her voice. "Yes, but on Monday nights it's kind of a comedy club, some singing, dancing, pretty eclectic. Lots of fun, everybody has a good time. Mostly locals, tourists don't get that far from Waikiki. Here, I got some passes, bring some friends." Betty pulls some tickets out of her purse and hands them to Jared, who glances at them and stuffs them in his shirt pocket.

"Well thanks, but I don't know if I'll be able to get anyone else to come if there's no strippers – I don't run in a very high-class crowd!" he says, with a bit of a smirk.

"Oh, don't worry," Betty says with a smirk of her own. "If you want raunchy I can do raunchy!"

Chapter 21

Jared enters the living room of his apartment and tosses his sweaty uniform hat on the first piece of furniture in range. Next on the checklist is to crank open the jalousie windows to get some air circulation. Like most residents in Hawaii, he doesn't have air conditioning, and without the cooling effect of the tradewinds, it is downright hot inside.

He stops by the kitchen and pokes around in the fridge. His reward is a half-full jar of dill pickles. He pulls out the pickles and trashes them, then tilts the jar and takes a big swig of pickle juice. This produces a pleasant grimace, sort of like downing a shot glass of whiskey, but without the furnace effect. A burp. More rummaging. Half a bag of beef jerky comes out of a drawer—perfect! A familiar routine, perhaps a bit lonely, but comfortable.

Ready to feast, Jared swings by the TV and stabs the on button. The distinctive music of The Twilight Zone theme, twangs from the TV as Jared flops on the sofa. Rod Serling emerges from the electronic haze and intones about yet another character flaw about to be discerned in some poor sap's soul. Seems most of the shows are variations of a genie granting wishes to a greedy man—Jared just knows it isn't going to turn out well. He is about to change the channel when he notices the blinking light on the answering machine. He pushes "play" and the device beeps to life.

"You have one new message," a man's artificial voice says. "First message..."

"Jared, hi, it's Lori. Just wanted to check to see what's going on. I hope you found out something. Anyway, I talked to the scheduler at your office and she said you will be off tomorrow. Can you meet me at the Pali Lookout, say about noon? I really don't want to say too much over the phone, so I'll see you tomorrow there unless you call and tell me different."

Jared pushes the button to reset the machine and turns his attention back to the TV and the pickle juice. He flips through a few channels with the remote, pausing at the weather report. "Let's see," Jared says, anticipating the forecast. "Temperatures in the high eighties, tradewinds at ten to fifteen, scattered clouds with occasional light showers." How hard could it be to become a weather forecaster in Hawaii?

Jared's reverie is interrupted by the phone ringing. He picks up and says, "Hey, Lori, is that you?"

"No, Jared. Raymond Tanaka here, just wanted to get back to you on the paper you brought by for analysis a couple of days ago. Hope I didn't catch you at a bad time..."

"Well, Professor, your timing is excellent, I just walked in." Jared picks up a pen and writing pad by the answering machine and settles back on the sofa, cradling the phone to his ear with a shoulder. "So, did you have any luck?"

"I did, I did indeed. Jared, understand this is somewhat piecemeal, but my guess is the paper is maybe a page from a ship's logbook because it describes sea conditions and there's a sentence about drifting and fuel. Then there's the part about currents and a bit of flowery talk about struggle and heaven."

Jared feels his pulse quicken. He scribbles notes as they talk. "Was there anything like a date, or was the name of the ship mentioned?"

"No such luck. If it was ever there, it's been obliterated. But over at the lab they were able to date the paper. It's a type and composition common in Japan and China about fifty years ago, which pretty much matches the other dating techniques I used. The stains and weathering make it look a lot older than it really is."

Jared jumps to his feet. "Dr. Tanaka, outstanding work! This really helps and I most certainly appreciate it. For sure I owe you one!"

"Glad to help out, neighbor, it was actually quite interesting. In fact I got inspired enough to write another haiku, this about man against the sea—a metaphor, of course. I'd be pleased to recite it for you when you come to pick up the document."

Jared's mood swings instantly. "Right... I'll drop by tomorrow and pick it up since I'm out that way anyway. See you then..."

* * * * *

Jared and Smitty, along with Craig, another flight instructor from Island Aviation, walk into the dim nightclub. The stage is well illuminated, everything else is in deep twilight. Betty and a local band are in full swing. A young crowd, mostly casually dressed locals, fills the room. Jared checks out the surroundings as his eyes adjust to the light — definitely strip club décor, well-worn at that.

Shoehorned into a sparkling silver gown cut to the navel, Betty belts out a spirited rendition of "New York, New York." She finishes up to good applause as Jared and his friends take seats at a table near the stage. Betty flutters a girly wave and a big air kiss to them. Jared waves back as a very well built blond in a short skirt and a tight top arrives and places napkins for each of them. *Guess that answers the question as to what strippers do on their nights off,* Jared observes to himself.

"Okay gentlemen, what'll it be?" the waitress/stripper says sweetly. She leans over enough to make sure her cleavage is appreciated.

"A couple of pitchers of Oly to start," says Smitty, eyeballing the waitress' attributes before she disappears with the drink orders.

Betty yells out a question. "All right! Everybody still doing okay?" The crowd responds with hoots and howls and some scattered applause.

"We're going to keep cranking it, taking requests all night," Betty continues. "Hey, anybody out there had any military experience?" A few guys raise their hands or respond with an "oo-rah!" Betty ignores them and waggles her finger at couple of young women at a back table. "Sorry girls, giving blow jobs to sailors doesn't count!"

Jared and his friends, along with the rest of the audience, laugh, groan or applaud. Betty turns to the band. "Hit it, boys!"

Betty and the band explode into a vigorous rendition of "The Boogie-Woogie Bugle Boy of Company B." Jared is amazed at the volume and range this little gal can produce — and her shameless vamping with the audience between songs.

An hour passes and several more pitchers of beer hit the table, with no let up on the high-intensity show from Betty and the band. They seem to be inexhaustible, especially Betty.

"Hey! You in the red shirt!" Betty barks, shining a flashlight at a couple seated off to one side. "Get your hand off her ass and pay some freaking attention!" The chagrined man holds up his hands in mock surrender while his girlfriend covers her face.

The beer pitchers are empty again at Jared's table. The band plays on as Betty croons, "I'm a Woman." Jared squirms from the pressure of too much beer. He leans over towards Smitty and Greg. "I've got to make a piss call. Be right back." He gets up and heads to the bathroom. There's no waiting and Jared sighs when he stands at the urinal as the beer leaves him.

Bang! The door flies open and slams against the wall. Betty and the members of her band rush in.

"All right Jared!" Betty yells. "Zip it!"

Led by Betty, the band emerges from the bathroom, carrying Jared on their shoulders like pallbearers carrying a casket. To the laughs and applause of the audience the band marches over to Jared's table and deposits him into his chair like he is a misbehaving two year old. The band members slap high fives and return to the stage, enjoying a standing ovation and delirious applause. Jared grins and shrugs. Smitty slaps him on the back, howling with laughter.

The band and Betty pick up where they left off. *"I am woman...!"*

Chapter 22

Jared pulls the Corvette into the parking area of the Pali Lookout, a popular sightseeing spot in the mountains overlooking the breathtaking vista of the Windward coast. Busloads of tourists, all armed with cameras, trudge enthusiastically to and from the lookout, leaning against the whipping wind. Jared searches for Lori as he walks towards the overlook. Unlike most visitors, he is dressed in running gear and a baseball cap. He keeps a tight grip on the cap – all headgear at the lookout is in constant danger of getting airborne, next stop the coastline miles below.

Jared spots Lori as she looks out over the Windward Coast. She is flanked by two very large HPD officers in aloha attire who size Jared up, wearing the expressions cops reserve for someone they doubt they can trust. No doubt, their colleagues have briefed them about Jared's proclivity for uncivil behavior.

Though still smarting from getting interrupted while giving the respect-for-property lesson to the surfer dude scumbag a few days ago, Jared makes the effort to be as pleasant as possible.

"Well, hello beautiful," Jared says to Lori as he approaches, having to shout over the wind noise. "Aren't you afraid of blowing away?"

Lori laughs, holding down her sun hat with both hands. "Hah! Not likely, as fat as I'm getting sitting around the house all day."

Jared takes Lori by the arm to walk her away from the overlook. The police officers follow about a dozen feet behind, discretely out of hearing distance of the conversation. The group pauses in a sheltered area away from the tourist throngs.

Lori glances around the area. "HPD has been keeping me informed about Trazer – still no sign of him. They think he's left the islands, maybe on his way back to Vietnam by now. But I get to keep these two Clydesdales a couple of days more, just in case." She waves a friendly gesture towards the two cops standing nearby. They smile and nod in response.

"Well... I hope I find him first. He needs to learn some manners," Jared says.

Lori says, "I guess I never thought about blowback from the traffickers – it's pretty scary..." She glances around involuntarily.

Jared gives her a reassuring hug. "Don't worry about Trazer – he's living on borrowed time. Anyway, I have some news on Rocky's document. Seems like it could be a page from a ship's log, probably from about fifty years ago."

"Really? What kind of ship? Where was it going?"

Jared shrugs. "Don't know – some comments about fuel and sea conditions, and maybe some problems the crew was having. But we do have some coordinates - out in the ocean off the coast of Kauai. That's good news, and also bad news. At least we have some place to look, but for what is just a guessing game. I made an over-flight to check out the location. It's a really big ocean out there. Can't just stick your head into the water to find things. Even with a good depth finder and the right boat it could take weeks, maybe months to survey the area. It's like looking through a soda straw for an airplane in flight." He pauses. "I really don't know what we can do with this information, Lori."

"What do you need to proceed?"

Jared makes a dismissive gesture with a hand. "Well, in a perfect world, what I'd really like to have is one of the Navy P-3 sub-chaser airplanes fly a search pattern in the area of the coordinates. They've got the equipment to find things under the surface — it's their mission, finding Russian submarines. Unfortunately, I've used up about all favors owed me." He looks at Lori, his expression grim. "Lori, it may be time to turn this over to someone with better resources."

Lori looks up at Jared, a stare of determination in her eyes. "You want a Navy airplane? No problem. I'll call General Hafferty tomorrow and arrange it."

Jared doesn't know quite how to respond. "You'll call... who?"

"General Hafferty. He's in charge of the Hawaii National Guard. If we need anything from the military, we just call him up. He's happy to provide."

Jared is still not convinced. "Uhh, who is 'we'?"

"Usually my father, but he'll take calls from me, too. This goes back to when Rocky was a congressman on the House Armed Forces subcommittee for quite a few years."

Jared looks at Lori with a new respect. "Damn, girl! You're playing in another league. Guess I'm still just a Texas hillbilly." Jared hugs her and gives her a quick kiss as the cops pretend to not notice.

* * * * * *

Trazer still remembers the stink of his breath, an oral exhaust of decay and cheap whiskey. That and the bleary, bloodshot eyes inches away from his face.

"Come on now, boy! Say it!"

Trazer stands before him, head down but quietly defiant.

At six foot four and built like a barrel of cement, the man is three times the size of the boy. The man leans over, hands on knees so that he can get in Trazer's face even more.

"Go on now, say it. 'Sir,' It's a simple little ol' word. Even a retard like you can remember it."

Trazer looks up at him. "You ain't my Daddy."

A bear-paw sized hand smashes into the side of Trazer's head, knocking him tumbling.

"Well, you're right about that, I wouldn't make nothing as sorry as you, you little shit. But long as you living under my roof and I'm screwing your Mama, you gonna say 'Sir.' And a lot more. Or I'm going to take you down to the cellar." He grabs Trazer by the throat and lifts him into the air. Trazer's feet flail, and his hands vainly try to pull the man's iron arms away from the crushing clinch. "You ain't going to like the cellar, boy, not one bit."

Then Trazer did something he was deeply ashamed of, something he swore he'd never do again. He cried in front of a woman.

"Mama, Mama, make him stop!" he begged in sobbing gasps. "He's killing me! Mama!"

Trazer's mother stood behind the kitchen counter. She reached into the overhead cabinet and pulled out a bottle of bourbon. She glanced over at Trazer, feet dancing in air, his face red, eyes bulging. She poured the whiskey into a water glass and added a few ice cubes, then sucked it down. Her eyes blinked rapidly for a moment, then she put the glass down with a clunk.

"I'm going to go out on the porch and watch the moon come up. Do what you gotta do to whip some sense into the boy. He don't listen much to me anymore."

The sound Trazer remembers is the screen door banging shut behind her as she...

"Awww!" Trazer grimaces as he puts out his cigarette on his forearm. Crude, but effective. It's his own little behavior modification program, used to bring him back to the present when the VCR in his mind went into auto playback. He surveys his scarred arm, now adorned with a new blister.

Going to have to have the dragon tattoo re-inked when I get back to 'Nam. Starting to look like a puking dog or something.

Trazer makes a visual sweep of the parking area. Across the lot, he spots Jared and Lori, plus a couple of plain clothes goons keeping them company. He slumps lower in the seat of the rental car and pulls the palm frond hat down to just above his eyes. He captures the scene in his mind as Lori and Jared exchange a good-bye kiss.

Well, how touching, a little puppy love PDA. That's going to make the payback so much sweeter.

There are two things that motivate Trazer: Money, useful for the drugs and whores it can buy, and retribution, or "payback." *Payback is revenge, plus interest,* as they used to say in the army. Like when he had his ma down on her knees begging for her life.

Should have killed the bitch right then and there, and castrated every drunken boyfriend she ever dragged home. That would have been a life worth living!

Instead, the Army drafted him out of the hell-hole that was his existence to that point. At first, he was thankful — the structure, the bright line rights and wrongs, and the disciplined harshness all appealed to him — at first. Gradually he came to resent dumbshit officers ordering him around, demanding to be called, "Sir." Especially that asshole platoon commander of his in Nam.

I saved the platoon, all of them, the ungrateful bastards, when I shot Lt. Rockledge. That fucking idiot was going to lead us into an obvious ambush, would have been a massacre! And he would have wanted me to "Yes Sir! No Sir! May I kiss your ass, Sir?" Right up to the last drop of my blood splashing into the dirt.

Loved the expression on his face when I pulled the trigger!

The ultimate payback to the Army was when Trazer switched sides — that was grand!

Trazer reflexively rubs the remnants of his mangled ear. He didn't kill Jared on the spot when he had the chance at his house in Saigon — another of his many regrets. That satisfaction would have to wait, or the State Department would have cancelled his passport for sure. But the time is coming. Soon.

Trazer surveils the area again. Jared climbs into a blue Corvette and gives a wave to Lori as he starts the engine. Trazer turns the rental car ignition key.

Wonder how many body parts I can shoot off before he pisses his pants and dies? And that bitch, the Governor's daughter! Running all over the place, sticking her tits in my business. Spent a million dollars getting everything set up for the plan, and she's got the President, the freakin' President, shining spotlights on everything! I'll be lucky to get half that money back, forget profits. Oh, yeah! I got some special payback for you, honey. I'm going to take away the most important thing to you in the whole wide world – and you're going to help!

* * * * * *

The trail winds along the top of the ridge, dimly lit in the prevailing shadows, only occasionally splattered by a ray of sunlight that finds its way through the tall hardwoods. It is refreshingly quiet here in the mountains, far from the continuous hustle and noise of Waikiki. Even the trade winds don't reach this far into the rainforest.

The isolation is the appeal for Jared — it isn't uncommon to spend a couple of hours jogging through the rain forest without catching sight of anyone, especially tourists.

Despite its rare use, the path is wide and relatively smooth, though who maintains it is something of a mystery. In all his trips to the mountain trails Jared has never seen maintenance workers, either government or volunteer. In any event, Jared doesn't care who to thank; he is more interested in generating sweat and working off stress. He is quite successful in both respects.

As he passes the trailhead parking area he glances at his watch — still time for another trip to the ridge crest, he notes, wiping the sweat from his brow. Three steps — breathe in. Three, more — breathe out. Repeat one thousand times per mile.

The silence is broken only by Jared's feet hitting the ground and his deep breathing — then, *crack!* Bark flies from a tree by his head. He instinctively ducks, then goes into a squat, looking for the shooter. Through the undergrowth he can see the trailhead parking area and a lone figure.

"Hey! You freaking idiot! You nearly hit me!" yells Jared, furious at the carelessness of this cretin.

Crack! Dirt flies from a near miss, stinging Jared's neck and face. He doesn't wait for a third shot, but does an acrobatic flip backwards, rolls into the defilade and flattens out.

"Okay, that was no accident," Jared grunts softly to himself. His heart rate, already high, trip-hammers so much he's afraid he's going to have a heart attack.

He grabs a handful of mud and smears the natural camouflage over his face, legs and arms. Some help, but not salvation if only twelve feet off the trail!

The repetitive crunch, crunch, crunch sound of gravel in the parking lot shoots another bolt of adrenaline into his already fried nervous system. Every step closer than the last!

The crunching sound stops. The trail itself is packed dirt, making for a soundless approach. Trying to move his head as little as possible, Jared searches for a way out. Uphill to the trail — no go, that invites a head-on confrontation. Downhill, yes, but that means fighting through the tangle of undergrowth to a cliff thirty yards distant.

Don't know how much fall there is from the cliff— really going to hurt, I know that. But it's better than a bullet in the head.

Jared takes a deep breath and tenses, ready for the sprint to the cliff and whatever lies below. Then he hears it — singing.

"If I die in a combat zone, box me up and send me home. Pin my medals upon my chest, tell my momma I done my best!"

Actually it is a chant, and Jared recognizes it immediately. He raises his head far enough to see down the trail. Jarheads! Or, more properly, Marines, six of them running his way in rhythmic synchronism. No doubt from Camp Smith, the Marine Corps base a couple of miles down the hill. They are decked out in combat boots, cami trousers, and sweaty green T-shirts. What a beautiful sight!

Above the chanting, he hears the sound of a tinny little car engine over-revving. A peek through the foliage reveals a small white car spewing gravel everywhere as it speeds out of the parking area and down the road,

Jared rolls over on his back, closes his eyes and sighs. "Man, I'm getting way too old for this shit..."

Chapter 23

L ori hates everything about the jail. It looks like a medieval fortress upgraded with chain link fences topped with razor wire, plunked down in a working class neighborhood in central Honolulu. Its proper title is the Oahu Community Correction Center, invariably called "O Triple C" by those unfortunate enough to live or work here. Even the innocent avoid approaching it, not certain they won't be swept into a cesspool of evil.

Even though she gets VIP treatment and her father is in the isolation unit, Lori hears the screaming of the deranged and feels the hot leers of the sexually starved. Her escort, a solidly thick Samoan corrections officer, seems to be quite capable of bench-pressing a Volkswagen, so she isn't physically afraid, but the display of wasted lives unnerves her.

The Samoan drops her off in the visiting area, where Rocky sits on his side of the long divided table. No one else is present, except for a corrections officer who oversees the area from a table in the corner. Rocky sits in his orange jail jumpsuit, eyes closed, silent. Lori takes a seat opposite him.

He's aged ten years...withered almost like a cancer patient.

A lump forms in her throat, and her words struggle around it.

"Hello, Father... It's Lori."

Rocky slowly opens his eyes and gives the slightest of nods. He retreats behind his eyelids again.

"Father," Lori continues, "you really need to meet with the lawyers, okay? They can help you, whether you want them to or not. But that's not what I came to talk about. What's important is all over Hawaii people support you. They're confused about the, uh, the situation, you know, but they believe in you, and are still so proud." She pauses, and creases carve channels in her forehead.

"Father, you are a great man, and everyone knows it... Let us help you!"

Rocky opens his eyes and fixes them on Lori for a long moment. "Lori, Lori... You look so much like your mother..." He pushes back his chair and rises abruptly, then bows formally. Without another word, he turns and shuffles down the corridor. Lori sits and stares blankly for a moment, then buries her face in her arms.

* * * * * *

At first glance, the bar is indistinguishable from any of the hundreds of small "Korean bars" that populate the islands. At second glance, it is still undistinguishable...the same neon signs in the Hangul language, a dark interior with Korean folk music piped in. This particular version is a block from the waterfront, which is convenient — most of its customers are crewmen from the many Asian fishing boats which make port in the islands.

Raymond Tanaka steps inside the front door, pausing to take in the scene. Only a couple of patrons present. Both are sitting with "hostess girls," no doubt buying them one overpriced "ladies' drink" after another. A few hours of this and they'll amble back to their boats, probably drunk, certainly much poorer, and possibly with a lower sperm count.

Reassured for the moment by the quiet familiarity, Tanaka makes his way to the bar, winding around the empty vinyl chairs and Formica table tops. He is scarcely seated before a young Korean girl, quite pretty in her long, tight red dress, sits down beside him and whispers something to him in Korean, finishing with a giggle. Tanaka doesn't answer, but makes an "away with you" gesture with his hand. The girl says something else, but this time her tone is not so sweet and lacks the giggle as she tramps away.

The bartender, a well-worn Korean man, nods at Tanaka, and without being asked pours him a drink. With surprising grace, he places it on a coaster and slides it over to the professor. Tanaka hesitates, then looks around the room. All is the same.

Hands trembling, Tanaka lifts the glass uncovering a key with a tag inscribed with the number five on it. His hand passes over the coaster and the key is gone. Tanaka slides two $100 bills across the bar, takes the drink and heads up the stairs behind the bar. The bartender impassively watches the soccer match on the wall mounted TV.

Tanaka eases his way down the dimly lit hallway. Room five. Another glance about. He gulps the rest of his drink, and takes a deep breath. His hand still shaking, he inserts and turns the key. He hesitates for a moment, then opens the door cautiously. In the dimness a very pretty Asian boy, not yet a teenager, sits on a bed, arms hugging his knees. The boy looks up, fear and resignation etched on his face.

"Oh, yes," Tanaka says in a low tone. His eyes gleam behind his rimless spectacles. "Nice...*very* nice."

He extracts the key, steps inside and closes the door behind him. The bolt clicks metallically as the lock falls into place.

* * * * * *

After being constrained in the gilded cage of downtown Honolulu and Waikiki, the Corvette craves open road, a commodity in short supply on Oahu. Ewa Beach is one of the rare undeveloped portions of the island. Sugarcane fields predominate and houses are miles apart, perfect to stretch the legs of the big 454 cubic-inch engine.

Pulling away from a stop sign, and with a straight open road beyond the hood, Jared hammers through the gears, feeling the G-forces on his back and the wind tugging his hair.

First gear: out of the hole—the Vette leaps forward, the front end almost coming off the ground, tires squalling. The tach whips towards red line as the car accelerates, the engine howling.

Second gear: after three seconds of first gear the engine demands second — Jared slams clutch and gear selector simultaneously and the tires bark as the power of all four hundred horses hits the pavement. The rpm's blast towards redline and sixty miles per hour. Time for a shift!

Third gear: Jared's hand and feet blur, and in a fraction of a second, the tach and speedometer swing wildly to the right. Ninety, then 95. Plenty of horsepower left, but not much road. Jared jerks the gear selector back through the pattern and stands hard on the brakes.

The nose of the Vette pitches down, but the sheer weight of the big block engine fights the deceleration. The flashing yellow intersection light is fifty yards away and the Vette closes fast. Downshift again, more brakes and the rear wheels lock. Jared muscles the wheel to keep the car straight. It slides to a halt in a cloud of dust and flying gravel, exactly at the white line marking the intersection.

Jared looks to his left as the dust cloud drifts away. The sentry at the gate to Barber's Point Naval Air Station eyeballs him with an icy stare. For a moment, Jared isn't sure whether he will applaud or draw his weapon.

Jared pulls up to the guard shack, sporting a big grin. "Just blowing it out a little," he offers. The guard, from his looks, is a career civil service officer who probably took customer relations training from the IRS Enforcement Division, is clearly not impressed.

"Drivers license, proof of insurance," he says without offering a greeting. Jared pulls out the documents and hands them over. The guard scrutinizes them for an inordinate amount of time, but unable to find anything wrong, he checks a list on a clipboard at hand. That done, he hands back the paperwork to Jared.

"Commander Parr is expecting you. Patrol Squadron One, take a right at the stop sign, first hangar on the left. And, Mister Scott," he adds with a glare for emphasis, "we take traffic rules very seriously here on the Air Station — very seriously."

In some other circumstances Jared would have invited the guy to please go have sex with himself, but now he was on a mission and not inclined to get thrown off the Air Station before getting to first base.

"Yes Sir, understand completely, Sir," Jared says with just enough fake sincerity to appease the rent-a-cop. He puts the car into gear and slowly eases down the road toward the hangars.

* * * * * *

"So you are Mr. Scott," the mission Tactical Coordinator, Cmdr. Parr says after the introductions, looking Jared over carefully. Parr is in his early forties, short gray hair, trim and compact. He looks very much the professional in his green Nomex flight suit, decorated with various unit patches.

Given spare time, Jared would love to take the opportunity to examine the plaques and memorabilia that decorate the ready room. The entire squadron history is portrayed via models of various airplanes, squadron commemorative deployment plaques with the names of participants carved in monkey pod wood, and original photographs of airplanes now found only in museums.

A twinge of jealousy begins to grow, but Jared subdues it and follows Parr up the stairs.

Sequestering themselves into one of the briefing rooms Parr and Jared face each other over a Navy gray metal table. Parr gets right to the point. "Well, to start off with, we didn't find anything at those coordinates we were given, nothing." He quickly continues, "However, about a half-mile away we did locate something that may interest you." He pulls a roll of what looks to be graph paper from his briefcase and lays it out before them. "See, here's those original coordinates, not even a wiggle on the Magnetic Anomaly Detector," he says, pointing to some lines etching their way down the paper. "But here, we got a reading, just a blip. To tell the truth, we missed it the first time around it was so small."

"How small is small?" Jared asks.

"Something in the range of 50 tons, may be 50 to a 100 feet long. We're used to looking for Russian nuke subs that displace 5,000 to 15,000 tons, so you can see why we almost overlooked it."

"Can you be sure it's a man-made object?" Jared asks, looking at the indecipherable squiggles on the graph paper, then over at Parr.

"Not certain, but the readings are consistent with refined metal, which gives a much sharper readout than naturally occurring ore deposits. See how clear this spike is?" Parr asks, jabbing his pen on a section of the return. "If this was natural it would be much more rounded and sloping."

"Any guesses as to what it is?"

Parr looks at him for moment and then says, "Well, I was hoping you were going to tell me that." He pauses expectantly, but receiving no reply, continues, "My guess is a large plane that crashed, or a sunken boat. Maybe a fishing trawler or an inter-island barge."

Jared ponders this for a moment. Cmdr. Parr hesitates, then asks, "Say, what's this all about anyway? We get a call on the secure phone from someone in government liaison at CINCPAC Fleet telling us to fly a search pattern without telling us why or what we are looking for, no hardcopy tasking or anything. What gives?" Jared can see him mentally folding his arms, awaiting an explanation.

Jared leans forward to whisper conspiratorially across the table, "Okay, I'm not supposed to tell you this 'cause it is really close hold, but since you've done such a good job, here's what it's about: last week one of our Trident subs launched a practice SLBM from about two hundred miles north of here. The missile was supposed to reenter at the Kwajalein test range, but it never got booster separation. Worse, the telemetry was screwed up and it didn't respond to guidance or self-destruct signals, but we tracked it on radar to near here. And now we found it. Damned lucky, too, can you imagine what would've happened if that thing had landed in downtown Honolulu?"

Jared leans back and says, a little louder for emphasis, "So, you can see why we've got a keep the lid on tight. Don't want to embarrass the Navy, do we?"

Parr, dutifully impressed with the revelations, swallows visibly.

Back outside, Jared jumps in the Vette and guns it through the gate, rattling the guard shack with a shower of gravel.

I may not be a soldier anymore but I can't pass an opportunity to lay it on these Navy squids!

Chapter 24

The *Mokoleia* plows through the blue swells, muscling them aside, if only for a moment, then passing to let them consume the frothy white wake that trails the boat. At 45 feet, the charter fishing boat is well suited for offshore, which is good, because that's where it spends almost all of its operational life. The engines make the hull vibrate to the core, and they change from a drone to a roar when the exhaust comes above the waterline. The splash of the bow wave adds to the constant background noise as Junior holds the boat on heading. He is on the flying bridge helm, glancing periodically at the compass to make sure they are on track. Junior is a classical local amalgamation of cultures, tanned dark brown, and proudly sporting a respectable beer-belly. Anyone who knows him describes him as a Hawaiian "good ole boy," a big guy with a constant smile and a relentlessly positive attitude. That certainly holds true today.

"J'ed, you bring da hi-fi, yeah?" he asks with a laugh and a grin, mangling Jared's name. "Gone play some Frank Snotra?" Junior is asking about the suitcase size metal box that contains a small dish antenna and a control board that Jared is unpacking and assembling.

"Naw, how you like *Twisted Sister*," Jared responds, and they both laugh.

Satisfied that his electronics are set up, Jared goes below and studies the ocean floor charts laid out on the table. Even though they are the best available from the University of Hawaii oceanography department, they are still quite sketchy when compared to dry land topographical maps. He rechecks Cmdr. Parr's coordinates one more time, but they didn't get any shallower. Forty fathoms – two hundred forty feet from the surface, more than sixty feet deeper that Jared has ever been on scuba before.

Definitely risky business, not the typical lobster and spearfishing dive!

He contemplates the chart, aware the mystery site is well beyond the limits that the U.S. Navy considers safe for scuba diving. Still, if he wants to keep this exploration as secret as possible there are few options. There are several deep water submersibles in the islands, but to get the use of one would've become a major bureaucratic wrestling match, involving delays and necessitating bringing many more people into the picture. The same applied to getting the equipment and expertise for exotic gas mixtures, such as helium – oxygen, to make a deep scuba dive safer. So in the end Jared decided to do it the way he did most things – by himself, to the maximum extent possible.

Hope there is something, anything, to be found that will help Lori resolve this conundrum with Rocky.

Junior and his eighteen-year-old son, Bobby, were waiting at the Princeville Airport when Jared arrived that morning. Together they loaded the diving gear and other equipment into the back of the pickup truck, then set out for the marina where the *Mokoleia* was waiting. Before leaving the dock, Jared made a couple of last-minute phone calls to assure both the local Coast Guard helicopter and the hyperbaric chamber at the University of Hawaii were serviceable and on standby, should the need for them arise.

Not that they are likely to do much good!

As they leave the dock, Jared joins Junior on the flying bridge. "Hey, J'ed, where you like go now?" Junior inquires.

"About six or eight miles down the Na Pali coast, I'll let you know more when we get near there." Jared had told Junior in general terms that he was going to do some exploring by scuba, just enough info to satisfy Junior's minimal curiosity.

When they approached the search area Jared unpacked an essential piece of equipment – a Collins SATNAV, satellite navigation set. With the signal sent from a commercial satellite in geosynchronous orbit over the Pacific, Jared could navigate to within fifty yards of the coordinates given to him by Cmdr. Parr. He had used it when making solo flights over long stretches of ocean, but this was the first time he had tried it from a boat. Fortunately, it seemed to be working as advertised and soon they had a range and bearing to the desired spot, a featureless expanse of ocean several miles distant from the mountainous shore of Kauai.

"Junior," Jared yells up to the bridge, "come about five degrees left." Junior complies and looks back down at Jared and the magic box.

"J'ed, you got genie in da box?" Junior asks.

"Actually, it's SATNAV receiver. Can tell us exactly where we are," Jared answers.

Junior rumbles forth a belly laugh. "Man, you *lolo!* Just ask Junior!" He squints toward the shore. "We now, mile and half offshore, six miles west Princeville. No problem!" He gives the "shaka b'rah" hand wave and grins again.

"Well, Junior, you got a good eye, but I need a little more precision today. This baby talks to satellites, gives a location to within fifty yards." Jared says.

Junior peers upward, as if looking for satellites. "I don't know, b'rah, all I see is seagulls…"

"Another couple of miles and we should be there. You keeping an eye on the fathometer, right?" asks Jared. Junior gives a nod and goes back to following the heading.

Ten minutes later Jared says, "Okay, just a bit more. See anything?"

Junior glances at the fathometer, "No, just flat."

"All right," Jared says, "start the search pattern."

With Junior at the helm, Jared gives directions and they begin a square search pattern starting where the SATNAV dropped them off. They proceed with ever-expanding legs until a given sector is covered, then repeat in an adjacent sector. It is monotonous, tedious work. Junior doesn't care however; he's getting paid by the hour.

Two hours pass. Then Junior calls out, "Hey boss, got some t'ing." Jared scrambles up the ladder to join Junior on the bridge. "Right here," he says pointing to a slight bump in the otherwise smooth trace of the fathometer chart. "Not much, maybe ten foot vertical."

"What's the depth?" Jared asks.

"About forty fathoms, two hundred and forty feet." Junior says.

"Okay, Junior, looks like this is it, or at least as good as it gets. I want you to throw the anchor exactly when I tell you. Let's reverse and come back across it again. We got to hit it near as possible. A miss of fifty feet is a wipeout if visibility is bad."

"Bobby! Standby with the anchor!" yells Junior.

"Here?" Bobby looks up from the deck below. "Anchor here? We got 'nuff line?"

"Yeah, not much current, we got enough. You betta hope the winch she be working, 'cause you pulling up by hand if need be!" Junior gives another laugh. Bobby doesn't look too happy as he heads for the bow.

Junior hauls the boat around and follows the wake back to the original position. "Standby, standby..." Jared calls, staring intently at the fathometer." Bobby struggles with the heavy anchor, trying to keep his balance as the boat rolls.

"*Now!*" Jared shouts, and Bobby heaves the anchor over the bow. It speeds towards the bottom in a cloud of bubbles with a rattling chain chasing it. Jared watches it until it disappears into the blue.

If we haven't found the right spot, that's all for today. Working these depths only allows one dive a day.

"What you looking for, Jared?" asks Bobby when he returns to the bridge. "Secret fishing hole?"

Jared shrugs. "I don't know... something...that's the question of the day."

* * * * * *

It is after noon, and Jared is anxious to get started. Even with a high sun angle, it will be semi-dark at forty fathoms, a dim twilight at best, so he doesn't want to lose any more natural light than necessary to a setting sun. He rigs a scuba tank and air regulator, then takes a couple of breaths to make sure it's functional. Satisfied, he waves over Bobby.

"Hey, Bobby, want to cool off?" Jared asks.

"Sure. We taking a break?"

"Looks like the anchor is holding. Think you can free dive this rig to twenty feet and attach it to the anchor line?"

"You got it!" Bobby gets on his mask and fins. He jumps into the water, almost losing his mask in the process. After fumbling a bit, he gets the water out of the mask, and Jared lowers the scuba rig to him. Bobby takes several deep breaths, inverts and starts down the anchor line, tank in tow. A couple of minutes later he reappears, spitting water and gasping for air.

"Tied off at twenty feet," he calls between gasps.

"Great, good work," Jared gives him a thumbs-up.

"Okay boy, back in da boat 'fore Jaws get a sniff o' you." Junior adds.

Jared helps Bobby scurry aboard and together they get Jared suited up for the dive. Junior watches with amusement as Jared struggles into a full-length wetsuit. "Jared, you need Hawaii boy skin — no need wetsuit!"

Jared laughs. "Yeah, I'm a cold water wuss and the water gets colder the deeper I go. You should install a hot tub for me, yeah?"

Not only will it be cold at forty fathoms, but the lengthy business of decompression stops will lead to a bad case of the shivers – a chill that makes getting the "bends," or decompression sickness, even more likely, a catastrophe Jared wants to avoid at all costs.

When Jared is fully dressed in his personal gear, Bobby helps him strap the cumbersome "twin ninety" scuba tanks to his back. The burden is immense, so heavy Jared is not able to stand unaided due to the weight and the rocking of the boat. Bobby helps him stagger to the rail and sit precariously on it.

Bobby's expression foreshadows his words. "Be careful down there, okay?"

"You got it," Jared replies, his expression mirroring Bobby's. He covers his mouth and nose with the mask and slides the regulator into his mouth. A deep breath confirms the device is delivering air as promised

This is it – all up to me. Flying solo from here on.

"Hey, good luck, b'rah!" Junior calls from the bridge, grinning widely. "You come back, see us, yeah?"

Jared doesn't answer, but rather sets his watch to the "start dive" position. He pauses for a moment, then gives a nod to Junior. Holding his mask to his face Jared rolls backward over the rail and into the water with a huge splash. He surfaces and Bobby hands him down another scuba rig. Jared takes it in hand and without hesitation turns and kicks powerfully away from the surface, into the blue void.

* * * * * *

Jared is relieved to find visibility is quite good, eighty feet or better. Even so, the sunlight fades quickly as he descends along the slanting anchor line. Since his decompression plan calls for only thirteen minutes of bottom time, calculated from the time he leaves the surface, Jared descends into the featureless gloom as rapidly as he can adjust his ears to the steadily increasing pressure. He pauses for a moment at fifty feet to attach the spare tank to the anchor line. Satisfied it is secure, he presses on with the descent.

Passing a hundred feet, Jared enters the twilight zone. At this depth he can no longer see the surface, nor the bottom, and there are no fish or other animals - he is totally surrounded by the gray-blue emptiness enclosing him, true inner-space.

Jared starts to fret when he passes two hundred feet: no bottom in sight! *What if the anchor has dragged off into deeper water?*

He switches on his dive light and is relieved the powerful beam finds the bottom about ten yards below. Mostly flat and rocky, with just a few coral clusters and small fish. The anchor lies in a small trench, firmly lodged.

Jared checks his watch and depth gauge, and then plays light around him, searching for a wreck, a crash... or something, anything! Despair rises within him. *All risk and no reward? Is there anything down here? Which way to go?* Looking at the anchor more closely Jared sees drag marks it made across the bottom before getting stuck. *That's as good of a direction as any.* His light leading the way Jared follows the scuff marks leading into the darkness.

At the end of the drag marks, the only thing in sight is a small ledge rising from the rocky bottom some distance away. *May as well start from a known point, and this is the only landmark around.* He starts for the ledge, mad at himself for risking his life in what is rapidly turning into a wild goose chase.

He stops short and goes bolt upright. Jared startles the fish by giving an audible hoot, releasing a cloud of bubbles which bursts from his regulator. There, unmistakable in the beam of his light, is what can only be a propeller protruding from the "ridge!" Jared checks his watch as he closes the distance; only eight minutes of bottom time left. *Have to make every second count.*

At first, Jared supposes the boat is upside down as he is looking at the smooth contours of its hull. As he draws up near the wreck, a realization: *This isn't a boat at all, it is what can only be a submarine! A midget sub, perhaps, but most definitely a military sub!* Jared cruises the length of it, recording the data in his mind and the scene with his camera, popping off flashes every few yards. She's about eighty feet long, lying on her side, with no obvious damage to the upper surfaces except for a peculiar dimpling pattern to the hull. Jared rubs his hand over the smooth metal; the black paint is intact, scarcely any marine growth.

Reaching the front end of the boat, Jared makes another discovery. There are two torpedo tubes built into the bow, arranged vertically, like an over and under shotgun. The lower one still has the snout of a very large torpedo projecting a few feet out of it. *The teeth of the tiger. From the looks of the missing torpedo, this tiger had taken at least one big bite.* Jared hesitates as the urge to examine this further grips him. He glances at his decompression meter, its indicator now deeply into the red section. *No time to spare, document and keep moving.*

He snaps a couple of pictures, the flash exploding lightning bolts over the scene.

The conning tower emerges from the twilight. Its periscope juts horizontally across the sand, the glass eye shattered. Jared moves closer with the light, illuminating the conning tower hatch. It is frozen wide open, daring him to enter. He briefly considers it, but the opening is much too narrow to accommodate him and his bulky tanks. Peering inside, he can make out the rungs of the steel ladder leading to the crew compartment, but little else is recognizable. A surprise: there's a current flowing from within the sub's hull!

Strange...

Jared pulls away from the hatch and swims over the top to the opposite side of the sub. It takes only a moment to find the answer: the submarine's bottom has been blown open along a 20-foot section, hull plates peeled outward by the force of an explosion. Pieces of what looks to be battery blocks litter the seabed nearby. Jason isn't a naval expert, but it's obvious to him what happened. *The midget submarine was scuttled, its bottom ripped open by a powerful internal blast.*

Swimming up to the ripped hull, Jared discovers it is just wide enough over much of its length to allow him access to what must have been the crew compartment. Much of the interior has been reduced to a maze of twisted pipes and jagged metal. Jared squeezes into it, tank clanging against protruding objects, his fins kicking up mud and silt.

Now I know why they call them midget subs, you have to be a midget to fit inside! Certainly a grown man would have been unable to stand erect, and two people could have gotten past one another only with difficulty in the narrow chamber.

Fully inside, Jared reaches the control room. A sweep of the light reveals nothing which looks like bones. He finds the bottom terminus for the periscope and the steering controls. He snaps off a couple more pictures, the burst of the flash blinding in the confined space. Finding a gauge that has somehow escaped unbroken, Jared wipes away the layer of silt surrounding it and examines it with his light. The *Kanji*, or Japanese characters, stand out clearly against white face of the dial. The camera pops another flash and the gauge is captured on film. *Well, that solves at least one mystery.*

Stirred by the scuba exhaust bubbles, silt rains down. Soon, Jared can't see three feet in front of him, even with the powerful light. As he starts to back out, he makes out an object, vaguely familiar, sticking halfway out of the mud on the bottom of the control room. He can just reach it, and with a tug, it comes loose. A sextant! An incredible find!

No time to examine it. He stuffs it in his dive bag. *Just get the hell out of here!*

The alarm on his watch sounds with a piercing screech, sending an adrenaline soaked jolt of fear through Jared's body. He must leave the bottom now or stay with the sub forever.

Time to go!

Only he can't. Backing out isn't working, his gear is catching on something behind him he can't see, something immovable. There's not enough room to turn around in this maze, and with every lurch the silt and mud fly. He gets hung up more tightly — it's now zero visibility.

Even if I can twist around I still won't be able to see what I'm snagged on!

A surge of terror washes over him like a wave, from head to foot, a scream from the primitive part of his brain which demands: Thrash! Fight! Break anything, even your bones! Escape! It takes *every* bit of self-determination Jared can muster to quell the feeling — to panic is to die, right here, right now, fighting until the last of the air, precious, precious air, leaves his mouth as he screams his last words: *"Oh, God, I don't want to die!"*

In the silt-filled darkness, Jared reaches for his dive knife. It's right where it should be — on the inside of his right calf, just below the knee. He gets a grip on it and yanks it from the scabbard with one hand, finds the tank strap with the other. Totally by feel he puts the knife blade to the tough plastic strap and saws away like a mad violinist. Vital seconds tick from his watch, every lost second a step closer to death.

I've got to be over my time! But if I don't free myself, time to get to the surface is the least of all problems.

Adrenaline pumping, Jared rips the knife through the last of the strap, and feels the constraining pressure release. He pulls his body from the scuba harness, the tanks no longer attached to his body. But the regulator is still in his mouth and he is clamped down on the mouthpiece so hard he is afraid he'll bite it in half.

Calm down, slow down! You're sucking air like a jet engine in afterburner!

When Jared squeezes out of the wreckage, the tanks come out with surprising ease. Jared doesn't take even a precious second to get the scuba rig on his back. He starts upward, regulator in mouth, dragging the bulky tanks by one hand. The anchor line comes into view, a precious link with the surface world. Air supply gauge check — *only three hundred pounds of pressure, maybe a minute, two at most — and the surface is five minutes away!* Shocked, Jared kicks upward, knowing the vertical speed invites the bends, but the desire to breath is too strong for rational thought.

He literally sucks the air from the tank now, pulling hard with his lungs to get every molecule with each breath! He is afraid to check again, but he does anyway. Air gage: zero!

Still can't see the surface! Not going to make it! The bubbles become fewer and fewer. Then they stop altogether — nothing left! Jared presses on. His motions slow, and the regulator drops from his mouth. With only baby strength left, his hand releases the tanks and they fall, in slow motion, away into the endless depths below.

The 50-foot tie-off tank is at his fingertips, swinging on the anchor line. Fighting to stay conscious, Jared grabs the regulator and frantically shoves in into his mouth. The flow is immediate - air, air, air! The most important thing in the universe, at least at this moment, is at hand. Every cell screams for it, his lungs collect it in huge, deep breaths, and his heart races madly to deliver it. Later, while he hangs on the line for a couple of hours, he will think of many things. Right now Jared cannot think. His only focus is breathing — air, air, sweet, beautiful air!

Chapter 25

Clutching a handful of mail and the bag containing the sextant, Jared juggles the keys to his apartment. He finally finds the right one and gets the door open. Still fatigued from the dive, his face is lined and his movements are slow and deliberate. He places the still damp sextant bag in the kitchen sink, but is too tired to start a cleanup. Instead, he flops on the sofa and relaxes, happy to be in a familiar, quiet environment.

He flips on the TV and idly browses through the mail, mostly sales promotions and time-share invitations. He always thinks it amusing people send him solicitations for whatever time-share "opportunity" he should jump on in the beautiful Hawaiian Islands. Didn't they look at his address before wasting the postage?

Jared turns over another envelope and stops cold. The writing is his own, addressed to Mrs. Evelyn Scott, 7122 Ridgeway Drive, Waco, Texas. Bold across the envelope are the familiar words: "REFUSED— RETURN TO SENDER." Jared contemplates it for a long moment. Then he tosses it aside.

As if gravity has doubled, Jared slumps deeper into the sofa. His head falls back and he stares at the ceiling without seeing. Ever so slowly, a single tear grows in the corner of one eye, wetly building, until its weight pulls it downward. Only one tear, never more, always silent, always there, waiting…

* * * * * *

Jared bumps around in the bathroom, still half asleep, driven awake by his over-stretched bladder. Relieved, he makes his way to the living room, navigating around the furniture by memory, since the apartment is dark as a cave. Steeling himself, Jared pulls open the window drapes, and squints painfully in the bright sunshine streaming in.

His landlady, Joyce, working on the flower bed outside, looks up to see a very unshaven Jared, hair going in every direction, standing in the window, wearing only his boxers and a smile. He gives a friendly little wave, which is not returned. Instead, Joyce gives him a steely look, grabs her gardening tools and is gone.

Jeez, do I look that bad? He makes a belated check to see if his penis is still in his shorts — thank God it is, or he'd be looking for a new place to live today.

He rummages around in the refrigerator. The milk he pulls out definitely doesn't pass the sniff test, and there is little else identifiable or not growing mold. Jared sighs. He keeps a neat home, but planning more than one meal ahead is not his forte. He finds a can of pork and beans in the pantry. He puts the can opener to work and is soon sitting on the sofa, a spoon in one hand and the can of beans in the other.

Just like the Army days, he muses. *Only nobody's trying to kill me.*

That moment of contentment is replaced by the memory of someone taking shots at him on the trail.

Well, hardly anybody! This brings a rueful smile only he can appreciate.

Slurping the last of the beans, Jared looks at the answering machine, which is blinking its red eye. A wandering thought surfaces in his mind: *Wonder why red is the danger color?* He takes a deep breath, holds it for a moment, then gives a sighing exhale. Thus prepared, he selects "play," keeping a finger poised on the "delete" button.

Beep! "Jared, it's Lori again. Look, can you please call me? Last I heard from you was from Kauai, you said you got big news. That was three days ago — you don't answer your phone, nobody at Island Air knows where you are. What's up? Are you okay? Please call me as..."

Lori, Lori--please don't turn into a nanny. The delete button gets a finger stab.

Beep! "Hello, Jared! It's Smitty — again — guess you didn't get the other messages. Hey listen, I gotta know what's going on. You missed three scheduled charters, and we were really slammed for pilots on Mother's Day weekend. Jared, the owner's not stupid. I can cover for you some, but...well, you gonna have to meet with him before I can put you back on the flight schedule. He's going to be flying in from San Francisco on Wednesday. I really hope everything's okay, I'd do anything to help you, but..."

"Well, shit." Jared says aloud, sighing. *More fences to mend – the story of my life.*

Beep! "Hello Jared. It's Melissa, from San Diego, remember? Hey, hope you're doing all right. Anyway, me and a girlfriend are going to be in Honolulu for a few days and I wanted to see if you'd like to come down and hang out with us. I got some, uh, enhancements I think you'll like. Maybe you can help me name them." A burst of giggles ensues. "We're going to be at the Royal Hawaiian, arriving..."

Tempting. Melissa is a classic honey blonde California girl with legs that can wrap twice around any man, but with way too much drama. *Got enough of that already.*

Beep! "Mr. Scott, this is Lucy Choi from First Hawaiian. I'm calling in reference to loan number, ahh...FL6838899SMT, which I believe is an automobile loan. That payment is two months overdue, which we are quite concerned about. We would very much like to keep you as a customer, but..."

Christ, can life get anymore complicated? He sits for a full minute, trying to get motivated, then finally picks up the phone and dials.

"This is Lori."

"Hi, it's Jared."

"Well, about time! I've been worried sick. Where have you been?" she demands.

"Right here, at home."

"At home? What in the world have you been doing that keeps you from making a simple phone call?" Lori asks, with no small amount of sarcasm.

"Sleeping."

Lori is incredulous. "Sleeping? You've been sleeping for three days?"

"Well not entirely, maybe sixteen, eighteen hours a day. I know it sounds bogus, but I get that way sometimes." He makes a weak effort at reassurance. "I'm feeling better now."

"And you couldn't stay awake long enough to pick up the damn phone and call? Jared, you need to get checked out," Lori says sternly. "That's not normal."

"What, and have the FAA pull my ticket? So I can be permanently out of work?

"Look, Lori, I'm a big boy, I can run my own life. Don't give me any shit, okay?"

There is silence at the other end for a long time. Finally Lori, very subdued, asks, "You said you had news. What's going on?"

"I think its time I talk to Rocky."

Chapter 26

He looks smaller than Jared remembered, and he seems to have aged a couple of decades since those proud campaign commercials of a few months ago. He doesn't stand when Jared enters the visiting room, not even when Lori bends over to embrace him. In a concession to his status, the jail officials have provided a private conference room for this meeting. Ostensibly, the meeting is to discuss a legal defense strategy, so guards are discreetly out of earshot.

Rocky acknowledges Jared's presence with a nod, but otherwise remains motionless at the table, hands in his lap, eyes once again closed. Jared and Lori sit opposite him, saying nothing for a few minutes. Lori glances at Jared and begins.

"Father, I know you may not want us to, but we've been trying to help you, we really have. You're a good man and it's killing me to see all of this happening to you, especially not knowing why. And you are not confiding in me, so Jared's been working hard to figure it out. Now we think we understand. But if we are wrong, we need for you to tell us." She nods at Jared.

"Uh, Mr. Konishi..." Jared has been on a first name basis with Rocky since they met, but the sudden formality is generated by Jared's acute discomfort with this meeting. He is extraordinarily curious, but satisfying curiosity looks to be painful.

"We are trying to help, you know, so I got the logbook page translated, the one you gave Lori..." At this Rocky's eyes open and he fixes Jared with a penetrating stare. His face is a mask, locking his feeling inside. "...and we, I mean I, made an exploration of the coordinates listed. I think you should see what I found." Jared opens the large manila envelope, and slides photographs across the table to Rocky. He doesn't pick them up, but leans forward a bit and looks intently at each of them. Expecting some sort of response or reaction, Jared pauses, but Rocky only closes his eyes and settles back in his chair.

"I know this must be painful for you, Mr. Konishi, but I should also tell you this was the submarine your brother, Masafumi Konishi, was aboard when he died. We know that because we found the sextant with his name on it." Jared reaches into a bag and brings out the cloth wrapped sextant placing it on the table between them. He slowly peels away the cloth. The sextant, now cleaned, still shows the effects of being underwater for forty years. At the base, Kanji writing is visible, and engraved in English: *Ens. Masafumi Konishi.*

Rocky stares at the sextant, mute, impassive except for the facial tremor beginning to form beneath the scar on his forehead. Jared waits, fearful of an emotional explosion. But once again, Rocky retains his composure. Lori rejoins the conversation.

"Father, is this it? Was this the reason Fujitta came to see you? Was he blackmailing you because he found out your brother Masafumi's war record? It's been forty years since the war. Father, it may be embarrassing for the new Governor to have a brother who attacked Pearl Harbor, but you were just a schoolboy at home in Japan! You're not responsible for him!"

Rocky opens his eyes and looks at the wall over Lori, then says softly, "Lori, I wasn't always 'Rocky.' My brother did not attack Pearl Harbor.

"I did. I am Masafumi Konishi!"

* * * * * *

Lori rocks back in her chair, mouth agape, but unable to form words.

Jared shares the silence for a few moments, then says, "I sort of figured it was a possibility, Mr. Konishi, but I didn't put it together until I found the old newspaper articles. I didn't tell you about this part, Lori," Jared continues, glancing at her, "because I didn't want to raise the issue until I could be sure."

Jared shifts uncomfortably in his chair, but resolve is in his voice.

"Most people remember the Pearl Harbor attack as a huge air raid, and of course it was. But there was also a simultaneous attack by five Japanese midget submarines, which were to penetrate the harbor and launch torpedoes at the battleships. Four were sunk in the battle and the fifth lost forever... until now. I did a lot of research at the library and found articles about the discovery and raising of one of the midget subs near Honolulu airport in 1960. That sub was intact and the crew missing. There was speculation they may have escaped and made it to shore." Jared pauses and looks square at Rocky. "Did they, Rocky?"

Throughout Jared's discourse Rocky had held himself motionless, his head bowed. Now he looks up and speaks in a flat, emotionless monotone.

"I suppose it is all going to come out anyway. As soon as I saw Fujitta walk into the office, I knew. So I guess you should know the truth firsthand. No, that crew must have drowned. But the discovery of it caused me a terrible fright, fear I would be exposed for what I am. The same fear I had when Fujitta appeared before me."

He looked straight at his daughter. "Lori, I have lived a lie for so many years it has become natural for me. I never wanted to burden you with the truth. Now you must know it all, for better or worse."

Lori reaches across the table and takes Rocky's hand as he continues.

"My father was a successful businessman in the 1920s and '30s. He owned several factories, along with his brothers and father-in-law. Unlike them, however, he had close ties to the Imperial government. So it was no surprise he was made head of the business section of the Japanese Consulate in San Francisco before World War II. My brother and sister stayed in Japan with relatives, but my father had ambitions for me. I lived in San Francisco the entire time. I attended American school and grew up speaking English almost as much as Japanese. My father was one of the few Japanese at the time who spoke English well, and was very proud of it. It was kind of a bonding statement that he had my name engraved on the sextant in English."

Rocky takes a drink of water from a cup at hand. His eyes focus far away. Gradually, the person he once was returns to his psyche and he speaks in an increasingly informative manner, as if giving a lecture.

"When relations with America worsened over the China incident in 1937, we returned to Japan. I was soon caught up in the war fever engulfing the nation at that time." Rocky remembers the large yellow chrysanthemum flowers tossed on the heads and shoulders of stone-faced soldiers by the women of Iwakuni as the troops marched through the city streets. Thousands of women, tens of thousands maybe, welcomed them, splendid in their colorful kimonos, joy and excitement on their powder-white faces. How could they not be proud to support the divine mission decreed by the Emperor?

"Everywhere parades and speeches wished our soldiers well as they went off to fight in Manchuria. The whole country was alive with a sense of destiny and invincibility, and I, as a late comer returning, was eager to show my patriotism.

"With my family's permission, I applied for admission to Eta Jima, the Japanese Naval Academy. Six thousand boys from all over Japan applied, but only three hundred were accepted. My family was so proud of me!"

Embarrassed by the pride that seeps into his tone, all these decades later, Rocky bows his head, unable to escape his memories. He had been so overwhelmed, standing on the crowded train station platform in his best suit, his father similarly attired. His mother wore her most formal kimono, appropriate for the occasion of turning her oldest son over to her country. The naval officer who met them seemed larger than life — tall for a Japanese, crisp in a dark blue uniform with shiny gold buttons. Rocky could not imagine himself ever looking the same.

"I arrived at Eta Jima on my eighteenth birthday. For the next three years we endured a harsh, you would say severe, program of discipline, training and instruction."

Japanese Naval Academy, 1938

Sweating rivulets in his wool suit and necktie, Masafumi Konishi jumped off a rickety military bus. He stumbled forward, his heavy suitcase plowing furrows in the dirt behind him. Like cattle in a round up, three hundred bewildered boys milled about, confused and scared, as upperclassmen and petty officers screamed orders and insults. The mob of new midshipmen, pathetically inept, scrambled and fell as they tried to form ranks. Masafumi wheeled around, eyes searching. He desperately sought something safe, familiar, in this surreal scene. Nothing.

"You! Cockroach!" Without warning a sweaty and red face beamed hate two inches from Masafumi's nose. A devil's face. The eyes bulged, and spittle flew as if from an oral machine gun. The First Class Midshipman splatters, "What is your name?"

"My, uhh, name?" Masafumi stammers. "It's, it's Masafumi Konishi."

Wham! The upperclassman slapped Masafumi's face so hard he fell to his knees, stars flashing through his eyes.

"The correct answer is Masafumi Konishi, *Sir!* You end every response with '*Sir!*' You got that?"

Masafumi struggled to his feet, fighting with himself to neither cry nor run.

"Yes...Sir!"

"Good! Now get in ranks before I crush you like the insect you are." Masafumi looked over the shoulder of the demon before him. The bus he arrived on rattled down the road and with it, any hope of salvation. His gut churned, but there was no alternative. He dashed to get in line.

Finally, in some semblance of rows, the neophytes shuffled off, straining to carry their overstuffed suitcases, every face grim. Masafumi looked up at the inscription as they passed through the massive ironwork gates. LOYALTY. DEDICATION. SACRIFICE.

Words of doom! What have I gotten myself into?

A shiver climbed his spine as the gates creaked, then clanged shut. Never had he felt such despair.

"Seven days a week we prepared ourselves for war. We ran and rowed boats until our hands and feet were bloody, and then studied our courses until our heads felt like bursting. Punishment for anything less than maximum effort was immediate and brutal, but we were self-motivated. We dedicated ourselves completely to serving the country and the Emperor. We even swore ourselves to celibacy so we would not distract ourselves from our preparations."

Rocky glances at Jared and permits himself a small smile. "Imagine that dedication in today's world."

Distant memories flood into Rocky's mind, long suppressed, now given new life.

His feet cooking from blistering asphalt, Masafumi rushed from yet another endless session of drill practice. Sprinting across the parade deck, he bolted through the classroom door just before the upperclassman closed and locked it. A moment later came the wails of a couple of slower classmates. Masafumi took his seat and ignored their pleas to unlock the door. They would be marching all night tonight!

Masafumi grabbed paper and pencil from his bag and prepared to copy every word the instructor said — a requirement, one not easy to meet with festering blisters on both hands. Some classmates liked the rowing training, but Masafumi hated it. He couldn't coordinate with the other rowers and was often lashed by their stinging insults. Nothing compared to the remedial training, of course. Many were the hours spent rowing solo between two distant buoys while his classmates got to play soccer or practice singing patriotic songs. His reflections took him from the class for a blissful moment as he imagined himself on a battleship, as far away from these stinking rowboats as possible.

The pain of trying to hold the pencil made him groan softly as he tried to grip the pencil in a less painful position. Ready to write, he suddenly noticed the room was now deathly quiet and the lieutenant on the podium was staring right at him! No, to his right. The midshipman beside him was sound asleep, his chin resting on his chest. Masafumi tried to kick him awake under the table, but found the chair leg instead.

In seconds, the lieutenant was upon the boy, along with the chief petty officer assigned as class monitor. With no warning, the petty officer jerked the sleeping midshipman from his seat by the collar and pulled him to his feet to face the furious lieutenant.

"You dare insult me, an officer in the Imperial Navy, by sleeping in my class?" he screamed. "You, a maggot not worth a single button on my uniform?" He swung hard and smashed his fist to the side of the midshipman's head. The miscreant gasped in pain as blood streamed from his ear.

"Perhaps a few years in the boiler room of the fleet garbage scow will improve your manners!" Sobs and plaintive wails echoed down the corridor as the unlucky soul was dragged away. Masafumi, like his classmates, stared straight ahead, glad misfortune fell on someone else that day.

Rocky pauses to fill his water glass again, his hand shaking slightly. His thoughts gather as he pauses, and he speaks a little louder as better memories come to him.

"After I graduated, I served briefly as a deck officer on a cruiser, but in the summer of 1941, I was selected for the Special Attack Force forming at Kure Naval base. Our weapon was a top-secret, miniature submarine, which could penetrate enemy defenses undetected and strike a blow without warning. We trained without rest for months as we learned to operate our subs, and several crews were lost to accidents. We were sad, but it did not deter us. At the end, the five best crews were picked, and I was among them. None of us were volunteers, but none thought to refuse.

"After the crew selection, we were given a week of leave. We still did not know our mission. We were told, 'You are going on a long maneuver. Say goodbye to your families.'"

Feeling like a military peacock in the splendid deep blue uniform of a junior naval officer, Masafumi picked his way along a busy street in Iwakuni, sword dangling at his belt. Women flashed him smiles and bowed at length. Several small boys pretend-marched alongside him, and men, even aged men, stepped out of his way, smiled and offered greetings. Masafumi tried to humble himself, but it was useless, given the adoration. Still, he was acutely self-conscious, blushing red more than once.

I haven't even done anything worthy, just the three years in that hellhole at Eta Jima! Please, save your praise for the heroes fighting in China! Those were his thoughts, but to verbalize them to the citizens would seem unkind, a reprimand, so Masafumi smiled and nodded with grace.

They were waiting at the gate. His father, mother, brother and sister lined up in a row, anticipation written on their faces. They tried to remain stoic, but emotion overcame polite manners and they applauded spontaneously as he neared. The fledging officer's face burned with embarrassment as he returned their bows of greeting.

Inside, Masafumi knelt across the low table from his father as his mother served green tea. His sister brought sweets, and then sat at his feet looking at him with big eyes. Saburo, his little brother, was awed beyond words. Timid as a bunny, he reached out to touch Masafumi's insignia and uniform. Masafumi offered his sleeve and Saburo rubbed his fingers along the single gold braid of an Imperial Japanese Navy ensign. Their eyes met for a long moment, then Masafumi playfully pushed him away.

"I shall have to excel," Masafumi said, grinning, "or you will outrank me someday!" The family laughed, and Saburo's words spilled from a huge smile. "You are the one destined to bring honor to the family name, Masafumi. You shall make us proud!" He scrambled to his feet and bowed as if for the Emperor.

Rocky shakes his head, the pain of his recollections heavy upon him. He buries his face into his hands.

"Pride and honor to our name? How was I to know a few years later I would not only steal Saburo's name, but his very identity as well." Rocky takes a deep breath and forces himself to continue.

It is a movie in his mind's eye, Masafumi's last day of leave. His family, dressed in traditional Japanese robes, labored up a dusty path. They carried armloads of flowers and bottles of saki, not for themselves, but for their long dead ancestors. It had been hot that summer day, and Masafumi recalled the welcoming breeze that eased their fatigue.

Their destination was a large stone crypt, half buried into the mountainside. Guarding the valley below from the cobalt blue of the Pacific was the distant sentinel of the thriving city of Hiroshima.

The clan gathered around as Masafumi's father unlocked and opened the heavy iron door. The patriarch removed a dozen large urns from the crypt, and lined them up in rows outside the door. The rest of the family adorned them with flowers, their fragrance competing with the earthy dankness of the tomb. With great reverence, food and drink offerings were placed in the crypt and everyone offered prayers for the many generations of deceased.

"Masafumi, come here."

Masafumi stepped up to his father, not sure what to expect.

"You are destined for great things, now and in the future. Our ancestors expect nothing less and they will help you succeed. When the way forward is difficult and despair is upon you, seek them out. They will take care of you. Do not forget this — do you understand?"

Not sure he does, Masafumi nevertheless stands at attention and gives the expected answer.

"Yes, sir, of course. I shall always be faithful to our ancestors and the family honor."

"A gift for you from the family. Steer by the stars to the heavens." A formal smile etched on his face, he presents a shiny brass sextant to Masafumi. He runs his finger along the name carved into the metal — *Ensign Masafumi Konishi*. The lump in his throat chokes any words, so Masafumi clutches the sextant to his chest and bows as far as he could, afraid the family may see his weakness.

The thought of his long ago tears brings Rocky to the moment that changed his life. All their lives.

* * * * *

His knees suddenly threatened to give way, as if someone punched him hard in the stomach. The other young naval officers, standing alongside in formation, looked at each other in similar shock and disbelief. Did they just hear correctly?

Before them stood Isoroku Yamamoto, Fleet Admiral of the Imperial Japanese Navy. He was resplendent in his dress white naval uniform, a plethora of medals on his chest clinking as he moved. His words resonated in the confined room: "You have been selected to strike a blow to the heart of the American fleet. Your target is Pearl Harbor, Hawaiian Islands."

"We had expected a battle, but this, an attack on the enemy fleet and its home base, was breathtaking! We were absolutely stunned, but our resolve was never in doubt. We began final preparations immediately.

"Also at this time, we were teamed with the other selected crewman in our two-man sub. This is how I met Petty Officer Fujitta. He reported to me at the dock where our sub was moored." Across those many years, Rocky can still see a young Petty Officer Fujitta approaching. He wore working coveralls, a soft hat and had a jaunty step to his stride. At precisely ten feet, Fujitta snapped a salute, followed by an appropriate bow. Masafumi returned the salute. Neither man smiled or exchanged pleasantries, nor were they expected to.

"Although he was the only crewman, because I was the captain and an officer, he was officially called my 'aide.'"

"'Your aide returns,'" Lori says softly, realizing the significance of the words for the first time.

Rocky nods, a grim look on his face. "Fujitta was capable. Not educated, but clever with machines and engines. We were united by our spirit and our mission and worked well together. Today I guess you would call it bonding.

"In November, 1941, the midgets were attached to the decks of the mother subs and we began our transit to Pearl Harbor. The midgets were 46-tons, just a fraction of the 3000-ton fleet subs carrying them, but we had two powerful torpedoes, and a top surface speed of 24 knots. Our main engine was electric, with a small diesel for auxiliary power."

Rocky clears his throat, his words tense with emotion.

"We were ten miles south of Pearl Harbor by the evening of December 6..."

Even forty years later, he can remember his heart racing when he got the message. "Sir, the captain wants to see you." Masafumi, dressed in his working overalls, looked up from the letter he was writing. He squeezed his way down the narrow passageway and to the mothership captain's open cabin door.

"Sir, Ensign Konishi reporting as ordered!" The captain, dressed in naval whites with a stiff choker collar, sat hunched over a small foldout table.

"Enter. Close the door behind you." His stare was as hard as cold steel as the ensign stood at rigid attention in the cramped cabin. Masafumi tried to read his face.

He wondered if he was worthy of the task?

Dispensing with any preface, the captain took a message out of a protective folder marked with a large red X.

"Admiral Yamamoto sends a message: 'The moment has arrived.' he read. 'The rise or fall of our empire is at stake. Everyone do his duty.'" Masafumi saluted, focused straight ahead, but inside his guts were churning. The captain barked a dismissal and Masafumi spun around, ducked out of the cabin, and made his way to the launch station. Perhaps triggered by the grim determination on his face, every crewman Masafumi encountered stopped and stared at him.

They knew. They didn't know exactly what, but they knew.

Fujitta was waiting for him at the boarding station, as was the launch crew. Masafumi nodded to Fujitta and without a word, the petty officer scampered up the ladder, through the hatch, and into the sub attached above. Masafumi was just as quick and in a few seconds, he was inside the midget. The air was pleasantly fresh, absent the foul smelling potpourri of human excretory functions that permeated the mother ship. It served as a good omen — air as pure as their resolve.

Masafumi looked down at the expectant faces of the crewmen of the mothership. "Banzai! Banzai! Banzai!" they shouted in unison. Trying not to think, Masafumi swallowed hard and closed the heavy hatch with a clang.

Chapter 27

In the sunrise twilight, the harbor was in an innocent rest. A few cars with their headlights on meandered along the shoreline road. Mostly the base was asleep, awaiting the sun. Here and there through the periscope, Masafumi could see a few sailors engaged in typical morning routines aboard the anchored ships. Only a couple of motor launches disturbed the otherwise tranquil Pearl Harbor waters. Slowly a line of battleships, moored two-by-two, came into sight.

"Battleship Row, Fujitta," Masafumi reported. "We are here."

Fujitta didn't reply, but took a deep breath and nodded.

Just as he was about to lower the periscope, Masafumi saw a formation of aircraft approaching in the distance. He jammed the periscope controller down.

"It's on! The attack is on!" he shouted. A moment later, the miniature submarine experienced a jolting *thud*, then several more in quick succession.

They raced to get the sub into firing position. Masafumi spun the wheel and willed the sluggish beast to turn faster, but the heading indicator crept across the compass card with the velocity of a slug on a cold day. Another *thud* rocked the boat, and Fujitta struggled with the bow planes to maintain proper depth.

Masafumi raised the periscope and swung it hard around. A great gray battleship, very close, appeared dead ahead. Sailors in various states of undress ran about on the decks. A few stopped to look skyward, then ran even faster. As Masafumi stared, bombers with the Rising Sun insignia swooped by in every direction. A smudge of black smoke emerged from the target's interior.

"Arm torpedo one!" Masafumi shouted.

Fujitta finished arming the firing circuitry and yelled, "Torpedo one armed, Sir!"

Masafumi made a last correction to the heading. "Fire torpedo one!"

Fujitta didn't answer - a boom of compressed air and the whine of the torpedo engine starting was more than enough response. Through the periscope, Masafumi peered at the streak of torpedo bubbles as it charged straight as an arrow toward the looming battleship.

Masafumi dialed in maximum magnification on the periscope controls. In the midst of the mayhem on the deck of the battleship, he saw a tall, redheaded sailor pause. He pointed to the approaching torpedo track, then started to run away. Before he got ten feet, the torpedo struck and the explosion sent him and a huge column of water rocketing high into the air. Then the ship crumbled and disappeared in a thunderstorm of flame and smoke.

Masafumi stared in disbelief, his elation with the attack replaced with the reality of war. The ship was a mass of fire and smoke; and bodies, hundreds of them, floated in the water alongside.

Yes, they were the enemy, but they were sailors, too...

Another *thud* brought Masafumi back to reality. He snapped down the periscope and consulted the planning chart prepared from local spy reports.

In a subdued voice, he informed Fujitta, "USS Arizona destroyed. Stand by for second attack, arm torpedo two."

"Aye, aye, Sir."

Masafumi cranked the wheel several turns to the left and waited a few moments for the sub to respond. Then he raised the periscope to find his target. He left the view of the Arizona and swung the periscope further.

A supercharged shot of adrenaline exploded through Masafumi's nerves. Destroyer! Headed right for the periscope.

"Dive! Emergency dive!" he yelled to Fujitta, and jerked down the scope. The thrashing sound of the destroyer propellers rapidly increased, as did the rising panic in Fujitta and Masafumi. They frantically struggled to get the sub deeper. The whole boat vibrated from the pounding propellers. Then — they heard what they feared most: two splashes, close at hand.

Masafumi shouted "Hold fast!" and both crouched down jamming their hands over their ears. A gigantic sledgehammer smashed into the sub, again as the second depth charge exploded alongside. Gauges shattered, paint and rivets flew off the bulkheads and the primary lights went out. Masafumi and Fujitta slammed into metal objects all over the crew compartment. Then — blackness.

* * * * *

"How long I was unconscious I do not know, but it was for several hours. When I awoke, Fujitta had restored most of the electrical circuits and bandaged my wound. I still carry the scar today." Rocky gestures to a silvery Y-shaped scar above his eyebrow.

"We rested and waited until dark, then escaped out the channel. There was still incredible confusion and activity, lots of fires and explosions, searchlights sweeping the sky."

"But where were you going?" Jared asks. "You couldn't make it back to Japan in that little sub, could you?"

"Well, no," Rocky says. "Our plan was to proceed to a rendezvous point near Niihau Island. There, we would scuttle the midget sub because it was impossible to mate them up again at sea." Rocky leans back in his chair a little. His voice softens.

"But our luck had run out. When the sun came up, we had to submerge and could make only four knots on the weakened batteries. We reached as far as Kauai that night, but we were far off course because of the strong current. Finally, our batteries and fuel were exhausted and we drifted for hours. It was obvious the submarine would beach by the next day. It was imperative that our secret weapon not fall into enemy hands, so I decided to sink it while we were still in deep water."

* * * * *

A beautiful sunrise warmed the eastern sky. We ignored it and made preparations to scuttle the sub, our tasks hampered by the constant rolling and pitching of the boat. I stuffed the logbook into a waterproof bag and carefully sealed it. I picked up the sextant from my father, stared at it with a smile for a moment, then placed it in a holder on the conning tower bulkhead.

"Are you ready?"

"Aye, Sir."

"Let's go." They grabbed life preservers, donned them and scrambled out the conning tower hatch. In the dim light, Fujitta looked at the roiling water and hesitated. He took off his shoes and looked to Masafumi for confirmation. Masafumi nodded and Fujitta took the plunge. He surfaced, spat water and started to swim for the mountainous coastline a few miles distant.

"Swim hard, I'm setting the explosives." Masafumi yelled. He reached down into the conning tower and started the scuttling fuse, then plunged into the ocean. Slowed by the waterproof bag, the two swam about a hundred yards, paused, and looked back. The little black sub, graceless as a dead whale in the rolling swells, suddenly emitted a resounding *whump!* Masafumi and Fujitta yelped as a gut-punch concussion reached them. The sub rose in a cauldron of boiling white water and an instant later disappeared beneath the surface. Only an expanding froth of bubbles marked its grave.

* * * * *

Who is this man who sits across from me?

Too respectful to scream her thoughts, nonetheless Lori is shocked and dismayed. Her stomach churns and threatens revolt. She could not be more stunned if Rocky had presented irrefutable evidence he was an alien from another planet.

Blew up the USS Arizona? Killed a thousand plus American sailors? Not exactly an entry you'd expect to find on the resume of the newly elected Governor of Hawaii!

Tears long gone, Lori manages little more than a grim silence as Rocky continues his disembodied narrative, as if recounting an incredible story in which he somehow found himself.

"We reached the island without too much difficulty, but then nearly drowned in the surf. We crawled up on the beach and passed out from exhaustion. When we woke, we found ourselves in what I now know was Kalalau Valley, one of the most isolated spots in the Hawaiian Islands. In those days it was uninhabited, home only to wild pigs and goats.

"For several days we hid, uncertain as to what to do. Eventually hunger drove us to explore the valley. We found bananas, breadfruit, coconuts; the papayas were abundant. Later we were able to trap animals. We only cooked at night in a sheltered area so no one would see the smoke. We did not believe anyone saw us come ashore, but we could not be sure. One thing we were convinced of, though, was that we would be tortured and killed if they caught us. Sounds paranoid now, but we truly believed that."

A faint smile crosses his face as he shakes his head.

"We built a crude shelter, and piled up wood and brush for a signal fire. But we never saw a Japanese ship. How could we know we would be there for five years! That I would end up as Governor? And killing Fujitta?"

Months pass, then two years. Our shelter was visibly improved, but we now looked very much like the castaways that we were - long hair, dirty and unkempt clothes, bleached and ripped in places. Camp duties became the focus of our lives, that and escape to Japan. But slowly our relationship changed.

I was weaving palm fronds into a carry basket. Fujitta husked coconuts nearby.

"Fujitta, forget the coconuts," I called loudly, glancing at the sky. "Help me with the weaving so we can explore the goat trail before it disappears again with the rains."

Fujitta didn't look up, instead continued to work the tough husk off the nut.

"Fujitta! Did you not hear me? Here at once!" I yelled angrily, throwing down the partially completed basket.

Fujitta looked up and glared at me without a word. He turned and sulked off to the stream to get some water, then sauntered back and grabbed the basket.

I stared hard at him for a long moment, uncertain as to what to do as Fujitta worked the fronds with deliberate slowness. We worked in silence for a while.

"To travel the goat trail is stupid."

"What did you say?" Masafumi responded, not sure he heard such impertinence.

"We have been here two years, have seen no one, and no one has seen us. To journey the goat trail, any trail, invites discovery. It is a stupid plan."

I jumped to my feet. "Enough! If you are too lazy I will go alone in the morning. We need tools, fishing equipment, news of our victories. You may stay and tend camp like a woman!" With that, I snatched away the basket and stomped off, blood in my face and anger in my step.

Chapter 28

In the early evening darkness, I laboriously made an entry in the logbook with the stub of a pencil, squinting in the faint light. Fujitta rocked in a homemade hammock a short distance away. "Fujitta," I called, "some more firewood, if you please."

Fujitta didn't move from his hammock. "I'm tired. Get it yourself."

I leaped to my feet, stormed over and upset the hammock. Fujitta hit the ground hard. He jumped up, fists clenched, ready to fight. We faced each other inches apart, eyes blazing.

"You are a lazy and insolent man!" I shouted into Fujitta's face. "It must be your poor upbringing and bad breeding! I should have you court-martialed!" Fujitta growled but said nothing. We continued to face each other, nose-to-nose. Our dirty faces blossomed with sweat, glistening in the flickering firelight. Fujitta's upper lip curled into a snarl, then he reached down suddenly — I jumped back, fists up to defend myself. Fujitta didn't draw a weapon, but rather unhooked the hammock. Without a word he carried it off into the dark, leaving me in a smoldering rage.

* * * * *

My woven palm frond hat did little to keep the misty rain out of my eyes, which made my steps even more precarious as I picked my way along the rut of a trail. I stopped to get my bearings and adjusted the carry basket strapped to my back. From my perch high on the side of the mountain, I could just make out pineapple fields far away in the next valley.

More than a day's trudge through this riot of jungle undergrowth. Still, an unguarded barn could make it all worth it. A good fishing pole and some real tools would put Fujitta in a better mood!

Balancing carefully, I inched forward along the near vertical mountainside. I looked down and shuddered.

A misstep here...

Without warning the sodden ground gave way and I plunged down the slope, bouncing off rocks and tree trunks. My yell was useless to slow the fall, so I grabbed for roots and plants that flew by. I picked up speed...

...until slamming to a halt on the unyielding rocks. Stillness...except for the rain of dirt and pebbles pelting me.

I tried to scream to drive away the massive hurt, but the wind was out of me and I could only gasp and sputter.

The pain! The pain!

I tried to move my leg away from its excruciating torture. Nothing happened — I was wedged solid in the rocks and could move but one arm, barely. My face was jammed against the rocks, too. No, it was softer than rock, strangely familiar...

It's...my foot. I can't move my head because my foot's hard against it.

From down the hall comes the clang of a cell door closing, followed by inmate curses and threats. Rocky ignores the distraction and continues.

"That was my lowest point ever. No matter what I did, I could not move an inch. All night I lay there, crying like a baby. I am not ashamed to say I begged for my mother to save me. Or anyone to kill me.

"Early the next morning I made another effort to free myself, but I was still hopelessly wedged into the boulders. I cursed my misfortune, my arrogance and my stupidity. Fujitta's words tormented my mind as much as the rocks did my body. *Nothing good can come of this.*

"How right he was! I treated him so shabbily, now he was my only hope in the world. Would he come looking for me? Why should he, after I humiliated him?

"I was beyond despondent, but in the morning light, I saw my last hope — my service knife. It was just out of reach, but if I dug away dirt from the bank, I thought I could get it to slide down so that I could reach it. With it, one strong stab to my jugular and my problems were over. I was ready, prepared to end it all." His tone was calm, matter-of-fact, but resolve seeped from his words.

"But then an angel appeared on the slope above."

Rocky reaches over and takes Lori's hands in his. He feels her tense.

"Lori, what I saw truly was from heaven. It was your mother, Keiko, looking down at me. She didn't say a word, then disappeared and a couple of hours later returned with her mother and father. Together they carried me back to their farmhouse, high in the mountain wilderness. That was when the second half of my life began."

Time has dulled the sensations, but Rocky remembered laying on a futon, sweating from the pain. Keiko gently cleaned his face as her mother stood nearby and watched.

"Thank you... very much...," Masafumi croaked weakly in Japanese.

"Who are you?" Keiko asked, also in Japanese, curiosity plain upon her face.

Masafumi grimaced and struggled to form an answer, but gave up and said nothing. Her upturned lips signaled a small smile of forgiveness.

Keiko's mother made tea in an ornate pot and passed a cup of it to Keiko. She helped Masafumi drink. Scanning the dirty, unkempt stranger lying before her, Momma San asked, "What is his name?"

"He seems to have forgotten. Maybe we should name him ourselves."

"Like a puppy? If we do, we may have to keep him!"

Keiko giggled and Masafumi managed a small smile, reacting as much to a soothing female voice as to the humor.

"Oh, since we found him in the rocks, maybe we should call him 'Rocky,'" Keiko suggested.

"As you wish, but we need to get him to a doctor. Your father will go down to the plantation tomorrow to get some men to stretcher him down the mountain."

Masafumi suddenly sat up on his elbows, eyes wide with fear, panic in his voice.

"No!" he screamed. The women recoiled as if stung.

Chapter 29

R ocky pauses, collecting his thoughts. "About this time, I realized they had been speaking Japanese. I guess I was in shock from the pain, but it began to sink in that these were *Imin*, Japanese immigrants brought to Hawaii since the 1880's to be field hands. Of course, you know all about that, Lori, you've heard your grandparents speak of it often."

Lori leans forward and nods. The frowns leave her face for a moment.

"When I heard talk about a doctor, the fear came. They could have done anything with me and there was nothing I could do about it. In desperation, I told them everything. About the sub, the Pearl Harbor attack, my family in Japan, my whole life story. Everything."

Masafumi, propped on the futon, faced Keiko and her parents. They listened raptly and from time-to-time, glanced at each other with disbelief etched on their faces. Exhausted, Masafumi finished and lay back. Keiko and her parents sat in silence for a few minutes, then filed outside to a picnic table visible in the yard. Masafumi could not hear their conversation, but it was soon clear they were arguing, evident by the animated gestures from each. Finally, Keiko hugged her father and they returned to the house.

"It was a difficult and very risky decision, but they agreed to keep my secret and take care of me. It was an act of true courage."

Keiko sat by the futon, a corncob in hand. She looked at Masafumi, who nodded, opened his mouth and closed his eyes. Keiko placed the corncob across Masafumi's teeth and he bit down on it. Keiko's mother and father quickly pulled Masafumi's broken leg into a set position. Masafumi screamed around the corncob and pounded his fist on the ground. He strained upward, but was held down by Keiko, the look of anguish on her face nearly matching Masafumi's.

"It was six months before I could walk without pain. During that time, I read anything I could get my hands on and was greatly depressed with the news of our defeat at the battles of Midway, Tarawa, Saipan. It was so frustrating to be flat on my back or hobbling around, unable to help my countrymen.

"But gradually I fell completely and deeply in love with Keiko." The memories of those days warm his words and he softly rubs his hands together.

"You know, in Japan love is not essential for marriage — or even hoped for. But after devoting my mind, body and soul to war for years, I was worn out mentally and physically. Love swept over me like a wave and I was unable to resist.

"It seems bizarre, given the circumstances, but those were the best years of my life." For the first time since Fujitta walked into his office, Rocky manages a genuine smile.

"It sounds strange to hear you say that, what with all the success you had later on," Jared interjects.

"I know, but happiness comes in many ways and there on the mountain top, I found love and contentment. There was only one thing that bothered me - immensely. That was the guilt of abandoning Fujitta."

Now fully healed, Masafumi packed a bag with travel items at the kitchen table. "Don't...don't go! You belong here." Keiko pleaded.

Masafumi hoisted the pack to his shoulder and gave Keiko a long, loving look. She gazed up at him with tearful, imploring eyes.

"It has been almost a year. I cannot abandon Fujitta to the jungle by himself. I am the captain and he is my responsibility. I must do the right thing." Rejecting further discussion, Masafumi turned and strode out into the morning mist.

"I brought canned meats and candy - delicious treats for a castaway. I wanted to win Fujitta over quickly and reestablish good relations with him. It took five days to reach the valley — my leg was not as strong as I thought. After two more days of searching I found him at a new camp some distance from the other."

Unseen by Fujitta, Masafumi emerged from the jungle and paused to take in the scene. Then he walked into the sunshine towards Fujitta and stopped a dozen yards away. Hairy and unkempt, Fujitta wore nothing than rags. He squatted, picked up a small handful of sea snails from a coconut shell bowl and ate them raw one at a time

"Fujitta-san!" Masafumi called out in Japanese, smiling broadly. "Your captain returns!"

Fujitta, startled, jumped up. He grabbed a large stick and whipped around to defend himself. Masafumi kept smiling and extended his open arms in welcome. Gradually Fujitta recognized him and lowered the stick. Still, he did not smile or speak.

"It took a while, but gradually he let me approach as I held out the food gifts. Fujitta was shocked to see me, he said, he was sure that I had been captured or killed. To him I was a living ghost. I almost cried when I saw the wretched condition he was in."

Fujitta and Masafumi squatted in the shade together. Masafumi talked as Fujitta ate from a Vienna sausage container. He took very small bites and chewed with exquisite slowness, licking his lips frequently.

"Fujitta listened silently as I told him of my accident and the family who nursed me back to health," Rocky says. "Then he asked a few questions about the progress of the war and my answers cast a shadow upon his face."

Fujitta finished the canned meats and licked his fingers thoroughly. His dirty, tanned face reddened as Masafumi detailed Japan's battle defeats.

Masafumi came to the part he dreaded. "Fujitta, the truth must be told – the war is lost for Japan."

Fujitta jumped to his feet and exploded: "Lies! Lies! Konishi, you are a coward and a fool! I am ashamed to have you as my captain!"

Masafumi started to rise to calm Fujitta from his rant. "Fujitta, I would not..." Without warning Fujitta hit a powerful blow to Masafumi's face with his fist. Masafumi sprawled backward, landing flat on his back.

Rocky shakes his head, the pain and disbelief still keen in his mind. "I was more stunned by the disrespect than the blow. After all, I was still an officer in the Imperial Navy, his superior, and hitting me was an absolutely unthinkable act."

Fujitta sprinted into the jungle. Masafumi rubbed his jaw, and then got up to yell, "Fujitta! Come back!"

"I searched for Fujitta for two days, but I could not find him. Nor could I find the sub's logbook that I had so diligently kept up. I suppose he had hidden it somewhere in anticipation soldiers might come for him. Oh, how I wish I could've found that book!"

Chapter 30

Rocky looks upwards without focus for a time, runs fingers through his hair and sighs. After a pause, he steels himself and continues.

"Eventually I went back to Keiko and the farm. I had terrific feelings of guilt for a while, but Keiko's love helped me overcome them. Then quite suddenly, the war was over. I was sickened by the news of a super weapon and the destruction it caused at Hiroshima — that was my family hometown! I was in a panic to return to Japan. It's almost funny — today it takes less than a day to get to Japan from here, but in 1946, it took me six months. I borrowed what little money Keiko's parents had and set off.

A kaleidoscope of memories floods Rocky's mind: Carrying a small suitcase and dressed in a cheap, ill-fitting suit and tie, struggling on his weak leg up the gangplank of a rusty tramp steamer; wet with sweat, crowding into a standing-room-only Korean train; limping along on a long and dusty Japanese road abutted by bombed out factories and homes. Ragged, rail-thin civilians and soldiers shuffling by, or sitting at the roadside begging for food; reaching a mountain overlook and gazing in horror at the devastated city of Hiroshima; walking slowly up what remained of a devastated residential street.

"I finally found where my family's house had been, but it was only a pile of ashes. I knew my mother, father, sister and brother's ashes must also have been among them. I was sick with sorrow." Rocky's nose wrinkles when he remembers the stench.

Physically and mentally weary, Masafumi walked among the burned remains of the family house. He carefully scooped some ashes into a blackened ceramic urn he found, and stood for a long moment with his eyes closed. His face a mask of pain, he bowed deeply to where the house had been and then walked slowly up the devastated road carrying the urn.

"After hours of walking, I reached the family crypt. Without the key, I had to smash the lock with a big rock.

"When I opened the crypt, I got a huge surprise. Gold, lots of it. Solid bars of gold, much of it with the markings of the Chinese and Philippine governments. How my father got them, I do not know. Perhaps it was legitimate payment from the Japanese government for his wartime manufacturing in those countries. Most likely, I am ashamed to say, it was loot from criminal activities in the conquered countries."

Lori abruptly shoves her chair back and stands up.

"That's enough! I can't take anymore!"

"Lori, please. It's too late now, but you need to know the truth."

"Lori..." Jared leaves the request unsaid.

She hesitates, but eases back into her chair, silent, emotionally spent. She rubs her temples for a while, and then settles for twirling a strand of her hair repeatedly, angrily.

"In any event it was soon evident that even bars of gold are worthless if there is nothing to buy. Japan was prostrate, just absolutely devastated. And I soon found that returning servicemen were treated with the utmost contempt and scorn. We were blamed for the loss of the war and the destruction it caused. I had people spit on me in the street - repeatedly. So different from when we first marched off to war!" He sighs!

Jared asks softly, "But how did you get back to Hawaii?"

Rocky shakes his head, recalling the difficulties. "Getting back was not as easy as leaving had been. It took two years and a substantial amount of the gold for bribes before I was able to return in 1947 – using my brother's identity. That part was simple – all the local records were destroyed by the bomb and officials just took my word for it when I went to apply for identity papers."

Rocky leans back and gestures expansively to Lori with his hand.

"You pretty much can guess the rest of the story. I got back to the farm and laid low for a few years, just to be safe. Gradually I realized my identity would not be challenged, so Keiko and I married and moved to Oahu and I moved in with them until I finished university. Then I used the remaining gold to start the construction company. It was tiny at first, but the timing was perfect. Statehood was just around the corner and the market just exploded.

"I settled into my new life, became 'Rocky' and forgot about Masafumi. Eventually I began taking an interest in politics. That was a mistake!" Rocky shakes his head, still amazed at his stupidity.

"I got too ambitious, too successful. When I was elected as the first Japanese-American governor, it made big headlines in Japan. Unfortunately, one of the people who saw it was Fujitta. He knew who I was right away – scar above my eye, the limp, and of course my family name."

"The only person alive who could have figured it out... what a shame," muses Jared.

Rocky continued. "Fujitta was an *obuyan* in the *yakusa* by then. I don't know how and when he made it back to Japan, but when he did, he found the same thing I did: ostracism and contempt, practically impossible to get any kind of work. So he did what many ex-soldiers did – he turned to crime. All this time he had saved the logbook, and with a page of it, he set off to see me. You know, I thought the time I spent crushed into the rocks was the worst day of my life. But the day Fujitta walked into my campaign office a few weeks ago was far worse..."

Rocky, in a fashionable aloha shirt and reading glasses, sat at his desk in the campaign headquarters office. Precisely hung photos of important people contrasted with a slew of papers piled haphazardly on the desk and nearby tables.

The common area and its multitude of staff desks and cubicles, was visible through the glass office walls. It was after working hours and only a few people milled about. Lori, dressed in jeans, collared shirt and wearing her hair in a ponytail, stood beside Rocky and handed over pages of the inauguration guest list they were considering.

The door to the office opened slowly. Rocky glanced up, just long enough to register a rather rough looking visitor, no doubt a job applicant, probably a Parks and Recreation guy.

The stocky, middle-aged Japanese man stood there motionless and silent, his eyes fixed in a burning stare at Rocky. His hair was cropped very close and a visible scar was carved into his jaw. Odd for Hawaii, he wore black slacks with a black button-up shirt and white tie. Multicolored tattoos covered his arms, revealed as he crossed them over his chest. Rocky gave a faint nod of welcome returned to his paperwork. Lori would find out his qualifications and send him to the appropriate staffer.

The man stepped forward.

"You cannot believe the terror I felt when I finally looked up and recognized him — Fujitta! Standing right in front of me." Rocky said.

"It was like seeing an evil ghost. I had put him out of my mind decades before, neither wondering nor caring what had happened to him.

"*Anata no shimobe ga modette mairimashita,*" Fujitta said in Japanese. "Your aide returns."

Rocky felt the color drain from his face. He took off his glasses, placed them on the desk and rose slowly to his feet. Never taking his eyes off Fujitta he said, "Lori, close the office and send everyone home. Do it now." Lori hesitated, then scurried out. She glanced back as she closed Rocky's office door behind her, doubt and anxiety on her face.

Uninvited, Fujitta flopped down in the chair across the desk from Rocky. Fujitta looked around at the awards and pictures of Rocky with important people. Rocky eased back into his chair, although the primal instinct part of his brain screamed, "Run!"

"You have done well for yourself, Konishi-San," Fujitta said, his voice heavy with sarcasm. "Or should I call you 'Governor?' Not bad for a piece of shit traitor!"

Fujitta offered up the most insincere of smiles. "I bet you never worried how poor I was when you were sailing around in your yacht, spending your father's gold, did you?"

"How did you...the gold, I mean?" Rocky could feel the wet stain of his armpits grow perceptibly.

"You think because you were captain, I must be stupid, yes? And you from good, patriotic family? Hah! Your father was just a well-dressed criminal, no different from the *Yamaguchi-gumi* he partner with to steal from Japan's conquests - gold was just part. Art, antiquities, jewels, anything of value. But your father only wanted the gold. When I was promoted to first level *obuyan* in the 1950s, I was sent to find the crooked businessman in Hiroshima, or more importantly, his gold. I never knew he was your father. Not until I see your picture in news couple of months ago, then I put it together. Pretty smart guy, huh?"

Fujitta again crossed his multicolored tattooed arms over his chest, jutting out his jaw. Smug satisfaction beamed from his face as he nodded his head in agreement with himself.

Rocky's stomach churned with nausea. He searched for the right words, but none came.

"Know what it was like in Japan after the war?" Fujitta lectured. "For those of us who didn't have bars of gold, I mean? Ever had old women and widows slap your face and curse you because of the disgrace you caused by losing? Or at least, by living?"

Rocky finally found his voice. "Fujitta, I did not ask for my good fortune! I made the best of what I had — you would have done the same!" His hands gripped the arms of the chair as if they were around Fujitta's neck.

Fujitta leaned forward and spat hatefully, "Shut up!" He continued in a snarl, "Now has come time to make amends, my captain, not apologies. You saw the 'Godfather' movie, yes? Well, I am going to make you an offer *you* can't refuse. We are going to become business partners..."

"No, I, I..." Rocky sputtered.

"Let's start with ten million U.S. dollars for your buy-in," said Fujitta.

"Impossible!" Rocky exploded. "I could never manage that!"

"Oh, yes you will," Fujitta sneered. "And here's why." Fujitta slid a weathered, handwritten document across the desk to Rocky.

"Remember that? The page from our sub's log with coordinates of scuttling — in your handwriting!"

Rocky recoiled in his seat as if Fujitta had tossed a live cobra in front of him.

Fujitta sat back, mirth dancing on his face. "How many Americans you kill on USS Arizona, Governor?" Fujitta laughed mercilessly. Rocky stared at the logbook page in paralyzed silence. The long forgotten words and numbers jumped out at him, stinging him with terror.

Fujitta continued his emotional torture of Rocky: "I'm going to need some guns and cocaine shipped to me — those are hard to get in Japan, you know? Hard for me, but the Governor can do anything!"

The fear level rose higher in Rocky's gut with Fujitta's every word. "It doesn't work that way here, you idiot! This isn't some third-world banana republic!"

Fujitta grinned cruelly and held up a three-fingered hand for Rocky to see. "Hey, be nice and maybe I let you keep all your fingers!"

Rocky glanced out to the common area. Campaign staff workers stared at the scene through the glass office walls. Lori reached the intercom and punched in numbers, glancing toward his office.

"Then I need your services for..., how do the Americans say it, 'money laundering?' Hah! Laundering! Know how many times in the valley that I had my laundry done while you were off screwing that *Imin* whore? What was her name? Keiko?"

For a moment, Rocky did not react. Then his adrenal glands injected a mega-dose of adrenalin straight into his nervous system. For an instant, his vision flashed red and time crashed into slow motion. He didn't think, couldn't think; instead he saw himself as if in a movie, his face contorted with rage and hate.

Rocky jerked his revolver from the desk drawer and leaped to his feet. He could feel the cold steel and textured wooden grip as he held the gun straight out toward Fujitta's chest. Without a word Rocky pulled the trigger, saw the hammer come back, then snap forward. Fujitta had no time to react. The pistol bucked in Rocky's hand and his eardrums *paingeddd* as the sonic shock wave hit them, but he felt no pain.

The first bullet was a gut shot — now it was Fujitta's turn to be shocked. The arms of the intruder flailed spasmodically. His face blossomed surprise, then twisted into a grimace as the second slug pierced him.

Rocky felt his jaw clench even tighter. He squeezed the trigger again as Fujitta frantically waved his vividly inked arms in front of him.

Another gunshot punished Rocky's battered eardrums as the bullet exploded through Fujitta's out-stretched palms and hit him in the throat harder than a major league line drive. He opened his mouth to yell, but the gurgling blood drowned the words.

Again and again, Rocky felt the recoil jolt his hand, saw the pistol hammer rise and fall, heard the *crack* of the rounds blasting out of the gun. His mind video-recorded the results: Fujitta jerked again and again as the bullets smashed him. Crimson mist airbrushed on the glass wall nearby. His chair tipped over backwards, propelled by his convulsions and the lead hammers slamming into his twisted body.

Finally the gun clicked on an empty chamber. The mind-movie ended abruptly. Rocky slowly lowered the weapon. For the first time he heard the screams and shouts of the campaign workers, felt the pain of his abused eardrums. Through the wisps of gun smoke floating in the room, he stared down at the bleeding but already quite dead Fujitta. He dropped the over-heated revolver to the floor with a clunk and the weight of the world settled onto his shoulders.

In the jailhouse conference room, new-found tears stream down Lori's face. Rocky staggers to his feet, his confession done. Lori hurries around the table to hug him.

The words drain from his emotionally exhausted psyche.

"I have betrayed two countries — Japan, the country of my birth I abandoned, and America, the country that gave me so much, but who I deceived. Lori, I'm so sorry..."

There is nothing more for any of them to say.

Chapter 31

As quietly as the angry exhaust pipes allow, Jared pulls his Corvette into the dark parking lot of Lori's apartment complex. It is near midnight and they are both exhausted by Rocky's revelations and the late hour. A convenient space beckons them and Jared shuts the engine down before the neighbors are roused to complain about the noise. They sit for a while, Jared with his hands still on the wheel, saying nothing. The engine plays its soft cooling jingle as the trade winds wash the scent of plumerias over them.

"Do you want me to come in?" Jared asks finally.

Lori sighs. "I'm not good company now, Jared. I need time to decompress, and right now I'd rather be by myself at home than anywhere else. It's all just so... overwhelming...," Lori says, her gaze focused a million miles away.

"Yeah, I know. It sucks, doesn't it? It felt like being gut shot to me. I can't imagine how it ripped into you. Call me if you need me. No kidding, whenever, whatever. I don't think I'll have to worry about being on the flight schedule anytime soon."

Lori shakes off her trance and turns to him, her black hair a jarring contrast to her face, bone white in the moonlight.

"Jared...thanks...I had no idea what I was getting you into. You didn't deserve to get wrapped up in...in this kind of family stuff." She leans over, kisses and hugs him tightly for a long time. She feels his physical and psychic strength flow into her, enough to enable her to get out of the car. Jared waits until she safely unlocks her door and then waves okay.

He returns the wave and she slips inside. A turn of the key brings the big engine back to life with a growl. The Vette pauses at the gate, like a lion wanting to pounce. No challengers appear and Jared and the car disappear into the night, its roar rising and falling through the gears.

Inside, Lori leans against the door, eyes closed, listening to the fading rumble.

He really has come through for me, the only person in the world I can trust to help me deal with this shit. I wasn't sure I could count on him — I was wrong.

Lori double locks the door and switches some lights on as she walks over to drop her purse on the dining room table. She looks around, seeing with new eyes. The furnishings are first class, the work of a professional decorator with a handsome budget. The community pool sparkles outside the sliding glass doors, kept company by ritzy lanai lounge chairs and pregnant banana trees.

Did this all come from the looted gold? All my privilege? Is that who I am?

Lori sweeps into the kitchen, still angry, and ignores the dirty plates and college textbooks on the counter. Yesterday's clothes and shoes sloppily decorate a convenient barstool. She doesn't care about that either. Her eyes fall upon a large poster pinned to the wall, adorned with the "Freedom Network" logo and President Jimmy Carter's signature.

At least I got that on my own!

Lori reaches to turn off the security system before the grace period expires. Her hand jerks to a stop in mid-motion and she stares, trying to process.

Why is the cover off? And what's the thingy attached by alligator clips? Did Maintenance...

A hand shoots over her shoulder and clamps over her mouth. Another rips her arms into a lock position behind her back. Panicked, she struggles and tries to scream, but the big hand crushes her face, squeezing it like a vice. She's never fought a man before and is shocked at how powerful he is, bone-breaking strength turned loose against her.

His nauseating body odor fills her nose as he cinches her body tight against his. The raspy breath right behind her ear adds to the stench.

"Don't fight me. I'm not going to hurt you if you cooperate."

Lori continues to kick and push away, but the man ratchets down the hold until her arms almost come out of their sockets. Worse: big hand, small face, little air!

"Relax, honey, relax," the man says, this time with sugar in his voice. "I just want to talk a little business with you and I'm gone — okay?"

Lori doesn't believe this for a moment, but in seconds, she won't be resisting anything. She nods as best she can and the man relaxes the grip on her mouth. Her heart pounding like a bass drum in hyper-overdrive, Lori gasps, "Who...are...you?"

"Trazer. AKA, your new best friend. Now sit down." He shoves her roughly onto the sofa. She is afraid to look at him, but dares to anyway. Glaring down at her is a scary monster with green dragon tattoos, stained and broken teeth. Dirty blond hair and only half an ear on one side complete the picture. To Lori, he oozes evil like an outhouse emanates toxic odor, and she is trapped in this horror movie with him. For some reason, perhaps because his hands had been over her mouth, she finds his dirty fingernails particularly repulsive.

"You can take anything you want, just get out of here," Lori manages to get out of her heaving chest. She knows it's a very long shot that's all it will take to make this monster happy. What were those self-defense moves she learned? Her mind freezes — the maneuvers she remembers were standing up, not cowering on a sofa! Trazer says, "That's sweet of you, Lori, but I'm a businessman, not a thief."

A jagged bolt of fear goes straight to the pit of Lori's stomach and she feels panic rising again. She visualizes a run for the door, then remembers it's double-locked. She'll never open it in time.

"How...how do you know my name?"

"Oh, I'm one of your biggest non-fans. You've been putting a little too much sunshine on my business lately." Trazer walks over and rips the "Freedom Network" poster off the wall.

"And now you even got President Carter hyperventilating for you — real fuckin' nice. I thought Fujitta was going to take care of this for me, but it looks like I'm going to have to do it myself."

Fujitta's name comes out of left field for Lori — this is getting as bizarre as it is scary! "Fujitta?" Lori asks, "I thought he was..."

"Yeah, Fujitta was my Japan connection for this little, how should I say it, sex trade business operation I had. I spent a million dollars setting it up and Fujitta decides to get greedy and cut a side deal with Rocky, the dumb shit."

Trazer shakes his head, disgust dripping from his words. "And, of course, your dad goes crazy and blows Fujitta away. Didn't see that one coming! *You're* not going to go crazy on me, are you?"

"What do you want from me?" she says wearily.

"I've got a gift for you," Trazer says, a hint of mystery in his voice, hands on hips. He picks up a gym bag from the chair where it has been resting and plops it on the coffee table in front of Lori. "Go ahead, but be careful, it's a bomb — a nuke, in fact." An obscene grin stretches his face.

Lori hesitates, looks at the bag, and back at Trazer, then reaches in. Her fingers gingerly search the contents, feeling the rough texture of a square object. She knows what it is before she extricates it - Rocky's weathered submarine logbook. Suddenly Lori feels as if all the strength has left her body, and with it, her will to fight. She has never felt so fatigued. Hands trembling, she holds the book, staring at it as if it was a Japanese version of Pandora's Box.

"Biggest bomb to hit Hawaii since, since...ha!..Pearl Harbor!" Trazer cackles uproariously at his own wit. "You get to keep it as soon as you do me a few favors," he adds, bending towards her, hand on his knees, malevolence on his face.

Lori musters the last ounce of her will. "I'm not helping you, not now, not ever, you sick bastard!"

Trazer's hand darts out, knocking the book aside and grabs Lori's throat with crushing strength. He slaps her face so hard, one of her eyes loses focus. She tries to scream, but the cry is dammed by the vice-grip on her neck. He locks his forehead tight against hers, assaulting her with his vile breath. She tries to fight, but there's no fight left, only fear. Shaking, crying fear. Then the ultimate humiliation — her bladder releases and she feels the warm wet spreading beneath her legs. But it's his words that scare her most: "Oh, yes, you will, Lori, if you love your father...and you want to save your boyfriend from one hell of a payback. There's only one way out, baby..."

Chapter 32

There are a hundred or more outdoor beachside bars and lounges in Waikiki, all patronized by people with at least one thing in common — they want to have fun. At one particular bar, however, there is an exception. Lori is having anything but fun, instead, living another reel in her personal horror movie. Her two new blonde friends, however, didn't come all the way from San Diego to mope around.

"So, when you going to introduce us to this millionaire?" Melissa asks over the din of the noisy clientele. "He's not, like, really old, is he? That'd be kind of creepy." The breeze catches her long hair and she sweeps it from her face with just enough head toss to make it dramatic.

"Who cares?" Brittany giggles. "A free moonlight cruise on a yacht - woo hoo!" She gives a fist pump. "There's gonna be Mai Tai's, right?"

"Yeah, all you can handle," Lori says, not nearly so enthusiastically. She wears her reading glasses and floppy hat low on her head.

Melissa slurps the remainder of her drink, jumps up and shakes her boobs back and forth enough to send her lei orbiting like a hula-hoop. She yells, "Awright! Let's get this party started!" - loud enough that people nearby give her the fisheye.

* * * * *

Lori leads Melissa and Brittany along the dark docks of the Ala Wai Boat Harbor, glancing back frequently to make sure the boisterous duo haven't stumbled off the dock or stopped to pee in the water. The enticing sights and sounds of the nightlife of Waikiki buzz in the background, competing with the endless clanking of rigging on aluminum sailboat masts. A soft, warm breeze complements the moonlight shimmering across the placid ocean to make for a picture-perfect night. This is lost to Lori, whose main objective now is to deliver the girls without throwing up.

The little group approaches a sleek red and white cigarette boat, rocking gently in its moorings. Trazer and a couple of his thugs await them, standing around smoking while rock music blares from inside the boat.

Trazer, *trey chic* in a multicolored aloha shirt, white slacks and deck shoes, is all smiles. "Ahoy, mates! Welcome aboard!" He touches his captain's hat brim in a mock salute.

Brittany looks over the gleaming vessel, a grin growing on her face. "So this is your boat? Far fucking out, man!"

"Yeah, 52-feet, 900 horsepower. Can outrun anything in the islands. We'll just do a slow cruise along the Waikiki shore tonight, though. Sound like fun?"

Brittany and Melissa harmonize their response: "Hell, yeah!"

"I wanna drive!" Brittany says, more a demand than a request. She sways a bit as she jerks an imaginary steering wheel back and forth. "And you got a Jacuzzi, too?"

"Sure, baby, whatever you want." Trazer intones, adding a couple of nods for confirmation. "Got to get on board first, though." A sweep of his hand directs them to the boarding stairs.

Trazer and a crewman help Brittany and Melissa board the boat, something of a challenge, given the girls' tipsy condition. Lori turns away and beats a slow, silent retreat down the dock. The dark hides her tears and trembling hands.

"Hey, you're kinda cute!" Melissa says to the crewman helping her. "What's your name?" she adds, her tone intimating getting laid later is a sure thing. "You are circumcised, aren't you?"

Meanwhile, Brittany grips the steering wheel and makes zoomy engine noises, interspersed with fits of laughter.

"Go on inside and I'll introduce you to the other girls," Trazer says solicitously to the blondes. He opens the cabin door and ushers in Melissa and Brittany. One of the thugs, pistol in hand, crowds in behind them. Lori turns her head, unable to watch.

From inside the cabin comes a confused voice: "Why are they all tied up? Is this some kind of joke?"

Chapter 33

The front door opens and Jared follows the apartment complex manager, Yuki, into Lori's unit. Yuki is the Japanese version of the proverbial little old lady, graying hair and thick cataract glasses, compression stockings gripping her legs. She has the kind of stub nose that shows the air holes conspicuously. Her neck cranes as she peers around, her eyes and ears searching like a radar/sonar unit.

"Miss Lori? Miss Lori? It is Yuki! You okay?"

No response, except for the soft humming of the air conditioning. Jared's breathing quickens and a sour feeling grows in his stomach, the kind he used to get in 'Nam. "Lori? Lori? Are you here?" he calls.

Yuki says to Jared, "Lieutenant Fong say you look fast, no touch nothing, nothing. Just look, okay?" She fingers each of the many keys on her key ring, kind of a makeshift rosary, as Jared opens the doors to each room in turn. He agonizes, not knowing whether to be relieved or more worried at not finding her. "I understand — it's just that I haven't heard from her in three days. That's not like her."

Usually I'm the one who disappears for days or weeks at a time. Now I'm seeing it from the other side, Jared thinks. Then realizes it's not pretty.

Jared pauses in front of the phone and his eyes fall on the call log. He looks at the last number dialed, and frowns, trying to make sense of it. He thinks, then thinks some more, and then pulls a business card out of his billfold and compares the numbers. Still he doesn't understand.

* * * * *

Professor Tanaka is in his dimly lit living room, staying up late, going through photos spread on the table before him. A small table light is the only illumination. Tanaka focuses with keen intensity on the images of the naked young boys. From time to time, he pauses on a particular photo and holds it up to get a better view. One of him with a particularly fine 12-year-old catches his eye, marked by a quick intake of breath. The exhale is just loud enough to mask the squeak of a door easing open.

Jared grabs him by the neck from behind and slams his face into the wooden table with a thud. Tanaka's glasses shatter and go flying. Pictures sail all over the floor. A smear of blood paints the tabletop.

"You really ought to lock your door when you go on a fantasy trip, you fucking pervert," Jared says, hate twisting his words.

Tanaka gasps and starts to moan, which rapidly becomes a plea. "Please..."

Jared jerks Tanaka upright and smashes him on the side of the head with his open hand, not hard enough to knock him out, but enough to make his ears ring. Wide-eyed, Tanaka gasps for air and sobs profusely, as blood sprays in a mist from his nose.

"Jared, I..." he blubbers.

"Shut the fuck up — I didn't come here to kick your cocksucking ass, but I might just do it anyway if I don't get some answers."

Jared jerks Tanaka out of the straight-back chair and throws him hard to the wooden floor. Tanaka rolls over into a fetal position, hugging himself, still crying, his tears washing streaks in the nasal blood.

"Kill me, kill me — I deserve it!" he wails.

"Maybe later. Where's Lori Konishi? Why did she call you?"

"She didn't. Trazer did, from her place."

It is Jared's turn to be shocked. "Trazer! How do you know Trazer?"

Tanaka continues to blubber pathetically. Jared kicks him in the ribs to get him focused again. A large gray tabby cat watches from the top of a bookshelf, impassive except for a twitching tail.

"I know it's wrong, I know it, I know it! I just can't..." Tanaka bawls between gasps. "We had a business arrangement, I gave him contact information on pretty young Caucasian women coming through the University going to the Orient, and he..." Tanaka edges away, arms protectively hugging his ribs. "...and he...gave, he shipped back...boys...in payment. I didn't know about the Rocky Konishi thing or I never would have helped you with the logbook." Weepy eyes look up imploringly.

"Where's Lori?"

"Trazer has her. He's forcing her to help him get some girls, there's a big fishing trawler just out in international waters waiting on them."

Jared doesn't attempt to minimize the disgust in his voice. "Tell me why I shouldn't just kill you right now? And enjoy doing it?"

"You...should..." Tanaka cries, shaking as if freezing.

"Maybe, but not yet. Keep talking."

* * * * *

The general aviation ramp at the airport is dark and quiet, except for the small black helicopter idling at the edge of the parking area. A limousine taxi wheels up to the gate, its lights sweeping the deserted lot. The driver clicks his way through the keypad and the limo enters as the swinging gate beckons him and the passengers inside. They stop near the helicopter and Trazer steps out, scanning in all directions. He tosses some money to the driver, then yanks Lori and the gym bag from the car.

"Don't let the driver go!" she says, gesturing at the limo. "Give me the logbook, my deal is done," she pleads.

"Not quite, sweetie." Trazer says, waving the driver away. "I need some travel insurance to get to the trawler, and you're it. Another thirty minutes and you fly back, bag in hand," Trazer says, without the slightest hint of apology. "Thirty minutes and everybody gets what they want."

Before she can protest further, Trazer grabs her by the arm and walks her to the idling helicopter, their faces illuminated by the spastically flashing white strobe light. The helicopter is set up for sightseeing, with the passenger doors removed for maximum visibility. The pilot is in the front right seat, helmet on, visor down, swaying in concert with the whirl of the blades. He gestures to the headsets on the rear seat. Trazer and Lori pile in, fumble around in the dim light to get the headsets and microphones in place, then snap the seatbelts on.

"Okay, let's get going," Trazer says over the headset intercom. "Here's the coordinates," he adds, passing the pilot a paper with the set of numbers on it. The pilot scans the lat/longs, glances at a chart and then clips both to his kneeboard. That done, he grips the control stick, and with the other hand slowly pulls up a metal bar that emerges from the floorboard. The helicopter shakes and the throb of the engine soars as the blades bite the air. Like on a mechanical magic carpet, they lift off, pause for a moment in a hover, and then swoop skyward. If it had not been under the worst possible circumstances, Lori would have been thrilled, imagining using her rudimentary flying skills on this exotic machine. Now, however, she is in a daze, mind racing a hundred miles an hour, but in a hundred different directions.

The thumping of the blades increase as the helicopter accelerates the climb toward the light bejeweled mountains. The H-1 freeway and sparkles of ten thousand homes slip below. Hot tropic air, cooled by the altitude, bathes them through the open doors.

Lori sits, eyes closed, fists pressed against her forehead. She had always prided herself in being a pretty tough cookie, but now feels totally defeated, a husk of her former self, worthless. No, worse than worthless.

She glances about. Three feet away the open door invites her, a breezy portal to another world. A better world...one she can fly to in just seconds. She sits staring as her hand slides along the coarse fabric of the seatbelt, coming to a rest on the cool, smooth hardness of the buckle. A moving rainbow of memories flashes through Lori's mind: A scary moment as Father lifts her onto a great white horse; her mother holds her hand as they dash house to house, daring tricks or treats; she shares the stage with President Carter, embarrassed but proud. She sheds the last tear she has left.

Trazer, perhaps relaxed by the rhythmic shaking of the machine, leans back and absorbs the vista below, as his scraggly blonde hair whips in the wind. Clearing the ridge, they start the descent towards the inky black ocean beyond.

"Ain't this a ride," Trazer says, as he peers down at the jagged ridgeline of the Kuolua mountains. "Brings back a lot of memories...most of them bad," he muses aloud. "Hey, pilot — got any 'Nam time?"

"Yeah, a little. Getting that adrenaline rush?"

Trazer laughs, "Nothing like going into a hot LZ to make you shit your skivvies." He returns his gaze inside. "What'd you say your name is?"

Jared raises the visor, looks back and locks eyes with Trazer. "Jared Scott. And let me introduce you to my friend, Colt," he adds, and aims the big pistol at Trazer's face. Trazer stares down the barrel of the forty-five, eyes big with surprise, shocked beyond words.

"Lori — get up here," Jared yells, gesturing to the front left seat with the pistol. Lori is only slightly less shocked than Trazer. She freezes, unable to react.

"Lori! Up here. Now!"

Her eyelids blink in a rapid and repeated staccato for a moment as her mind re-engages. Then she scrambles out of her seat belt and works her way up into the cramped area of the co-pilot's seat, losing her sandals to blow out the door. Jared hands her the gun. She is surprised how heavy it is, never having held one before. *And how do you aim it?*

"If he tries anything, just shoot his balls off to get his attention. We should reach the cigarette boat soon." Jared checks the coordinates again and makes a slight correction as the helo bounces through turbulence.

Trazer softens his posture and not as much white is showing in his eyes. "Well, ain't this sweet?" He shakes his head in mock disbelief. "Dudley Do-Right and his gook girlfriend cook up a surprise. Nice, real nice. Guess I get the dumb shit award for tonight. But hey, I got surprises, too." A gargoyle grin grips his face. "Have a look." Trazer kicks the gym bag towards Lori. She hesitates, then zips it open while she struggles to keep the gun trained on the leering Trazer. She reaches in and pulls out...a Honolulu telephone book.

Teenage hormonal excesses excepted, Lori has never truly hated anyone. Not with the black, primal, mind-searing emotion that now erupts from deep within. In an instant, she understands, *really* understands what her father felt when he grabbed the gun from his desk drawer. Hate trumps every other emotion in the deck. Love may make the world go round, but hate can make it spin backward, maybe even explode.

"Where's the logbook, you bastard!" she screams. She aims the automatic with both hands as best she can, trigger finger quivering.

"Sitting on the editor's desk at the Honolulu Advertiser unless my buddy back on the island gets an all-clear radio message from the mothership." Trazer mouths a kiss at Lori. At that instant, the thing she wanted most in the world was to wipe that obscene grin off Trazer's face. Whatever it took. She closes her eyes and begins to squeeze the trigger, uncertain as to how much is enough. But instead of a jolt of recoil, she feels Jared's hand pull her arm down.

"We don't have time to worry about that now," interjects Jared. "We got a job to do."

* * * * *

Jared puts the helicopter into stealth mode, strobes and exterior lights extinguished. Only the soft glow of the instrument panel keeps him company in the cockpit. Unless it passes directly through line of sight with the moon, the helo is quite invisible. And unable to be heard as well, Jared knows, over the scream of the cigarette boat's big engines.

With his night vision goggles on maximum magnification, Jared spots the sleek boat as it pounds across the wave-tops, throwing a white wake that gleams in the moonlight. As the helicopter closes the distance, he can make out the crew as they hang on as best they can and peer through the dark, looking for their destination. From his vantage point, Jared spots the mother ship, a large Vietnamese fishing trawler, still a few miles distant in international waters. One of the crew points ahead as the trawler's lights emerge over the horizon. With the goal in sight, the driver throttles back so that the boat thrashes around a little less and the two other thugs go below.

Jared urges the helo onward as he discerns the crew haul out the girls, six of them, wrapped and bound by heavy chains. They lay them out on the cockpit deck like game fish that have been pulled over the transom. Even at this distance, Jared can see them thrashing about, fighting their captivity.

The crew of the trawler scurries about as they ready for the transfer. A deck locker is popped open and they pull out a cargo net and a hoist line.

Jared assesses the situation. He takes a deep breath and slips off the NVG's. He yells over his shoulder to Trazer. "Okay, here's the plan. I'm going to fly low above them and you call them on the bullhorn." Jared points to the bullhorn stashed under the co-pilot's seat. "Get 'em to stop, unchain the women. We'll put out the rope ladder and once we get them on board you can get off. Fair?"

"Sure, Jared, whatever you want," Trazer says, relaxed and indifferent. He leans back, as half-smile dances on his face. Jared glares at him, then flips on the million candlepower landing light, which sears the speeding boat with the ultimate "gotcha" beam. He glances back at Trazer. "Get ready with the horn. And no bullshit."

The boat crew, stopped in their tracks by the sudden appearance of God above, stare up between shielding fingers, paralyzed into inaction. Then the captain shouts words unheard and they leap to obey. They swiftly attach iron weights to the chains wrapped hard around each of the girls.

Don't let it be that, oh God, no!

Jared turns to Lori, who still holds the forty-five on Trazer, but her gaze is turned to the scene below. "Lori! Don't look!" But he knows she will.

As they see the helicopter approach, the girls thrash and kick and stare into the light, imploring, begging with their eyes. The thugs only tighten the bindings around them. That done, they stop and look at the captain. He glances up at the helicopter one more time, then gestures a command. The crewmen grab each squirming, sobbing girl in turn and without hesitation, hurl them overboard into the churning wake like so many sacks of potatoes. In an instant, the girls disappear, one at a time, as they twist into the endless black water below, their screams soundless trails of bubbles which disappear vertically into the depths.

"No! No! Noooo!" Lori screams, as the unbelievable horror of the scene registers on her face.

"Make them stop! Now, goddamn it! Make them stop!" Jared screams as he pounds the bulkhead.

Trazer glances out at the boat below as the last girl splashes. Her blonde hair streams behind her as she plunges for the bottom, kicking, twisting, a thousand feet of seawater between her and her final resting place. Her broken lei bumps away in the churning wake.

"Well, looks like it's a little late for that. Did I forget to mention to you about the recognition signals from the light gun? Just to verify everything's okay?" A snicker. "If not, goodbye evidence!" Trazer laughs with genuine pleasure as he kicks over the gym bag to display the signal light gun.

Jared tears off his seatbelt. "Lori! Take the controls!" Lori is jarred back to the immediate. She looks at him, wide-eyed, not believing his words.

"But I don't know how to fly a helicopter!"

"Well, goddamn it, learn!" Jared yells and yanks off his helmet. Lori drops the pistol and grabs the helicopter controls. Immediately the helo gyrates in all directions as she wages war with the controls. Finally, she grips the stick with both hands and the oscillations begin to dampen out. Jared breaks free of his seatbelt.

Trazer offers another taunt. "Hey, Dudley! Didn't you learn anything in 'Nam? Everybody is expendable, especially women!" Trazer unsnaps his seatbelt, but Jared is on him and showers him with hammer punches, limited in ferocity only by the cramped quarters of the helo cabin.

Trazer shields himself with his arms like a boxer on the ropes, then kicks Jared hard in the chest and knocks him back. Jared growls like a dog and re-attacks, his fists fly as he tries to pound Trazer's face through the bulkhead. Trazer, a veteran of innumerable street fights, kicks him away with his heavy boots.

Lori glances between the fight and the inky black darkness outside. At that moment, Trazer hurls a stunner of a blow to Jared's face. He reels back crashing into Lori, knocking her headset off. The helicopter lurches upward and then slews sideways as she struggles to push Jared off enough to regain some semblance of control. Lori's feet find the rudder pedals and a shove skids the helo so hard Jared is afraid the tail will break off. Trazer grabs the front of Jared's flight suit and yanks him to the deck, then he kicks and pushes him toward the open door.

"Time for you to go flying, Superman!" Trazer snarls through gritted teeth, and then slams a boot in Jared's chest and pushes with all the might he can muster. Jared's hands and arms flail, but he can't find a grip. He slides up to and then...falls out the open door.

* * * * *

"Jared! Oh God," Lori screams as Jared vanishes. At that moment, Lori never felt so alone. Panic washes over her like a tsunami. She doesn't really know how to fly, much less how to land the helo, and there is a murderous madman just behind her. She can't make her brain think. Think! But her conscious, thinking brain is overwhelmed by primitive, instinctive, irrational compulsion. Lori lets go of the controls and the helo instantly returns to wild oscillations. Then genuine hysteria sets in — Lori tears at the seat belt and shoulder harness. Only one escape: Jump! No matter that they are hundreds of feet in the air, and the black water below will smash her like concrete, jump!

"Lori! Grab the controls! Fly the helicopter!" Jared screams at the top of his lungs, but Lori can barely hear him over the engine and wind noise. She jerks around — a miracle! A resurrection occurs as Jared's head reappears, then his shoulders and arms. Jared hauls himself up from his precarious perch on the life-saving skid and fights the G forces to climb back in the cabin.

"Oh, you came back for seconds, huh?" Trazer spits and renews the attack of the boot heels. Jared takes a couple more slashing blows to the face. Caught by the wind, blood sprays from gashes ripped into his scalp, but Trazer still pounds him with a furious blitz. Jared wobbles on the skid, about to fall.

"Should've killed you in 'Nam, but this'll have to do. Adios, motherfucker!" Trazer's leg is poised, cocked, ready for the *coup de grace*. But at that moment, Lori gets the helo back to straight and level. A second of stability, Jared takes a chance and lets go with one hand, long enough to reach under the seat and grab the portable fire extinguisher. The Velcro fastener comes away easily and in an instant, it's in hand. A frosty blast of spray smacks Trazer's grinning face. He falls back as Jared scrambles back aboard.

Luck is with Trazer. Lying on the cabin floor, he reaches for and finds the pistol underneath him, whips it up, finger reaching for the trigger. Jared blinds him with another gale of white fog as the .45's muzzle explodes, twice, shattering the twilight, assaulting the eardrums. The flash-bang of the pistol startles Lori, as do the new holes in the Plexiglas in front of her.

Jared heaves the empty fire bottle like a shot-put, smacking Trazer square in the forehead as he struggles to get up. He falls back, dazed, and slides completely out the open door, arresting his fall with a death-grip on the skid with one hand, waving the pistol with the other. His fury abated, Jared scurries over, flops prone on the floor and looks over the edge of the deck. Trazer stares up at him, his face contorted, twisted black with emotion. Hate? Terror? Rage? Just like so many years ago, Jared and Trazer lock eyes.

"Drop the pistol! Jared yells, then reaches down and grabs Trazer's wrist in an iron clinch. "Drop the pistol and I'll pull you in!" Trazer, out of luck and out of options, hesitates, opens his hand and the pistol falls away. With only Jared holding him, Trazer swings with the wind, feet pedaling thin air.

No mistaking his expression now—pure unadulterated fear. He reaches up to Jared, the fear on his face beseeching salvation.

Maybe he is human after all. Maybe he even has a soul. Maybe he is me.

"Did you forget about me, Trazer?" Lori yells down at him, then jams the control stick to one side as hard as her adrenalin charged system can muster. The helo wrenches violently and Trazer's forearm smashes against the skid just below Jared's death grip. With a *snap* the bones break, and before Jared can react, Trazer's flesh fails. His arm separates with a sickening rip, and suddenly Jared only clasps the wrist and fist. Trazer falls away from the helicopter, clawing at the air with a hand no longer there, transfixed in the helicopter spotlight. An unheard scream tortures his face. Jared watches him growing smaller, shrinking, a slow motion nightmare receding into the abyss. He takes a long time to disappear, years, in fact.

With Trazer's fist still in his clutch, Jared shoots a look at Lori. She meets his gaze, her face blank, an expressionless mask. Her eyes — he has seen these many times before — the sightless eyes of the newly killed being loaded onto his helicopter. Eyes without soul.

Jared feels the hand twitch, and as he watches, horrified, Trazer's middle finger relaxes and points skyward.

Okay, I was wrong...

He releases the hand and it follows its owner into perdition.

Chapter 34

R ocky and Lori kneel on a white blanket laid on the broad expanse of grass in the backyard of Rocky's mountainside home. Swaddled in the traditional Japanese robes of the head of a household, Rocky's plain kimono is a soothing contrast to the splash of color that is Lori's close fitting Hawaiian print. They are silent, lost to their private thoughts, but Lori is certain that Rocky is as acutely aware of their surroundings as is she — the fragrance of the flower blossoms, the tingle of every breath of breeze, dogs barking, and car horns in the distant valley. Every sense is amped, hyper-energized and recording in high fidelity as the sun completes its long arc to the horizon. The twilight is upon them.

Rocky nods and then casts his gaze upward for a moment. With both hands and great deliberation, Lori serves him *saki* in a polished stone cup. Rocky holds the cup in his lap with both hands for several minutes. Then he drains the contents in one long swallow and puts the empty cup down beside the remnants of his *sukiyaki* dinner.

Lori stands, bows deeply and kneels a few yards behind, the gentle rays of sunset warming her face. From inside his kimono, Rocky extracts an annotated sheet of rice-paper, a *haiku* poem. He recites it in Japanese, so softly that Lori can't hear. It is, after all, to him, from him.

Returning the poetry to the robe, Rocky picks up the brass sextant that Jared recovered from the sub wreck. It glints golden in the last rays of the sun. Rocky closes his eyes and touches the metal, feels the unique curves and angles. His fingers find the engraving and linger there. Lori knows the words:

Ensign Masafumi Konishi

The sextant finds its way from his hands to the blanket beside him. Only one more item is left untouched. His eyes fix on the gleaming, razor sharp blade of the *tanto* and its carved ivory handle, which sit on a wooden serving plate. Leaning left, then right Rocky slips the kimono from his shoulders, careful to tuck the sleeves under his knees.

The last crescent of sun disappears into the Pacific. The wind quiets, silence reigns. Rocky picks up the knife, grasps the handle firmly and wraps a small cloth around the upper blade so he can grasp it firmly with both hands. He closes his eyes, sits motionless for a long moment, then raises the knife and plunges it directly into the left side of his abdomen. He gasps aloud in pain, but it does not deter him — he rips open the soft flesh and organs of his belly, sweeping the blade from left to right.

Lori is glad she can't see his face. The twilight deepens, like a curtain coming down.

One final act. Rocky twists the knife and yanks it to his breastbone to complete the *hara-kari* ritual. He jerks the dripping knife free and it tumbles away, leaving a red smear on the blanket. He gasps once and covers his face with his hands.

For several minutes, Rocky sits, not breaking the silence. His muscles seem to relax in sequence and he slumps, moment by moment. Finally, without a word, he topples over, twitches a couple of times, and is still.

Lori stands and waits for a few minutes, taking in all of the sensations around her — the beautiful view of the lights of the valley below, Venus in the ascent, the grass cool and tingly beneath her bare feet. She doesn't think, just records, with all of her senses. Then she takes a large white sheet and drapes Rocky's body with it. She kneels beside him, making sure to avoid the spreading crimson stain.

She opens a small bag and extracts her mirror, checks her reflection from several angles. In a practiced movement, she releases her long, silky black hair from her pony tail, shakes it out and drapes it over her shoulders. A thick cord is at hand and Lori wraps it several times around her kneeling legs, binding her calves to her thighs.

Lori reaches over and gently places one hand on Rocky's still warm shoulder. She stares sightlessly into the distance for a long, long moment. Her contemplation done, she picks up the revolver, places the muzzle to her head, closes her eyes, and atones for her sins.

* * * * *

Jared rests on one knee at the grave. It lies in the incredibly beautiful and peaceful Punchbowl Veterans National Cemetery, just a few miles from Waikiki, but entirely a world apart. Row upon row of soldiers, sailors airmen, and Marines lay at rest, their marble tombstones lined in perfect symmetry. It is peaceful here, eternally peaceful. His hands tremble as he reaches out and touches the letters, now barely visible in the growing dusk, with his fingertips. He lingers, then stands. Abruptly he raises his hand to his head...

"Nolan, I love ya, buddy, but it's time to move on. Rest in peace, my brother." He executes his very best salute. Then he turned and walks away among the headstones into the dusky night.

THE END
(See also alternate ending)

Lori stands and waits for a few minutes, taking in all of the sensations around her — the beautiful view of the lights of the valley below, Venus in the ascent, the cool tingly grass beneath her bare feet. She doesn't think, just records, with all of her senses. Then she takes a large white cloth and covers Rocky's body with it. She sits down beside him, reaches over and places one hand on his still warm shoulder and stares sightlessly into the distance for a long, long time.

* * * * *

Jared sits onthe low rock wall that circles the parking area overlooking Makapuu Point. Six hundred feet below the sheer cliff, the surf crashes onto the rocks, the white froth illuminated by the silver rays of the moon. At this late hour, there is no traffic, nothing to distract; just Jared alone with his thoughts, which are a muddle, at best. He still isn't sure how to tell Lori, but for once, he isn't going to slip out the back door. He dreads facing emotions, but takes some solace in the fact he has somehow found the courage, some would say, courtesy, to end a relationship in an adult manner. It isn't much to feel good about, but for Jared it is a major accomplishment.

Lori drives her car onto the overlook and eases into the spot next to the Corvette, headlights stark against the night. She takes a while to get out, then walked around to Jared. Neither says anything. Lori looks out over the water, the wind on her face, strands of hair dancing around her head.

Over her shoulder, Jared says, "I heard about your Dad."

"Yeah. It was sad."

"Are you going to be okay?"

"No."

This is going to be the all-time worst break-up ever. I really picked a fine time to find some courage! Jared reflects.

Lori turns to face him. He reaches out, and they hold hands as their eyes meet.

"Jared," Lori sighs. "It won't work. I'm broken in a way that you can't fix. And you are broken in a way that I can't fix. As much as I wish it could be different, we're no good for each other. I don't know who I am anymore, and you won't face yourself."

Jared rocks back as if she slapped his swollen and scabbed face. The world seems to stop turning as he scours his brain for words. As usual, they aren't there.

"I don't understand," Jared murmurs lamely. His thoughts swirl, but can't find their way to clarity.

"Yes, you do. How can either one of us possibly hope to give ourselves to another person? We are so broken. Jared, I love you, but I can't be with you because I don't know who you are. And neither do you. The only real emotion you have is anger. Go fix yourself. I'll try to do the same. Maybe some day we can be whole again, but right now I can't even imagine that far ahead. Go get better, okay?"

There is a long pause as Jared searches her eyes in the moonlight, looking..for what? Something to fill the void he now feels? Absolution? Hope? Forgiveness?

Her eyes, those big, beautiful expressive brown eyes that once danced a lighted path to her soul, are empty, unrevealing, dead, and he knows, beyond doubt, he knows... He leans forward so that they touch, forehead to forehead. A tear drips from his face onto hers, mixing with one of her own before they are carried away into the night by the wind.

"Are we good for anyone at all?"

"I don't know. I hope so, Jared. I really, really, hope so..."

* * * * * *

Jared lets the dust settle around the rental car, then scans the weathered memories. The old place is pretty much as he remembers it, only the weeds are higher, the paint duller, and the old chinaberry tree with the tire swing is gone. A couple of chickens scout for worms and seeds, mostly in the tree shade in deference to the blistering sunshine.

Jared half expects his old dog, Lefty, to come flying off the porch to love and greet him, but Lefty should have long since gone to dog heaven, no doubt enjoying an endless supply of rabbits to chase.

Jared grips the wheel, stares straight ahead, takes a deep breath and waits for his heart rate to slow to the low triple digits. Finally he steps out, facing a blast of hot Texas air and looks over the car roof toward the house. Just visible are the notches on the porch column that marked his growth. His would be the one on the right, indices marching higher and higher, eighteen in all. He doesn't look at the left column.

With all the enthusiasm of a condemned man ascending the gallows, Jared trudges up the steps in slow motion and knocks on the door.

"Just a minute, I'm coming!"

The warped wooden door swings open with a scraping rasp. Jared's visual registers immediately fill: mid-fifties, but looks at least ten years older in spite of her modest attempts to look like someone starring in *Dynasty*. Hair shot through with gray, pulled back into a convenient bun. A simple print dress, unmistakably homemade, completes the picture. She wipes her hands on her apron as her face reveals a progression of emotions.

First, the big eyes of shock and surprise; next, the wrinkled brow of puzzlement; last, a squinting glare. The look was searing.

"Mom..." he says, hopefully.

The door makes a scraping rasp again, this time capped by a loud bang.

"Please, come back here!"

"Go away, Jared. I don't wanna see you."

"Mom! This isn't fair! I've come all the way from..."

The door flies open, this time testing the strength of the hinges. Jared stumbles back and nearly falls off the porch. His Mom is madder than the proverbial wet hen, shaking a finger at Jared with one hand, the other a fist jammed onto her hip.

"Isn't fair? Honey, life ain't fair! You think it's fair to have your youngest son die uselessly in a war we didn't want or need? You think it's fair to be all alone for the past ten years? Not having a soul who gives a damn if I wake up in the morning? No! Don't you dare come here and tell me life ain't fair! Now get yourself off this porch, mister. Go on, now, git. Go back where you belong."

"Mom, I'm your son, too..."

"Well, you sure don't act like it. Where were you? Where you been? Too drunk to show up for your own brother's funeral? Easing your guilt in liquor and loose women? Never come to visit me, never come to comfort me in my grief and sorrow. You left me all alone."

Her voice softens. The blood in her face cools, ever so slightly.

"You were all I had left and you couldn't even come to visit, or call. I could forgive you for Nolan's death, the Good Lord seen fit to take him and I've made my peace with that. But what I can't forgive you for is how you deserted me in my time of need. You and that worthless father of yours. Now, git on out of here," she scolds, sweeping a finger at the rental car.

"I'm sorry, okay? I have tried." Jared offers the palms-up gesture of supplication.

"You haven't taken my calls..."

"Too little, too late."

"...and my letters come back unopened. I was hurting, too. I still am. I didn't know what to do with myself, who to be, how to atone for what I've done. And I just gave up. I'm sorry for that. I'm sorry, Mom, I'm so sorry."

He is six years old again, begging forgiveness for breaking her grandmother's favorite vase. He turns away, tears blurring the dusty landscape.

A fracture appears in her glacier of hostility.

"I still need you, Mom. I hope you still need me. And I want to be here for you."

He lifts his chin a bit. "I'm here for you now..."

The wall of ice collapses. Jared feels the gentle touch of her hand on his shoulder. She dabs her eyes with the fringe of the apron.

"I can tell, honey." They share a hug and a moment of exhausted silence.

"Come on in and rest a spell. We'll have a glass of iced tea, and then there's somebody we need to go see."

Chapter 35

Jared walks slowly up the dry, windswept hill, alone with his thoughts. In the distance a lawnmower hums, but except for that small intrusion, silence surrounds him like a blanket. The sun reaches for the horizon, giving sunflowers the last daily dose of its warmth.

Jared moves among the markers, notes the names, and finally comes to the one he has been looking for: Nolan Anthony Scott; PFC, U.S. Army; 1950-1968. It's there...it's always been there. For the first time, this is a place he is not afraid to be. He kneels down beside the grave, the lump in his throat making it nearly impossible for him to breathe. His hands tremble a little as he reaches out and traces the name with his fingertips. *Nolan Anthony Scott*, forever age eighteen. Jared can't hold back a sigh. He reaches into a pocket, extracts his old dog tags, holds them tight in his hands for a moment. Then he slowly presses them into the sod below the headstone. He stands, and raises his hand to his head.

"Nolan, I love ya, buddy, but it's time to move on. Rest in peace, my brother." He executes his very best salute, a slow motion arc of his hand that sweeps across the all the lost years. He turns to face his mother. She nods to him.

"Come on, Jared. It's time to come home."

THE END

www.ingramcontent.com/pod-product-compliance
Lightning Source LLC
Chambersburg PA
CBHW020843260626

47169CB00003B/1109